Six Dreams

ABOUT
THE

Dreams

Train

AND OTHER STORIES

Maria Haskins

TREPIDATIO

PUBLISHING

ISBN: 978-1-68510-005-6 (sc)
ISBN: 978-1-68510-006-3 (ebook)
Library of Congress Control Number: 2021944435

First printing edition: August 13, 2021
Printed by Trepidatio Publishing in the United States of America.
Cover Design: Don Noble | Cover Layout: Scarlett R. Algee
Edited by Sean Leonard
Proofreading and Interior Layout by Scarlett R. Algee

Trepidatio Publishing, an imprint of JournalStone Publishing
3205 Sassafras Trail
Carbondale, Illinois 62901

Trepidatio books may be ordered through booksellers or by contacting:
Trepidatio | www.trepidatio.com
or
JournalStone | www.journalstone.com

For mamma and pappa, my mom and dad, who gave me life and books, and then let me loose upon the world.

TABLE OF CONTENTS

Publication History

Acknowledgments

About the Author

Six Dreams About the Train

and Other Stories

INTRODUCTION

IMAGINE YOU'RE LYING IN A boat, drifting, staring at the stars, trying to pick out the shape of Orion or Taurus, Gemini, anything really. You're wondering what those ancient astronomers were on when they named the constellations and mapped them out. You wonder if you can get some whatever-it-was now.

Above you, with no warning, a dragon flies over.

But it's not your average dragon.

It's made of starlight and metal, of melody and screams, of breath and cobwebs, of water and the crash of waves. And, frankly, it *might* be a dragon or an eight-legged horse or a creature of the deep; Hell, it might even be a spaceship.

That's what reading a Maria Haskins story feels like: the unexpected dragon in the sky.

Why am I here? I'm here to introduce you to Maria Haskins—although, honestly, I'm pretty sure you already know about her. You're here, right? And if you've got any sense, you'll skip over this introduction. If you're here, in this book, you've come looking for a Haskins tale and you already know what you're doing. Well done. Come back when you're done with the stories—they're the main event, after all—come back then and see what nice things I say about Maria's words and worlds.

If you're here for fairy tale and fantasy, it will be found in the deepest darkest part of the woods—and the wolf is not always your enemy and your family are not always on your side.

If you're here for science fiction, it'll be not just out in the stars, but beneath the oceans, written with enough tension and pressure to give you the bends.

If it's horror you're after, well, buckle up: zombies and cleavers and pastries, oh my!

There's a range of lengths to choose from—if you're time poor, then mainline "Good Dog," "When Mama Calls," "Ten Things I Didn't Do," or "Silver and Shadow, Spruce and Pine."

Got more time on your hands? The kids are away, spouse out of the house, it's a long weekend and you've got a bottle of good whiskey and a packet of your favourite cookies? Then settle into the hammock with "Deepster Punks," "Dragon Song," "Tunguska, 1987," or "Cleaver, Meat, and Block" (which is one of the finest zombie stories I have ever read).

There are horizons and guiding stars, there are good dogs, and fairy tale girls slogging their way towards the light, there are women and men earning redemption. There are parents and children, running towards each other, and away. Trying to communicate across time and generations, trying to give and get understanding. There are devils to make deals with, and things from other worlds—things that just want to go home.

In this, the Year of the Plague, when the world seems to be in freefall, fiction is the sanctuary we need more than ever. Any bleakness in this collection pales by comparison with the beauty of these stories. Yes, they are hard-times stories. Yes, they'll tear at your heart. But there's always hope. There's always an aesthetic of kindness. There is always also an element of song to these tales, something old and essential and bardic and wise.

So, off you go: the dragon's waiting.

Angela Slatter
Brisbane, Australia
29 July 2020

WHEN MAMA CALLS

LIV IS ON HER BACK, on the forest floor.

Above, white clouds and blue sky make a patchwork quilt. The moss is thick and soft, and the air trembles with the sticky-sharp smell of pinesap. A spiderweb is strung between the swaying branches overhead and drops of dew are threaded on the filaments of silk like iridescent beads.

Liv's dream was cold and deep, like winter, but it's gone now, and Duke is here. His nose tickles her face, making her giggle. Liv gets up. Duke wags his tail, ears flopping as he runs. Liv runs with him, towards home.

She shouldn't have fallen asleep. She's done it before: walked too far, stayed out too long, and she knows Mama will be worried.

In the meadow, grass and flowers bend in the breeze, tickling her outstretched hands. Liv runs so fast she doesn't just feel the wind and sunlight, she is the wind, is the light—glow and warmth. She runs so fast even Duke cannot catch her.

Home is grey wood crouched beneath dark spruce, red geraniums peeking out the windows, door hasped. Liv slips inside, treading softly on warped boards.

It's cold beneath the swaybacked roof. Not a gleam of embers in the iron-stove.

Mama is abed, curled up small beneath the blankets. Her hair is grey, not black, but Liv recognizes her anyway.

Mama's eyes are open.

"Hello, Mama," Liv says. "I'm home."

Mama doesn't answer, only breathes, slow and shallow.

"She can't hear or see you, not yet," Duke says, and lies down on his rug by Mama's rocking chair.

Liv sits on the floor with Duke and waits. Outside, the forest whispers her name. "You forgot your bones beneath the moss," it murmurs, but Liv doesn't need her bones right now. She only needs her Mama.

Shouldn't have stayed out so long, Liv thinks. *Should've come back sooner. Before her hair turned grey.*

Liv and Duke wait together while the forest hums a lullaby outside.

They wait for Mama to fall asleep. They wait for her eyes to close so she can see them.

TUNGUSKA, 1987

1929

ALEXANDER WAS RUNNING THROUGH THE snow. The rifle and the pack of squirrel-skins pounded against his back with every step. Realization seeped into him as he ran: he had shot a Metallic. Its shiny armor hadn't protected it. After all these years of living in fear, it had been that easy to take one down: one shot, straight into its midsection, and the hovering thing had cracked apart and fallen to the ground.

He'd peered inside the broken remains and seen nothing but metal and wires. Nothing living hid inside. Ajax dead beside it, a mess of black and grey fur and curled tail in the snow. So much blood. The torn ear, where the neighbor's dog had ripped into him as a pup, had been the only recognizable part of his head. Best damn squirrel-dog anyone had ever had. Best damn dog anyone had ever had. And that Metallic had fired like it meant nothing.

Alexander's heart raced as he ran. Was this what rebellion and resistance tasted like: tears and bloodied iron on your tongue, the sting of gunpowder in your nostrils?

The squirrel-skins on his back tumbled loose. He scrambled to collect them. Added to the pile of skins at home, it would have been enough to keep them fed through the winter, maybe even get some new shoes. Thirty gråskinn, greyskins, squirrel winter-furs, two Swedish crowns apiece, money under the table, free and clear. Better pay than hauling logs or working in the mines for the Metallics. Even with the bans on hunting and firearms, the money had been worth the risk. At least until today.

Hunting squirrels required not just skill with a rifle, but patience, and preferably a good dog, too. And he'd had Ajax, who would sniff out a squirrel anywhere, then wait quietly as Alexander lay down on his back beneath the tree—silent minutes, muscles tight, breaths withheld—until he could take his shot: one bullet, right through the tip of the squirrel's nose so as not to ruin the skin. As he ran, the first seek-and-destroy patrol shot overhead. The Metallics were fast, but not as fast as he'd feared. He'd somehow thought they would be there as soon as the shot fell, blasting him into oblivion from the sky. Like they'd done in Umeå, during the uprising of 1910. That had been only two years after the Metallics had invaded, when people didn't know what would happen if you fought back.

Alexander knew. That's why he ran, hoping the tall pines offered enough cover, knowing they probably didn't. He wanted to run home, to Lappvattnet, to Mother, to Katarina, but with the patrol overhead, the Metallics would surely know who he was and where he lived by now. If he could shake them off, he'd spend the night in some neighbor's root cellar, then hop on the horse-coach going north in the morning. Hopefully, his friend Kurt would be driving and wouldn't ask any questions. Not much of a plan, but it was all he had.

Katarina would tell him he was an idiot, that he'd be killed. That he'd be leaving her and Mother to fend for themselves. She'd be right. He'd always kept away from the Resistance, not wanting Katarina or Mother to have to pay for his convictions. Now they'd end up paying anyway.

The patrol shot overhead again, the oblong vessel skimming the treetops, the engine-sound sizzling in his ears as it passed. He prayed as he ran:

Don't turn. Don't turn.

Katarina would have laughed at that: him, praying. She was the one who'd quote preachers and scripture, while he'd preach revolution. "It's 1929!" she'd say. "War and strife are banned, so what kind of revolution are you imagining?"

Don't turn. Don't turn.

The patrol turned.

1987

Sometimes I dream of a different world. Different, yet always worse than the shithole we're in now. How's that for hope? How's that for rebellion? 1987 is a bad year for hope and rebellion, even if you're eighteen years old, have just wrapped a chunk of malleable bio-explosives in an old shirt, and placed it in your duffel bag. The eightieth anniversary of the Metallics landing in Tunguska is still a year away, but the world is already being pulled between official celebration and futile protest. Not even the news coming from our government-issued radios and electro-pad newspapers can hide that. There's unrest in the Ottoman and Austro-Hungarian enclaves, and on the Korean peninsula. Feeble riots in the big cities. Metallics descending to punish and contain. There are group suicides in far-off jungles, and in basements down my street: three kids from my high school take poison together and die a week before graduation. "Life's shit," their note spells out.

It's bad, but it doesn't equal the purges in 1933 or 1942, the old folks say. Because no matter how bad you have it, old people can always one-up your misery. This is the perfect world the Metallics have given us. A world where every human life is kept small, hemmed in by regulations and restrictions. Safe and sound. Like it says on the sun-powered glitterbanners mounted on every public building: "Eight decades of peace, progress, and prosperity!" The best of all possible worlds. Even Voltaire knew that was a joke, and he's been dead for over two centuries.

I'm standing in my room on the second floor of my parents' house in Skellefteå, Scandinavian enclave. All I've ever wanted is to leave this goddamn town, take the train, even a bicycle, or hitch a ride on a motorized transport on the Metallics' express-roadway, though that would mean risking jail or worse. Never mind the travel permits. I want to see the Mediterranean, Egypt, Spain. I have visions of temples along the Nile, faded paint thousands of years old there for me to see and touch, gateways to a time when this world belonged to human beings, not metal husks.

Instead, I've been drafted. I'm going to Tunguska, the holy of holies, up the hind-end of the Russian enclave. "Selected for Advance Development Program," says the hand-delivered note I received yesterday—short notice so I won't have time to run. Ink printed on real paper: a rare luxury. No mundane electro-voice transmissions for this message. Soon, I'll be sitting in a flying ship for the first time in my life. I've hit the motherlode.

It's June. Summer night. No real darkness in the sky this far north. And there it is. I see it: hull of steel and light, descending on the other side of the river, disappearing into the newly unfurled foliage of the birch trees. My ride. Onwards. Upwards. Anywhere but here.

I know it's all wrong. It's not supposed to be this way. Not my life, not this place, not this world. I can feel it, I've always felt it, every conscious moment of my life. It's like a nightmare, but I was born dreaming it, born asleep. Maybe a massive explosion will wake me up. It's worth a try.

Mom's standing at the door. Dad is off in the ore-fields on his mandatory work-rotation. He won't be home for another month. Not like he could do anything but say goodbye anyway. Grandpa isn't here to say goodbye. His room downstairs has been empty for a year, but still smells of contraband tobacco, urine, and medicine. Proof that not even the all-powerful Metallics can prevent or cure all diseases. All Grandpa can do is watch me from the photo on the wall: him and his sister Katarina in 1927, outside the old house in Lappvattnet. He's wearing a suit that looks too big; she's wearing a dress, a coat, and an old-fashioned fur-collar. Ajax the dog is sitting between them. The house and village were leveled in the 1950s to make room for a protein-manufacturing facility.

Grandpa is dead. Katarina and Ajax are long gone. He hardly ever talked about them, but then he rarely talked about anything at all. All those years when he lived with us after Grandma passed away, he was more absence than presence. He spent his life doing carpentry and growing potatoes in our residential plot, and if you asked him anything beyond that, he'd say, "Let the world be." Sorry, Grandpa.

Before I leave, I check that the package is tucked safely in the middle of my bag. I'd carry it on me, close as skin on skin, but I'm afraid they'll frisk me before takeoff. Mom hugs me, holding tight, not crying. Neither one of us is much for weeping.

"Evelina."

She says my name as if to conjure, as if to summon, as if to protect. Just like Grandpa said Katarina's name just before he died. I heard it: a whisper, a breath. Later, perhaps, when I'm gone, Mom will breathe my name like that into the empty rooms.

"I'll be back," I say. She nods.

We both know it's not true.

1929

The blast burned into the snow next to him, turning ice crystals to steam, knocking Alexander off his feet and into a gulley where a small creek wound its way through the forest in summer. He fell hard, snow in his mouth, and got up with his hand clamped down on the metal wire looped through the noses of the skins, holding them together. Not ready to let go of that money just yet.

He stumbled, rolled into the creek, felt ice and rocks crunch beneath him as he got up and kept running. Another blast hit the pines: a tree catching fire, flaring up with a crackle. Smell of smoke and sap. He'd seen the Metallics burn forest before, to flush out the Resistance. It was said that in Tunguska, they'd leveled and burnt a huge swath of forest when they arrived: an almighty blast of heat and sound. Just to show they could. The Czar had made obeisance within a week. Then Europe, North America, Africa, South America...the whole world toppling.

Another shot. Alexander was thrown off his feet again and felt his arm twist when he landed. Scramble. Up. Run.

"Why did you shoot?" Katarina would have asked him that. After all, the Metallics were only working for the betterment of humanity. That's what the preacher told them from the pulpit every Sunday, that's what kids were taught in school. And he knew Katarina at least half believed it.

He was thrown off his feet once more, felt the heat of the hit singe his cheek. This time he stayed down. He tried to get up, but his boots felt like lead and rocks, his sweater was almost ripped off his body, he smelled wet wool and sweat and tasted his own blood. It was hard to see through the mist of smoke and pain.

There is no need for revolutions. So he had been told. No need for war and struggle. No need to change the world.

He tried to get up again. Failed. He rolled over on his back. Above, so close it was almost touching the trees, the patrol-ship hovered—hull of steel and light. He expected another blast to finish him, but instead the round, shiny head of a two-legged Metallic bent over him, blue glow-eyes staring down. A second patrol must have landed nearby. Like one wasn't enough. He tried to see what was happening to his body—saw the blood in the snow, dark and plentiful, and knew he wouldn't live. Then he died.

1987

The six-horse wagon picking me up is transporting high-tech parts to some place up the coast, but making a detour for me doesn't seem to bother the driver. She clicks her tongue and snaps the reins to get the horses moving. Mom is standing in the summer twilight on the porch. I turn away; I don't want to see if she's crying. Instead I peek into the wagon behind the seat: shiny metal, colored wires.

"What is this stuff?"

She shrugs.

"Who knows? It's high-tech. Mechanical electro...you know."

Meaning: it's restricted. Meaning no ordinary human peon gets to find out what it is, except, perhaps, the ones who are drafted for the Advanced Development Program. Like me. Like two other teens from our town who were taken five years ago. Your family is treated special if you're taken: better accommodation, better food, better pay, some groveling from the local politicos at special occasions. Everyone else just hates your guts. At least I'm leaving town.

"Your grandpa killed a Metallic, right?" The driver glances at me as we pull in near the Port.

"Yeah."

"And lived."

My family's claim to fame.

"Yes. Otherwise, I sure as hell wouldn't be around."

She doesn't even crack a smile.

"Do you know why they spared him?"

That's always the question, but who knows why Metallics do anything? It was 1929, and the Metallics were busy tightening the screws of domination, turning the world into a secure cage. A cage for pets, or cattle? No one really knew the answer then, or now. They spread across the globe: punishing disobedience, stomping out insurrection, yet curing children, and handing out new technology. Mercy or annihilation? You never know with Metallics.

The driver is still looking at me. She thinks I have an answer. I shrug.

"No idea."

I jump off the wagon holding my bag close. The driver sniffs, disappointed, and is off, hooves clopping in the gravel. In front of me, the entrance to the Port building slides open. I try not to think of the package in my bag when I stop for the obligatory body-scan, passing between two heavily armed Metallics hovering on either side of the door. They do not stop me.

1929

"What did you do?"

Katarina's voice. It was the first thing he heard when he came back to life. He was lying on a table. The room was dimly lit, but he knew he was home. A two-legged Metallic was in the room with them: blue glow-eyes turned on him, chest-piece blinking slowly—yellow, red, white—its six extendable extremities hanging limp. Katarina was standing by the window, lips moving silently as if in prayer, holding the fresh bundle of greyskins. She had always loved the feel of that soft fur. The first skins he ever got, she had sewed into a neck-piece for herself. She still wore it to church every winter Sunday.

The Metallic remained silent and still. No blaster at the ready, no warning message being broadcast. Looking closer, he realized that the tips of its upper metal limbs were bloodied.

"It saved your life," Katarina said, staring at the Metallic. "Stitched you up. And it did something to your heart, I think, and you came back. You were dead when that Metallic carried you in here. When it laid you down, I thought I saw..." Her voice faded.

"I couldn't have been dead if I'm alive now."

She shrugged.

"Why would a Metallic save me? I just shot one of them. One of them killed Ajax. I couldn't..." This time, his voice faded.

Katarina trembled, shoulders hunched, hugging the bundle of skins tight. Alexander heard the sobs, ripping through her. His sister, the one who never cried. He closed his eyes, thought of her playing with Ajax in the yard, thought of her saving the beef bones when she made soup, thought of the way she'd bandaged the puppy's torn ear.

"Sometimes I dream of a different world, just like you do," Katarina whispered. "A world without Metallics. But it's just a different version of hell. In my dreams, I see dead bodies piled high, like firewood. Pyramids of skulls and bones, neatly stacked. Children scrounging for scraps in ruins. Fields turned to mud beneath booted feet."

She had that same hunted look as always when she spoke of her night terrors.

"Those are just nightmares. You know that."

"Maybe. But they feel real. Like they should have happened. Like they might happen."

"That's your fear talking. You know there must be better ways to live than this."

Katarina shook her head, unconvinced.

"They're taking me away," she said.

The pain of that was almost like dying again.

1987

The windows on the ship are small and round. I can barely see anything through them, but then there's not much to see: miniature houses, small lakes, tiny trees, and more tiny trees. There are solar panels everywhere down there: on roofs and hilltops, glinting in the first shreds of dawn. "Global solar power goal achieved!" That was the good news headline about a decade ago. Because peace and prosperity is all the Metallics want for us. Fairness. Equality. Sustainable development. Catchwords hammered into us with metal fists.

In my dreams, the world is different. There, I see this world through a glass darkly, unfamiliar shadows moving across familiar landscapes. When we studied history in school, I felt a whisper of it as I scrolled through the decades on my electro-pad. Something missing. Excised. Scrubbed away. No stain to mar the Metallics' world and its predetermined, prefabricated perfection.

The world cracked in 1908, said the first Resistance flier I found slipped into my high school locker. I used to think it was a figure of speech, but sometimes I can almost feel the crack that winds through the world, can almost run my fingertips over it: a seam, a scar, a lie. Chafing, wrong.

I'm not alone on the ship. Three of us got on board in Skellefteå and we've landed twice, picking up passengers in Sundsvall and Vasa. Twelve of us now, strapped into our seats behind the robo-pilot. There are ten seats on either side of the center aisle, facing each other, the curved hull behind our backs. All of us just out of high school.

The others are talking. They're like me: scared and insecure, arrogant and intelligent, conceited and stupid. Watching them, listening to them make awkward conversation, I already know what they're feeling because I feel it too. That ever-present yearning for love and sex and understanding. That ache to get somewhere where we're not told what to do and who to be every single day. That longing for new places where we can become someone else: someone unknown, someone unseen, someone unheard of.

Vain hopes. We're all stuck in a world where everything is as it should be. Nothing to fight, nothing to change. No one to become except what the Metallics wish us to be: peaceful, prosperous, safe. It's enough to make you scream, or kill yourself. Or kill someone else. Life is a pointless, worthless pile of refuse, and I have the explosives to prove it, provided by the Resistance. The local group was only too happy to recruit me: thanks to you, Grandpa.

"I heard they landed on the Moon. And Mars."

"That's impossible."

"No it's not! Metallics can go anywhere. For all we know, they came from Mars."

"Shut up!"

He does.

"There are human-shaped Metallics," one of the boys says. "The two-legged ones. I think it's a suit, not a machine."

"You don't know that." The girl next to him shifts nervously and changes the subject. "I'll probably be doing physics. Supposedly they have some of the world's best physicists at Tunguska. Some have been holed up there since the beginning."

"Doing what?"

"Who knows?"

"My parents think they're going to kill us."

One of the girls laughs at that, a sound sharp and unexpected enough to jar all of us.

"They can kill us anywhere. They don't need to put us on a flying ship to do that."

Her Global has a Finnish lilt. I look at her: dark braids, dark eyes, shadows beneath the cheekbones like hunger, like someone who also feels the chafing of that crack, that seam, that lie running through the world. I like her already.

"I wonder if we'll get to see them," she adds. "You know, the real Metallics. The aliens."

Everyone goes quiet so suddenly that I have to stifle a nervous giggle. It's been a while since I've heard someone willfully "spreading disinformation and fomenting unrest." We all wait for someone to come and shut her up. No one does.

1929

Katarina put the bundle of greyskins on the table. He remembered the crunching of the bones when he cut the feet off the last squirrel and skinned it, turning it inside out to dry, feeding Ajax the innards. Him and Ajax. Just a few hours ago. The silence beneath the pines, a day like any other. And then the unexpected whir of the Metallic approaching, Ajax barking, snapping at metal limbs. The blast. Ajax never liked Metallics. Most dogs didn't. Father's old army rifle from 1875 was already in his hands: bullet at the ready, no chance to miss at that range.

"Are they taking you because of what I did?"

"No. I got the note yesterday. I just didn't tell you."

"When do you leave?"

"Tomorrow. Early. Soon. Mother already knows."

"No one ever comes back once they're taken."

"I know."

Alexander thought of Ajax dying in the snow. Thought of himself, dying in the snow. He thought of the brief taste of revolution and freedom, already gone stale and bitter.

"What will they do to me?"

Katarina's eyes glimmered.

"They let you live. What else can they do?"

1987

It's dusk when we get to Tunguska, sunset shaded by cloud as we follow a small, wheeled Metallic across the landing field to our quarters. Everyone is bunking together—narrow beds, stacked three high—bathrooms and showers in an adjoining building.

"Official welcome ceremony in one hour." The electro-voice message comes from a tiny radio device in the corner. We can see it already: the holy of holies. It seems to cover half the world, rising out of the ground, spreading towards the horizon. A vast complex of metal and concrete: domes and antennae, towers and pinnacles. And it's even bigger below ground, if the rumors are true.

"I can't believe we're here."

"It's still in there, you know."

"What?"

"The ship, the one they came in."

"I heard there was more than one. An armada."

"Everyone knows that. They were landing everywhere within a month. All over the world. Obviously they had more than one ship."

"Yeah, but the first one, it's still in there."

While everyone is talking, I remove the package from my bag and slip it inside my shirt, stuffing it into the waistband of my pants. I want to blow up whatever it is they treasure in there. I want to punch a hole in this worthless world and let in the light and air so I can finally breathe. I want to be free—free from the Metallics, free from the cage—even if it's just for a brief moment.

We're brought to a meeting room. A man talks for a long time. He's the first human we've seen so far. No sign of any other beings, though I can tell the girl with the dark braids is expecting them. The man speaks the usual nonsense: world government, peace and prosperity, using human and natural resources efficiently. Finally, the punchline:

"You will become a permanent part of this astonishing machinery for progress."

And by the way, no one gives a damn about you and your human desire to be free.

When the man leaves, a woman enters the room. She is old. Silver hair cropped close. Dressed in a standard-issue work outfit: blue denim coveralls, orange seams. But around her neck lays a soft garland of grey fur. And walking beside her is a grey and black dog, tail curled on its back, one ear torn. Something catches in my throat when I see them, and the wrapped package feels like it's burning through my skin. She is looking only at me—at least that's what it feels like—and there is something about her: an ease, a presence, like nothing I have ever encountered before.

She is free, I think, watching her. I don't believe I've ever seen a free person before, and I'm not even sure what it means that she is free.

"Two things." She speaks Global with a barely noticeable Swedish accent. "One. None of you will go back to your lives as you know them. If you try to leave without permission, you will be killed. Please don't. Two. You will learn many things here that will seem strange to you. But perhaps the strangest thing you will learn is that there are no Metallics."

She lets that sink in, then repeats it.

"There are no Metallics. No one landed here in 1908: no ships, no...aliens." Her eyes rest a moment on the girl with the braids, amused. "Best way I can explain it to you right now is that a gateway opened, and a group of people came through. Human beings, like you and me."

We breathe that in, suddenly cut adrift.

"They changed the world. They have saved millions of lives since 1908. That's not propaganda, that's fact. They are the reason we are here, the reason you are here. As you will learn, there is a plan for mankind, and our task is to implement it. It is not without cost. Humanity has had to sacrifice many things in order to guarantee long-term survival. You have all been chosen to come here because you are special, and because we need you."

We are confused as hell, but we all like the sound of that, much as we might pretend we don't.

"Some of you are here because of your considerable scientific talents. And some of you are here for the same reason I was brought here: because you have an unusually high sensitivity to the distortions caused by the temporal adjustments implemented since 1908."

That last sentence hangs in the air: rippling, bewildering.

"Are you saying...Metallics...time travel?" It's a whisper from the back of the room.

"In a manner of speaking, yes."

Her gaze is on me: sees me, sees my hand on my shirt where the package is still burning through my skin.

"A sensitivity to temporal distortion is a useful skill in our work here, but not always easy to live with elsewhere. Some of you might have spent your whole lives thinking something was wrong with the world. Most people do. You might even have felt the need to right those perceived wrongs. But trust me, there are no Utopias to be had. The alternatives have been explored and rejected." She searches our faces, and I wonder what she finds in mine. "Our work requires skill and patience. While the technology here makes many things possible, its use is severely restricted. Even changing one detail, saving one life, correcting one mistake, preventing one death, altering the course of one day," the blue gaze pierces me, "can have significant repercussions that may take years, even decades, to be fully realized."

Her hand rests on the dog's head, but her eyes are still resting on me. The words are saying one thing, but her face is saying something else. It is saying: listen to me, hear the spaces between my words, the gaps between the things I've said.

1929

Katarina was standing on the porch. She'd already said goodbye to Mother upstairs. He hadn't wanted to be there for that. Now he was leaning on the doorframe, too weak to stop her, too weak to help, too weak to change anything.

"Anything I have from now on is owed to them," he had told her last night. "But I've paid, too. They took Ajax, and now they take you."

The sleigh was waiting on the road, horses steaming in the cold.

"I saw something," she whispered when he hugged her. "Last night, when that Metallic brought you home."

He turned and looked at the Metallic standing by the road, maybe waiting to see Katarina off, maybe set to accompany her wherever she was going.

"What?"

"I saw... I saw it...saw inside... I'm not sure. I can't figure out what it means yet."

The Metallic watched Katarina get on the wagon. It turned as the sleigh pulled past, and for a moment Alexander thought its posture and bearing seemed familiar, like a reflection or an echo of something else. Katarina waved. Then she was gone. He never really saw her or the

Metallic leave because of the way the blinding sunlight flickered in the snow.

1988

Sometimes, at night, I dream of a different world. Millions dead, bodies piled like firewood. Skulls and bones neatly stacked. The shadows of children burned into walls by an unknown conflagration. Countries turned to mud beneath booted feet. The oceans dying. The air killing us. Death and destruction stalking us. I know it's the truth. I know it happened. But not to me, not in this iteration of the world.

We're the plan's newest acolytes, its chosen, its latest prisoners: not yet wise or trusted enough to be brought before the gateway hidden deep within this hold of concrete and steel, but we are learning. Multi-branch history. Temporal distortion analysis. Mass-psychology in a controlled society. Astrophysics. Quantum theory. Temporal mechanics. How to design artificial, mechanized intelligences for enforcement and communication. How to use and maintain bio-enhancement suits. We are taught that while the universe might appear infinite to those who study space and time, it is not. For us, there is only this world; the best of all hells, designed by those who escaped the wreckage of the future to save the human race from self-destructing.

But Katarina's presence tells me something else. The grey squirrel-skins around her neck whisper of resistance. The dog by her side is a murmur of revolution. There is a crack in the world, and she has gone through it, letting in a glimmer of light. I can feel that light, the warmth of it, the possibility of change and freedom, whenever I bury my hands and face in Ajax's fur.

"Was it you?" I've wanted to ask her. "Was it you who dragged Grandpa home through the snow, that time he died and lived again? Did he understand that, in the end? Is that why your name was his last breath? Did you go through the gateway to save him, like you went back and saved Ajax, bringing a dead dog with you to the here and now?"

I still haven't asked her. Maybe because I don't really need to hear the answers anymore.

Every day I think of the package stashed under my mattress, still wrapped up in an old shirt. But I can wait. I am awake now, and I am patient. And maybe, just maybe, there's something better in store for me.

SEVEN KINDS OF BAKED GOODS

LEYRA HAS OFTEN TOLD ME that life is a cruel joke played upon the living by gods or chance. I can certainly see her point, after being stuffed in a sack, flung downstairs, and slung across a horse at bedtime. Maybe she has the Northern true-sight after all, much as she'd deny it if she were here.

The smell of mould and winter-stored potatoes chokes me as I dangle across the high-cantled saddle; the coarse fabric of the sack chafing my face and hands, the rag stuffed in my mouth ensuring I can't even complain about the bumping and the bruising.

Yet even now, even here, I wouldn't change a thing about the life I've lived, if the chance were given. After all, it has to count for something that I'm the only Dwarven crafter ever to cause more deaths with flaky pastry than a well-honed blade.

It's true that no one will ever herald my baked goods the way they would have hailed my metalwork, had I stuck to that, but at least my revenge was always sweet: sweet as almond paste and chocolate glazing, sweet as macaroons and spice-cake, sweet as seven kinds of baked goods laid out on a platter, served to the high and mighty for justice and revenge.

**

First and last sword I ever made I called Bleeder. I even etched my name into the steel: *Crafted by Disa Rockbottom*. These days, it hangs on the wall in my room above the bakery, and it's a right gorgeous piece of work, straight and true, hilt all a-sparkle: the kind of weapon a hero might wield to fell a great beast of evil. Only thing is, you can never hit a damn thing with it. That's how I made it: speaking my Dwarven craft into the steel as I folded and hammered it, as I held it in the flames, as I pumped the bellows, as I forged and tempered it, bonding the craft deep and true. A sword that will always miss, no matter how sure and skilled the hand that wields it.

A young warrior bought Bleeder from my family's shop. He swung it once or twice, seemed pleased with the way the garnets and the crystals sparkled in the hilt, and paid handsomely for it. Never saw my parents as proud as I saw them that day: proud of me, of my craft, of my skill. Proud of the money I'd made them. It lasted all of one day.

Next day the warrior came back, so irate he could barely speak, besides the cursing. To demonstrate his grievance, he swung the sword at me, and though his stroke was straight and well-aimed, the edge turned aside and cut into the workbench. I didn't even flinch.

Next, I made a dagger. Fang, I called it. Prettiest thing you ever saw with a straight-true edge, a hilt of blackwood bound with silver, blade so sharp it would bleed you just to look at it. Except I'd made it so that whatever it cut would also heal. My father liked the looks of it, and told me to show him that it worked, so I did. Cut my hand right then and there, almost severing the fingers. Fuck me, did that hurt! But worth it, for the look on his face. Took a few minutes for the flesh and sinews to heal over, and another minute for the skin to come in right.

My father wasn't much for jests, especially not those that were made of craft and steel and iron. Still, he didn't kick me out until he caught me in the act one night: blouse open at the neck, skin blushed, hair frizzled from the heat, sticky hands rising from the soft mound in front of me.

"Disa's baking again!" my brother Malen shouted, pointing at me, his mouth ajar.

That louse. Never got a good word or deed from that runt. They'd come back a day early from the Crafter's Meet, and I was stood there, elbow deep in bread dough, freshly baked raspberry hearts cooling on the counter betwixt the tools and ore, where Mother liked to hone an axe-edge.

Father shouting: "Ten generations...!" before his voice gave out. As if to summon each and every smith before me into the room, to stand in judgment of my actions. Not even one lowly tinkerer or jeweler among them; only steel and iron, hilts and pommels, helms and shields.

"I *am* a crafter, Father. Don't you see how well you taught me?"

And he saw then. He saw the Dwarven craft I had spoken into the dough beneath my hands, the craft he'd taught me to use in the blacksmith's forge now rolled into the sugar and the butter: glamour, fortify, and bliss, soon to be digested.

I'm still surprised he didn't kill me, but he threw me out right then and there, Mother helping with her boot up my backside, screaming "Sacrilege!" and "Blasphemy!" Wasn't even allowed to bring a stitch or coin with me, just Bleeder, Fang, and most of those raspberry hearts.

I hopped a potato wagon to the city the next morning, to seek my fortune. Turned out my fortune was sleeping in the alleys, begging and pickpocketing, and fighting off the other scroungers when I had to. So it went, until the day Leyra snatched me by the braids.

***

There's the sound of a rickety old door kicked open, the smell of a fish-oil lamp being lit, then I'm rolled out of the sack onto a warped and drafty floor. I find myself in a dark and dirty hovel, likely on the outskirts of Oldtown, near the harbour, a place I might have slept in a time or two when I still roamed the city streets.

As the oaf tightens the ropes around my ankles, I wonder if Leyra has been taken, if she's still alive. She was at the tea-traders, staying over-late as she sometimes does, and it worries me that the oaf has not asked about her once.

He peers up from the ropes to look at me.

"You're wondering about the Northerner." A perceptive oaf. "Wondering if she'll come to save you, or if I've already shanked her between the ribs and sunk her corpse beneath the pier."

"You'd need a bigger sack to haul her, dead or living," I mumble, and just manage to pull my scrunched up bustier out of my armpits with my tied-up hands before he binds my wrists behind my back instead.

I tamp down the anger, breathing patience slow and purposeful into my lungs, letting my mind wander off to other things. Like the oaf's crossbow leaned against the wall. Like the bundle in the corner that clanged like metal as he threw it down. Like Leyra eating sugar-dreams, pouring tea and smiling.

***

First time I met Leyra was on the street when I checked her pocket for loose change. She slapped me right over the head with that big hand of hers and held me by the braid when I tried to get away. Should have known to tack my braids down tight, but you don't always find good hairpins in the offal heaps and gutters.

"You'd be that Dwarven sneak-thief I've heard tell about," she said. "It's said you've got a knife as won't kill anybody."

I guess I'd stuck enough people that word had gotten 'round, and when I told Leyra about Fang and Bleeder she laughed so hard she had to sit right down.

"What else can you make?" she asked, and it might have been the way she laughed, or the fact that she'd shared a dram of Northern spice-wine with me, but I told her everything: up and down, inside out, the story of my life.

When she heard I was a scuttled baker, something lit behind those freeze-blue eyes.

"I run a tea shop," she told me, and I saw the gleam of something darker sunk deep in her eyes right then, heavy stones of grief and pain, gone right down in the depths, but I chose to ignore it for the dazzle of that smile. "I could do with hiring a baker. But you should know it's not the teas I make the money on, not really. Most of the profit's in killing people. Which means you'll get a life of naught but disrepute and danger."

"What kind of people do you kill, would you say?" I wondered, sipping on that spice-wine, and she said they were mostly the kind that had murdered old women, swindled widows, and were known to beat up children, pups, and kittens.

"Deserving, then?" I mused. "I'd be handing out some justice. Working for a just cause."

A sideways glint, the smile widening enough that I could see the hunger lurking just beneath.

"Always."

***

"Where would a Dwarf learn how to bake?" the oaf asks as he secures the ropes around a wooden post, left behind from when this building housed cows or horses. "Never heard of such a thing."

He is talking more than seems prudent for a henchman, and I wonder if he might have pilfered some of my cinnamon buns from yesterday before he grabbed me, the ones sat cooling on the counter, with a smidge of swagger murmured into yeast and sugar.

"I watched the baker next door to my parent's smithy," I reply, wriggling my fingers to loosen up the knot. I think of old Kirra with her grey hair and bent back who let me watch her work, even though she knew my parents would never have allowed it. I think of the book of recipes she handed me one day, written out in her own hand. That book is still in my possession, dog-eared pages stained by lard and eggs and melted butter.

"Why'd you not leave town already?" he asks me next, almost as if he really wants to know. "You can't have thought you'd get away with seven-fold murder, right here in the city?"

"We like our shop," I answer, thinking of the gilded sign above the door, Leyra in her red-white apron, stood behind the counter, weighing loose-leaf tea on brass scales, using silver tongs to place pâtisseries into boxes.

"Well," he says, drawing out his knife, and I can tell he doesn't like the look on my face right then. "You've lost all of that now."

He seems more for cutting flesh than breaking bones, and as he works me over, taking out the gag to let me speak every now and then, I tell him different things, but nothing that he wants to hear. I know he wants a confession of seven-fold murder, and a list of accomplices, but mainly he seems interested in extracting pain before he kills me.

"You should have stuck to smithing," he tells me when he takes a break from cutting. "Decent profession, that. Respectable. Good money, too."

"I have a sense of humour," I answer, spitting blood and puke. "Steel and iron make worse jests than pastry. Also, dough and batter please me in a way that anvils and hammers don't."

I look at him, taking in the scarred face and the muscled arms.

"Why do you do what you are doing? This...henchman...ing?"

He shrugs and wipes the knife clean on his britches.

"Good pay. Hard enough to get work now that the war's over. And I don't mind serving justice and a just cause."

I catch my breath enough to laugh at that.

"Who pays you?"

He gives me a long and quiet look. Considering. Deciding I won't live long enough for the truth to matter.

"The highest." Meaning, the Princeps of the City. Meaning, Leyra and I are both damned and doomed no matter how this goes. "He does not like having his men nipped away by poison."

***

Once Leyra took me in I set to baking. Most days I made whatever took my fancy, while Leyra stood in the shop and sold the baked goods and the teas. I breathed just a hint of craft into my wares, enough to make you come back for seconds and for thirds, though not enough that you'd know why.

Special orders came through a man in Oldtown: some old swashbuckler who pretended he dealt in secret death and judgment, when he mostly dealt in beer and chewing tobacco. He passed assassination-orders on to Leyra, and I'd bake up something special for delivery, speaking my craft as I stirred and whipped and glazed, while Leyra added her philtres to dough and frosting.

Most often I'd use the fortifying crafts—the same kind you'd talk into the metal to toughen up a blade or shield—to make the eater live an extra day or two, hushing up suspicions. It is a testament to our skill and our discretion that never once in those years did we ever draw the attention of the shirriffs, but I admit that not all those days were rosy.

"Have you ever seen it, Disa?" Leyra asked me once as we sat and picked through the leavings of the day after the door was shut and locked: pastry crumbs, pot of tea, a flask of spice-wine, sleeves rolled up in the oven-warmth. "A house, torched and burned, with all the people still inside. Door barred. Most likely soldiers stood outside with their pikes and spears. No escape. And you see it as you come walking up the path, home from market. You smell it before you see it, but you can't believe it, you don't want to see. And then you see it anyway. Animals burnt and charred. Flesh and beams still smoldering. The house reduced to naught but heat and rubble. Small hands reaching for you out of the wreckage."

"No, I've not seen anything like that."

"Strips you clean. Leaves you always wanting. No matter what good you may have acquired since."

She looked at me, and I saw the heavy stones of sorrow sunk deep into her eyes, long ago. I had no words to stir her smile.

"I trained to be a seer, did I ever tell you that?"

"Only every time you're drunk," I remarked, but quietly, so as not to disturb her brooding.

"Didn't want to. Didn't want the lonely life with herbs and prophecies. Didn't want to see things true. So I chose my own life. Husband. House. Squalling babies. All burned now. So much for choice."

Another slosh of spice-wine.

"Did you ever think you were meant for something else," she asked. "Something other than cakes and teas?"

"Not lately. But before I left the smithy, I thought that maybe I should make armored underwear for ladies. Nicely fitted, easy to slip on underneath a gown or cloak, offering superior support and comfortable protection."

Leyra kept her face straight, sipped her rum and tea.

"There'd be money in that," she offered.

"A fortune."

"I'd buy a bustier myself, if you were selling."

"Let me take your measurements so as I can write up the order."

That made her laugh, and for a moment the darkness lifted up its wing. But most times she would not be talking when she drank, just carving names into the table with an old skinning-knife. Children's names. Same names she has tattooed on her arms, twisted round with runes and leaves. Northerns do that, so I've been told, paying tribute to beloved dead.

***

The oaf has taken a break from cutting me, and he's rambling now, about the money he's to get and what he'll do with it. First off, a fancy horse, then a property with fertile land and livestock, servants, wife, all lined up before me as he rambles, as he cleans the blood off his fingers, as he wipes the sweat out of his eyes.

Listening to him babble between the times when I've passed out, I've guessed the truth: that Leyra's man in Oldtown got a taste for gold and drink, letting something slip. Not enough for a trial or the gallows, but enough to hire someone with a sack and blade.

"You're a dreamer, henchman," I rasp. "More than likely the Princeps will have you hung to sweep his own trail clean."

I can see his face, can see he fears I speak the truth, and I drag another feeble breath to keep life flowing through me a while longer, still thinking about Leyra, and the waters beneath the pier.

***

For two years we made a good living, and we hung our sign above the door: "*Northern Delights—Baked Goods & Blended Teas*" all scrolled about with golden leaves and flowers. The bakery itself gained in fame and popularity, even in the highest lordly circles, until the Defender's Council, the seven high lords with jewelled chains hung around their necks, wanted a platter of our wares for a private feast.

That's when Leyra let me know her plan, the one that had been steeping in her mind since before I'd met her: a brew so strong and dark and bitter that it would choke the rich and mighty.

"It was the war, not men, that took my husband and my little ones, people would say to me. But I know who gave the orders of rape and plunder. I know who sent the soldiers out into the countryside. I know who wanted the deed done: seven warlords, sitting now on Council chairs because peace is come and past misdeeds have all been swept aside."

"I understand if you do not want to help me," she went on. "This will surely drag you down even deeper into danger and disrepute."

"Disrepute and danger is what I chose the day you snagged my braid. I won't choose any different now."

She smiled at that: a flick of it, soon gone.

Seven kinds of baked goods, that's what we would serve them, as was customary on fanciful occasions among the Northerns: cookies, cakes, and pastries, accompanied by cups of strong and aromatic tea.

Seven men, seven kinds of baked goods, seven poisons. I liked the symmetry of that.

***

I wonder now about the number seven. It takes my mind off how the oaf is cutting through my left index-finger with his knife. Why seven baked goods, particularly? One for each day of the week perhaps, or one for each of the seven sisters among the stars, or maybe one for each of the seven heavens up above, and the seven hells down below. Though that'd make it fourteen, and besides: that's a Dwarven view, likely not an influence on Northerners.

***

How I baked for that, how I mixed and stirred and whipped, thinking of Leyra's children; thinking of her, bent and broken amidst the rubble of her life, every step out of that fire leading to the here and now. Meringues, silken-skinned and lustrous. Lemon pastries, baked in fluted tins, filled with luscious lemon cream. Vanilla puffs, dusted white with powdered sugar. Chocolate mousse pâtisseries, brushed with cocoa glaze. Bite-sized rhubarb and strawberry pies with woven lattice crusts. Dark chocolate biscuits, rolled out thin as leaves. And Northern sugar-dreams, Leyra's favourites, creamy white and tender-brittle at the touch.

With so many men so highly placed, all at the same occasion, it was utmost in our minds that they not all drop dead at once, or in the same way. The seven poisons were the key, because results would vary depending on what and how much each one ate. I spoke ample craft into those seven baked goods: to toughen up the eaters' constitutions, reinforcing guts and organs, adding a whisper of desire to make the councilmen crave more.

Leyra paid a servant girl inside the castle to tell her how it went. They all ate, we heard, and not a crumb or crust was left behind. Then Leyra watched them closely, counting down the lives.

One man died on his way home right after the feast, stumbling off a bridge. An accident, so it seemed to most. Two died some months later once my craft wore off their innards, and their livers finally gave out. The last four died within eight months, from accidents and ailments that were the leavings of our work: organs weakened, veins stiffened, hearts made brittle. Natural causes, more or less.

Seven men, dead within a year. Struck down in their prime by a woman peddling teas and a Dwarven baker. We raised a glass the night the last man died, and Leyra looked deep and long into the fire, fingers tracing the names inked and twirled around her arms.

***

Morning light comes through the boarded-up windows. The oaf seems tired of cutting, and I feel none too good myself, what with my skin scored and bleeding, and half a finger missing. Can't see too well either with my eyes caked shut.

He checks the ropes and says he's going out to get the horse tacked up. Says he must deliver me this morning. Seems my confession is not required, nor a detailed list of accomplices and poisons. It would have been worth a little more, that much I understand from the way he glares: another bag of coin perhaps, or a younger wife.

Soon as he steps outside, I busy myself with my bustier.

The bustier is my most recent joke, and never has it seemed funnier than here and now. I crafted the metal springs and rods and braces, then had a seamstress sew the silk and cotton over top: a fine piece of armor-craft I guess, though it was fiddly work compared to baking. It fits me like a second hide, padded soft and reinforced, lined with silk and thinly felted wool, accommodating both my bosom and a hidden blade.

Flexing my left bicep, I squeeze the spring-loaded contraption hidden in the silk, and Fang pops out of my cleavage. I've practiced the trick a few times, but it's harder when you can't see straight and your hands are bound. Worse still when someone's outside, wanting to kill you.

I wriggle. The blade slides across my thighs and towards my bound hands. Another wriggle and I've got a feeble grip, managing to snick the ropes—wrists and ankles freed—before the blade falls from my hands. Then I run: blind, out the door, no time for clever plans or subterfuge, just hoping he's gone far enough to give me a head start. No such luck. Soon, I hear him behind me, chasing down the alley. The alley's narrow, barely wide enough for one, lined with empty houses, barred doors, brick walls. Far ahead in the dusk before dawn I see the docks. Too far.

I hear him coming, heavy thumping feet closing in, and then he's got me by the arm and neck.

"You should have stuck to smithing," is the last he whispers in my ear, before he cuts my throat, and goes off to collect his bounty, or maybe to get a sack and shank for Leyra.

I think of many things as I fall, none of them important anymore. Fading stars above are glinting softly, just a hazy mist between me and them. I think of Leyra, of danger and of disrepute, my life laid out on a platter: each day devoured, every crumb, and come to naught but death in the end. Then I follow the stars up into the deeps.

***

It's Leyra who pulls me up. Should've known she'd come, dead or otherwise. But no one's ever come for me before.

"Who will bake my sugar-dreams if you don't?" she says when I wake up, and I pretend not to see her crying, grateful that she repays the favour.

I touch my neck, the blood soaked into my blouse and bustier, pooling beneath me. But the skin's all healed, no seam or scar.

"Next time I make a dagger, I'll blunt the edge somewhat," I say, and try on a smile, though it falters.

"I came home and every room was empty and your room a right mess. Figured our luck had just run out. But it held a bit: some scroungers saw a man passing into Oldtown with a twitching package slung across his horse."

"Did he come for you?" I ask.

"There was a man. Just now. He tried to grab me when I was looking for you in the alleys. I pulled an axe on him. He pulled a sword on me. A fancy sparkly one. Not sure where he might have gotten it."

A length of steel wrapped in a bloodied cloak lands at my feet with a heavy clang. Then Fang lands there too, my own blood still dripping off the blade. Leyra laughs, and I laugh too, because once in a while, even life tells a joke worth laughing at.

"It's the Princeps as was paying him," I say when the laughter starts to hurt too much. "He'll want us dead again."

Leyra thinks on it. Not long.

"I hear the western cities are parched for proper tea and poisons, pastries, too, seven kinds and more."

"Any chance of disrepute and danger?"

"Always," she grins, and even now, after my throat's been cut, that smile still leaves me dazzled.

DRAGON SONG

Kettil

ONCE UPON A TIME, BEFORE the World Tree Yggdrasil took root and grew between them, sky and heaven were one. Once upon a time, it was the same with men and beasts; sometimes, it still is. That's what Mother used to tell him long ago, back when her stories still mingled with the music of Sigrid's lyre, when Tekla's hands still smoothed his hair down if he woke and whimpered in the night.

How long since Sigrid's strings fell silent? How long since Mother left with the ships again, sailing west-ways? How long since the homestead burned? How long has he been *here*? A month, a life, forever: each day and night devoured by fear and hunger.

The shuttered longhouse reeks of rot and dung, of fear and pain, but even with all the living bodies kept in here, the air is cold, like a larder. His breath gathers into mist, into ghosts, writhing in the pale sunshine seeping through the smoke hole far above.

He longs for Mother's voice, for Sigrid's songs, for Tekla's touch, but they have all turned to smoke, to ashes, to shadow.

***

When the door to the longhouse opens, everyone scrambles away from the daylight, tripping over chains and ropes. A tall, hunched shape enters, mouth and eyes a-glimmer, heavy breaths, heavier feet, iron claws glinting on its hands.

It is a man, and he stalks through their stink and terror, then stops. His back is covered in shaggy white fur, chest traced with swirling ink, head shaved and scarred. He looks well-fed and sated, because the meat he feeds on in this place of want and hunger is plentiful.

"Who are you, boy?" The child cowers on the ground, wincing as the knife-sharp metal claws rake his skin, drawing blood. "*What* are you?"

Once upon a time, he had a name. Once upon a time, he was a boy. What is he now?

When the iron claws touch again, he shivers, as though a fever burns through the marrow of his bones. All his fear and hunger turn into a blazing flame beneath his flesh. The heat of it flares through hide and muscle as the change ripples over him, as brown fur bristles down his spine and ribs, as his limbs bend into new joints, and there is no Tekla here to smooth it down and soothe him.

"No," he tries to say, but he has no words anymore.

"You shouldn't have let me see that, boy," the man whispers. "Now, it's the cage for you. Now, I'll eat you first."

***

Astrid

The dragon has come for me at last, and it is not the pale barrow-wyrm that claimed Beowulf when he grew old. No. My dragon rears up against the sullen clouds above the distant shore. From my ship, I see the blue ice-shimmer of its scales, the hoarfrost twinkle of its hide.

I have dreamed of this dragon for so long that it seems no strange thing to finally see it in the flesh, beneath the sky of the waking world.

One hand gripping the railing, the other on the hilt of my sword, I steady my footing, bracing for the onslaught of claws and fangs. The boat heaves in the dark water. My hird is at the oars, twenty strong backs turned so they cannot see the dragon taking flight, wings glistening azure and pale cerulean, its form slipping into the brightening sky. Only Garm watches with me, sharp teeth bared, hackles raised along his back.

Then it's gone. There is only the shore and the wind and the rolling waves.

The crew is singing while they row, my nephew Thorvald urging them on as their palms blister and their muscles tire. Twenty good men and women, but too few, too young, too green.

All I've got.

My old, callused hands clench into fists, grasping for things that aren't here; for everything I've lost.

Kettil.

I hold his name and the memory of his face in my mind: like an ember, like a wick and flame. Kettil, waking in his bed under the sheepskin covers: stirring, turning, laughing.

Gone.

"When did you first see that dragon, Astrid?"

Tekla's dark eyes peer up at me from beneath the heavy folds of the bearskin cloak. My cloak. The only thing left now of the trove of treasure I won in my long life. Before we set out, I gave it to Tekla as payment to help me find Kettil. My crew frowned to see a thrall receive such a gift, but I would have promised anyone any measure of gold and silver, yet all Tekla wanted was *this*.

You can give me coin later, she said, but I saw in her eyes even then that she knew my end, and that it did not lie far ahead.

"There are no dragons anymore," I answer, keeping my voice low to dull its edge.

"And yet this one will come for you."

"When?"

She shrugs.

Peering down into the depths I think of Sigrid. Almost, I see her face in the water, pale and wavering, as though the drowned woman is following the ship, clinging to the current below the keel.

Sigrid was no great blade-wielder, though she'd pick up shield and sword at need, but she wielded a different kind of power with her lyre. She used to sing to us of Odin's halls while we waited for landfall and battle on days like these. She'd sing of the Valkyries, of drinking horns overflowing, of Odin's Hall, and a roof thatched with gold. Now she's dead. Drowned in a storm two seasons ago. Sunk to the bottom of the North Sea without a weapon, or her lyre, in her hand. No Valkyries to carry her aloft.

She didn't want to come aboard that year, said the cold was creeping up her bones.

"Who will watch over me if you're not there?" I jostled. "You've been my nursemaid at sea since we learned to row and sail."

She laughed because it was the truth.

A wave took her when my back was turned, and whatever was left of my heart after that, disappeared with Kettil.

Garm stirs at my feet, nose tucked between forepaws. Crouching, I touch his head, rub his soft, notched ears between my fingers for a bit of comfort in this gods-forsaken place.

Tekla is stroking the cloak's silk lining: bits of fabric in every colour beneath the sun—scarlet and sienna, saffron and indigo, royal purple and ashen rose—priceless scraps I brought back from Miklagård in another life, stitched together by Sigrid, working by firelight one winter long ago when we were still young enough to be vain and lovestruck. I always hated the bulk and weight of it, the roughness of the fur against my neck, yet I wore it everywhere—to please her, and to impress. My father was a skin-changer—the songs say he fought the Danes in bear-shape—and Sigrid knew the worth of summoning that history, as did I.

"It makes me feel like a queen," I told her the first time I wore it, already scratching at my skin under the collar. "Reminds me why I don't want to be one, too."

Looking up at the sky, I search the clouds, but the dragon is gone.

There are no dragons anymore.

"Do you think of Beowulf when you see the dragon?" Tekla asks. Her hooded brown eyes framed by soft black lashes remind me of Sigrid, and her gaze is sure and unafraid. She is a seer, so Thorvald tells me, even though she's been naught but Kettil's keeper since she came to me ten years ago. "What was he like? The man, as he was and lived—not the story others tell of him."

I turn away.

How many times have I answered that question? Often enough that the tale as Sigrid and I told it in the years that followed is woven together with the truth even in my mind.

"He was the strongest man I've ever known," I say, wincing from the familiar pain in my right shoulder and arm. The old scar twists as if teeth and blade are still digging into it. "There are none like him anymore."

I think of Sigrid, of her fingers gently rubbing warmth and softness into my scars. The touch of her dark hair on my face when she bent down, loosening her braid. The supple welcome of her body beneath me.

I shrug off the memory. I cannot bring her with me, not here, not now. Not while Kettil is gone.

"How long since you were here?" I ask instead, nodding at the approaching shore.

This time, it is Tekla who turns away. "A lifetime."

"And you are sure this is where the raiders came from?"

"I might have run off to the woods that day, but I know what I saw. Men painted white and black like bones and death manning the longships. Burning your homestead, stealing your treasure, killing your people, taking your son. Led by one who thinks himself a beast, covered in a white bearskin, wielding claws of iron, stalking halls and fens, hungering for men's flesh."

"And he is here?"

"It is his island."

"Why would he travel so far to take what's mine?" I've asked myself that question every day since I found Kettil gone. Glancing at her, I add, "Perhaps he came for you."

Her laugh is a gull's cry, brief and sharp. "No. Not me." She shrugs. "He raids far and wide, just as you have in your life to take that which belonged to others. To barter, or pillage. What distance did you travel to buy me from the Danes, trading amber and furs for thralls?"

The boat dips in the swell and Garm whimpers between my feet. He's never loved the sea: not as a pup, and certainly not now there's grey around his muzzle.

"Why are you helping? You have no love for me. No fear, either, far as I can tell."

"I am not helping *you*. I am helping Kettil." Her eyes glint through the salt-tousled hair, and streaks of sea-spray wet her cheeks. "To you, I am a thrall, no matter that you've trusted me with your child since he could barely toddle. To him, I was a sister and friend."

***

We make landfall at midday, pulling the ship up the pebbled shore. The stones roll and slip underneath our boots, and there's a cold wind that finds its way through wool and leather: a damp, hoary chill that sinks deep into guts and marrow.

I watch as Thorvald helps Tekla disembark: the way his hands linger on her slender hips, the way she smiles when he grasps her waist.

Thorvald is a good man, I remind myself. He has always followed his own counsel, ever since he came to me, orphaned at the age of twelve, after my sister died. A warrior through and through. Not reckless or foolhardy like most men, but bold: the kind of leader others follow because his confidence gives them courage. The kind of leader Beowulf was when Sigrid and I followed him. The kind of leader I was, once.

At the water's edge, Tekla stands rigid, gazing inland with mingled hate and longing. Until this moment, I was not convinced that she came from this place, but I know that look. Returning to where you came from and loathing the mere touch and smell of its earth and air.

"Where are they?"

Tekla pulls the bearskin close to ward off the chill.

"I told you. North, up the coast a ways. Small but fortified stronghold near the shore. If we land any closer, he'll know; the best approach is from here. With only one ship..."

"I know," I growl, regretting that I spoke. Old age is a sly beast, making your mind wander and fret.

The crew readies their gear, and Thorvald hefts his axe, fastens his cloak: dyed-blue wool trimmed with wolf. He is the only one who does not seem bothered by the cold. Some whisper he is a skin-changer, like my father, his grandfather. Here and now, I might believe it myself.

Further up the sloping shoreline, where the sand ends and the tufty grey-green grass begins, there is a narrow ditch scarring the ground. The soil in it is black, and though it is no wider than a footstep, we stop. Thorvald crouches, touching the earth with a shudder.

"Ashes. Crumbled bones."

"Human," Tekla says, face flushed. "Burnt flesh and dirt."

I am standing on a precipice, and this narrow trench is the abyss, glinting with splintered skulls and crushed teeth.

"And if we cross it?" I ask.

Her tone is flat. "Then we cross a line of ash and dirt and bone."

Some of the men and women in my hird grasp the bronze and iron hammers around their necks, mumbling staves and runes.

"It's a curse, then," Thorvald says.

"No curse." Tekla's voice is defiant. "No curse, because he has no craft."

"How'd you know?" one man asks.

"Because he tried to kill me once. Because I stopped him. I was just a girl, but even so, what little power I had frightened him. That's why he sold me."

"How far does the ditch reach?" I ask.

Tekla's eyes are pools of night, distant stars sunken in their depths.

"All 'round the island."

I think of Kettil's face, the only flicker of light I have left to guide my steps in this bleak and endless darkness. Then I step across.

Thorvald is next, then the rest: slow and hesitant, but they follow. Tekla walks on ahead, and I realize that she crossed before any of us. She did not hesitate, just stepped over and kept going toward the treeline.

***

Kettil

He is in the cage, face down, with the taste of bile and blood and beast on his tongue.

"Can you hear it?" a woman whispers, so close the words stir the hairs on the back of his head, but he does not open his eyes. He has seen enough ghosts.

"Can you feel it, then? In the ground." The voice is Tekla's now. He keeps his eyes closed, but turns his head, flattening his cold and aching body into the dirt, and there it is: a tremor, distant and faint.

"Someone's coming." It's Mother's voice but Tekla's touch, smoothing his matted fur when he whimpers. "We're coming for you."

He opens his eyes, but the cage is empty. No Tekla, no Mother.

His heart slows, his breathing falters. Soon, he will be less than smoke, less than ashes, less than shadow. Soon, the door will open, but no one is coming for him except White Bear.

***

Astrid

We make camp beside a stream as the leaden sky darkens. There's a stillness in the air, between the stunted, twisted trees, that makes my gut twist and my blood quaver. We took too long, I know that. A month and more to get here, with Kettil alone in this place that seems to teeter at the edge of the underworld, with the serpent gnashing at the roots of the World Tree under our feet.

Thorvald sits with me, and our eyes drift to Tekla by the small fire. The others sit in a rough circle, tending to weapons, talking in low voices. Some glance at the trees around us, on guard.

"You're bedding her."

He shifts his weight and grins. "For a year or more."

"Not that you ever told me."

"I've never told you of any woman I've bedded. It only bothers you because you don't like her." He gives me a sideways glance. "Or perhaps, you like her too much. Your bed's been cold since Sigrid."

A look makes him fall silent. "I need her help. It's hard for an old warrior to need anyone's help, let alone the help of a nursemaid." I watch as Tekla stares into the flickering heat as if deciphering the glow and flames. "Does she truly have the sight and craft?"

He shrugs. "I've seen her read the dice and bones. Like any seer, she sees true with the Mother's help."

"That is no small thing. Sigrid and I saw women wield the Mother's craft in the south, near Miklagård. They were strong. Her priestesses wore necklaces made of men's balls."

Thorvald's grin widens. "No one takes my balls unbidden, for necklaces or otherwise."

We listen to the night for a while, to the breath of wind in grass and stunted trees.

"That ditch," I mutter, not sure if Thorvald hears me. "The ash and bone. It reminded me..."

"Of Grendel?"

I nod, but in truth, I am thinking of Grendel's mother and her lair—that yawning pit of ancient shadows below the world, that stench of rot and sickness. None of those who follow me now have seen such darkness. They do not know it lurks ever beneath them, and within.

"Tell the story."

Thorvald's voice stirs me from the gloom.

"What?"

"Grendel. Tell the story."

"I've told it a thousand times since you were a boy."

"Yes. But it's a good story. And you tell it well."

There's a childish eagerness in his face, and in the crew's voices, even Tekla's, as they call support, and finally I acquiesce. I trace the tale, like I trace the ragged scar on my shoulder, memories etched in flesh and skin: King Hrothgar's welcome, how uneasily we slept in the hall that first night, Grendel ripping through us before Beowulf snagged him on a spear and took off his arm.

Tekla's eyes are on me while I speak, and for a moment, I can almost fool myself into thinking it's Sigrid sitting there, ready to strum her gilded lyre.

I've heard the tale told differently in some parts now: that Grendel was a monster, a beast; that Beowulf alone dared follow Grendel's mother into the dank horror of her den. But I remember how it was. I remember Grendel's pale eyes in the firelight, his howl as he scorched his bleeding arm-stump in the embers. I remember his mother, crouching low in the hall when she came for us, her blond hair a nest of twigs and grass, hands as strong as roots and tide. I remember leaving even Sigrid behind, and following Beowulf into her lair. There, Beowulf and I fought her, and she was stronger than anyone I've grappled with before or since.

It smelled like death in that cave, *our* death: mine and Beowulf's. Yet in the end, it was the wyrm that came for him. And when it did, he would not let me follow; it had come for him alone. *Go home to Sigrid*, he said. *Live, grow old.* And I have.

When I stood with Sigrid by Beowulf's pyre, I thought I wanted to die the same way: grasping a sword, its edge bloodied and blunted, bound for Odin's halls. But since Sigrid left and took her songs with her, I've wondered: What if the halls are empty? What if there is nothing beyond the dark? What if there is only the pyre, if I'm lucky? What if there are only crows and ravens picking my carcass clean, if I'm not?

***

In the night, a shadow leans over me. I see its face: Sigrid.

Sigrid, who has followed the waves and currents, who has crawled up from the bottom of the sea, her soul still clinging to her unburned corpse. She digs into my ribcage, sodden fingers clawing for my heart. Her face is so close that I can see the empty sockets, smell the seaweed and salt, so close that I can peer right inside her skull—picked clean beneath the sea.

Bony fingers clutch me, hard and merciless, and Sigrid's jaw is moving, as if to speak, whether to warn or curse me I do not know.

"Astrid!"

Tekla wakes me: a tangle of stars and rent clouds above her head, her voice a hiss. The chill of Sigrid's touch lingers.

"Someone's here."

I shake her off. There is a stifled cry nearby, flashes of iron, and a blade scrapes my side, slashing through cloak, tunic, skin. Garm growls and snaps, and I see them: two men, maybe three, tearing through the camp, silent daggers stabbing where they can, my hird scrambling for weapons of their own.

All is mayhem, until Tekla speaks one word, barely more than a whisper. Arms outstretched, fur and silk shed, wearing nothing but her linen shift, she is suddenly aflame: tongues of fire flickering in her hands, unbound black hair a blazing crown. The attackers flee into the night. Some chase after them, but Thorvald calls them back to avoid an ambush.

The flames die down as Tekla lowers her arms. She is shaking but unscathed, steadying herself when Thorvald wraps her in the bearskin cloak.

There's a searing pain in my ribcage, and Garm is limping, licking blood off his paws. Only one man is seriously injured, Egil, the youngest. Tekla tells us to lay him down beside the fire, and to bring a skin of mead. I watch as the crew obeys her with a newfound quickness.

Egil shudders, blood gushing from his throat and mouth. Too much of it, too quickly.

"Drink," Tekla says, holding the mead to his lips, making sure Egil's hand is grasping a sword. "The Valkyries will give you the second cup when you sit in Odin's hall."

She leans over him, singing softly into his ear, something only he can hear.

It doesn't take long. He shudders, then it's done.

Afterwards, I watch her moving among the crew, tending wounds, directing Thorvald to feed the fire for light and warmth: no need for stealth now. In the pale dawn glow, the fur and silk of the cloak gleams like burnished treasure. I thought her foolish, asking only for that garment, but the way she wears it, the way it holds her up, the way she moves in it, the way the crew looks at her now, I understand.

When she comes to me, I am stripped down to my skin, rinsing the wound on my side with water from the creek. I've already washed Garm's paws and legs clean and found no cut or tear, but the dog won't stop limping.

Her gaze rakes across my aged and worn body: the scars scored into my skin, the sagging flesh, the blond and grizzled hair unravelled from its braid. I stand before her, laid bare as the years have made me.

"What do you see?" I ask.

Her eyes glitter with what might be either regret or pity. I want neither.

"I see you, Astrid. As you are and as you were. I see your beginning, and your end."

I rub my shoulder, feeling the old memory of jagged flint digging into joint and sinew as Grendel's mother tried to slay me. "What did you tell Egil as he died?"

She does not answer. Instead, she opens the jar of healing salve she carries in the pouch at her waist. It smells of pinesap and sun and childhood summers—my own and Kettil's—and it is almost more than I can stand. All the grief and glory, all the sweet and bitter days of my life, are in that scent.

"The fire...*your* fire," I say, voice unsteady. "Did Kettil know?"

"I could hide nothing from Kettil," she says, a smile reaching her lips before it fades. "Nor he from me. When you first tasked me with looking after him, we were both children. He followed me everywhere, even when I told him it was not his place to trail behind a thrall. Sometimes, if no one was around to see, I'd snap flames up between my fingers just to make him laugh." Her voice and fingers are firm and sure as she applies the salve to my skin. "I asked him never to tell anyone, not even you, and he never did. He kept my secrets, as I kept his."

"Never saw anything like it in all my days."

"It's dangerous for a woman like me to show anyone her power. Better to use it where it isn't seen, unless the need is great. A man who sees a woman with such power might try to break her. Or own her."

She puts the jar away, wiping her hands on the shift beneath the cloak, and her gaze strays to Thorvald. He is throwing wood on the fire, and the smell of burning brings back the reek on the wind the day we returned to the homestead. We sailed into the smoky haze veiling the shore, Thorvald jumping the railing, wading chest-deep in the water, bellowing at the ruin of it all.

My own body, then, was heavy as rock and iron. Sinking.

The dead had been thrown into the well. We pulled them out, and I looked for Kettil's tunic, for his blond hair, for his boyish hands, among the corpses, but he was gone. Carried off while Tekla hid in the woods and watched my home burn.

"Why'd you not help them when the raiders came?" Rage and bitterness burn my tongue while I get dressed, and I taste salt and iron, grief and pain. "Why'd you not wield your fire then? Why'd you not save them?"

The bearskin cloak hangs limp and heavy around her, too long for her slight frame, its bulk weighing her down rather than holding her up. For a moment she is neither thrall nor seer, but only a girl.

"I saw *him*. I saw White Bear, and I was afraid... Afraid he'd take me back here."

She keeps her eyes on Thorvald, speaking low so he won't hear.

"White Bear butchered my mother when I was five. Then he laid me on the block. Said he knew I had a power in me, that he would devour it to make him stronger. I burned him. Didn't even know I could wield the fire then, but I did it. After that, he kept me in a cage until he sold me." She scratches at her skin under the furry collar. "I had two brothers and a sister. Their bones are in that ditch we crossed. I've heard their whispers since we set foot on the shore."

I shiver, old and spent and tired. "What end do you see for me? Speak true."

"I see the dragon. Nothing else."

What does it mean, I wonder, that I don't doubt her?

"When?"

"Soon."

I breathe out my sorrow and rage.

"Good. There's not much left to do, then."

***

We reach the village in early morning, though the sky is so dark it might be dusk. From a hilltop, we look down on thirty longhouses, sod-roofed, horses grazing, pigs rooting, forty armed men within, give or take. Garm trembles beside me, and Tekla shivers beneath the cloak.

"Where would he keep Kettil?"

She points at one of the longhouses: no smoke is rising from it and it has only one door, barred from the outside.

"Wait." Her voice is soft, but I sense the power gathering about her, sense it in the ground, through the leather of my boots. It's in the air, too, a far-off rumble like a storm approaching, as if air and earth and sky are twisting in her grip. When she spreads her arms, a mist rises, rolling in from the fields and dells.

She murmurs a word, and her hands and hair flicker, red and yellow flame.

Below, a man is brandishing a spear: we've been noticed. A shaggy white skin hangs down his back, pinned around his shoulders. He is shouting, but I cannot make out the words because the storm is breaking. Grim clouds swallow up the world. Rain like ropes lashes the ground, turning dirt and grass to mud. Lightning crackles above and below, the force of it clawing at my hair and skin.

Thorvald bellows at the crew and we run down the slope, boots slipping in the muck. I am running blind in the streaming rain, waiting for a spear or arrow to take me.

I am glad Sigrid is not here for this. This is no battle for songs or tales. This is death. My death.

By the time we get to the wall we are roaring with battle fury. Thorvald bursts the gate off its posts with nought but his axe and body, or maybe it shatters from the lightning, or maybe Thor himself rips it off its hinges. I can't tell. The defenders fall—screaming, dying—and there is an almighty clap of thunder that splits the world and sky, from the roots of the earth to the vault of heaven above. For long moments the world is white.

When I regain my sight, men are scattered on the ground, the smell of burnt flesh mixing with the rain.

"Lightning!" Thorvald yells, a feral grin on his face, blood in his beard, the beast he hides inside peeking out beneath his brows.

Garm is beside me, tearing armour and flesh. My own sword is bloodied, but I do not recall how many I have slain.

Our enemies flee and fall and die as the storm empties itself into the world. And when the rain lets up, there is a moment of stillness as the sun breaks through, as the light glitters in the puddles, in the dirt, in the entrails and the blood.

At last, I am standing with Thorvald in front of the house Tekla pointed out. We do not speak. Thorvald lifts the bar and pushes the door open.

I step inside, into the same smell of filth and rot I found in the lair of Grendel's mother. Shapes are moving, scrambling towards me, past me. Children. Small and pale. Hobbled and bound. Cowering in the sun, weeping in the light when they see our faces.

None of them is Kettil.

"What is this place?" Thorvald's voice is quaking. He has not seen the pit below the world before. He has not seen the darkness that lurks ever beneath our feet, within ourselves, until now.

The longhouse is empty, so I think. But as I pace further inside, I know it isn't so. In the inmost part is a cage of wood and iron. Small and low.

Something moves inside.

"Light, Thorvald."

Thorvald does not reach for a torch or candle, he busts through the wall with his axe: two strokes to crack the lumber, clay, and straw.

The thing in the cage moves again. It is small and furry, grunting in the rays of sun. Before I can get closer, Tekla rushes past me, the bearskin rustling. She has taken Thorvald's axe and wields it with a fierceness that belies her slender frame. The stroke falls and splinters fly, metal, wood. Another stroke, then Thorvald is beside her, shouting at her to stop, yet she manages a third stroke, and the small prison shatters. Thorvald pulls the axe from her grip, but she is already kneeling in the remains of the cage, shedding the cloak and throwing it over the cowering, whimpering thing. A small creature, that might be soothed by the thick pelt, by the scent lingering in the silk.

I cannot tell what it is, and yet I know.

"Kettil?"

Tekla is speaking to Thorvald, close and quick, words I do not hear, and he picks up the cloak and whatever is inside it.

"Kettil."

No answer.

"I have him," Thorvald tells me as he carries the bundle outside. "I have him, Astrid."

"Take him home," I say. Or maybe it's just a whisper. Or maybe I can't speak at all, but I catch sight of Thorvald's face and his expression is as good as any oath sworn by fire and blood.

Something else moves, then. Bursting out of the dirt, out of the rags and wood in the corner beyond the broken cage.

White Bear. Man-eater. Child-killer. Beast. Monster. *Man.*

His wrists and hands are festooned with leather straps holding iron claws. A soiled white bear skin hangs down his back, teeth and claws strung around his neck. He is the biggest man I have ever seen. Half again as tall as Thorvald, flesh inked with runes.

"Astrid!"

Thorvald is at the threshold, still holding the bundled cloak. Beyond him is Tekla, and the glance she gives me carries everything. I know. She knows. And it will be all right.

Go home, I think as I shove Thorvald out the door and kick it shut. *Live. Get old.*

I turn to see Garm—fur matted with dirt and blood—leaping out of the shadows. Teeth bared, jaws open, ripping into White Bear's arm. Iron claws slash, Garm whimpers, and there's the thud of bones hitting the wall.

White Bear's face is bruised and bleeding from lip and nose. His mouth speaks, but I am in the silent space between light and dark, between sky and heaven, between this side and the next. I am the Mother, come to claim my due.

He lashes out, claws reaching for me, but nothing can stop me because there is no life to hold on to anymore. Nothing tethers me to this world except this fight, this vengeance, this death. There is only me and him, there is only this sword, this final stroke, that takes White Bear in the throat. There are only his cold and stained talons stabbing through my belly, and in that moment the dragon comes for me. I see it clearly through the shadows and blood: the blue ice-shimmer of its scales, the hoarfrost twinkle of its hide, its wings spread above me like the vault of sky and heaven, one and the same.

I hear its voice, and it is Sigrid's voice, singing words only I can hear.

Carry me, I think, whisper, scream.

And then I soar.

***

Kettil

Tekla sings as Mother burns. She sings of the Valkyries and Odin's hall, of the drinking horns overflowing, of a roof thatched with gold. Kettil listens. The cloak is warm: Mother's cloak with the smell of her still hidden in the folds of fur and silk, underneath the smell of fire and smoke and Tekla.

Once upon a time, he was a boy. Once upon a time, he was a beast. Here and now, he is neither.

He lets the sun wash him clean, strip him bare. Its light is pure and harsh and unforgiving; healing, comforting, cleansing. It shines on him and through him: he sees right through himself, right through Mother's pyre, right through Tekla, too. Through sky and heaven into the everlasting darkness on the other side.

Once upon a time, before the World Tree Yggdrasil grew between them, there was sky and there was heaven. Once upon a time, they were one. Once, they will be again.

LONG AS I CAN SEE THE LIGHT

"DO YOU REMEMBER THAT NIGHT when we saw the light?"

She asks this as they're sitting on the balcony, and he turns to look at her. When he meets her gaze he can see the thing that lurks within her now—the presence that isn't really her—look back at him, peering out through those familiar blue eyes. A cold trickle of fear runs down his spine, and he almost gets up, he almost runs away from her again, but he has been running for so long already. He's too old to run, too tired.

What year is it? What month? He has to think about it for a while, and when he eventually remembers, he realizes that it's almost exactly forty years since he ran away from her the first time.

He inhales deeply from the cigarette, knowing it's his last smoke: a filthy, hand-rolled, slim and rather bitter stick of something that is supposed to resemble tobacco, but doesn't really. She asked him about that: where he got the cigarettes, why he started smoking. "No one smokes anymore," she said. "No one even manufactures cigarettes." And of course that's true enough. He could have told her that he picked up the habit in recent years when he lived rough in the alleys downtown. He could have told her that there are times and places and situations when sharing something, anything—even a lousy cigarette—with a stranger is a way to feel a connection, however briefly: a fragile tendril of community and communion. But in the end, he said nothing at all, just shrugged.

"Do you remember?" she asks again, prodding him. As if he could forget. As if that one memory is not his everlasting, never-ending nightmare.

He remembers it very well. He remembers sitting with her, with Lisa, in the park that night, in that small suburb outside Vancouver.

They sat next to each other on the blanket he had brought and spread out in the grass near the baseball field. The blanket was just for sitting on. It wasn't like he thought they'd be making out or anything like that. It wasn't like that between them, not then or ever. And that was fine, because Lisa was his friend. His best friend. His only friend, really, when he thinks about it now.

They were born the same year and grew up in the same cul-de-sac: they went to the same preschool, the same school, eventually the same high school. Through the years, Lisa stuck with him, even when other kids laughed at him and called him crazy or stupid. The doctors and his parents used words like "neurological disorder" instead, of course. Whatever that meant. All he knew was that he noticed some things that no one else seemed to see, and that he couldn't understand some things that others found self-evident. But Lisa never seemed to care about any of that. Lisa simply remained his friend.

The night when they saw the light, he had asked her to come with him to the park after dark, saying he wanted to show her something. Maybe she thought he'd bring his telescope and that they'd look at some planet, or the moon. They used to do that back then because they were both into science and science fiction and astronomy. He didn't tell her what he had seen in the park on the two previous nights: he just wanted her to come with him, because if she could see it too, then it had to be real, and not all in his head. She kept asking: "What is it? What is it you want me to see?" And he remembers saying: "You'll see. It'll be worth it."

She was always kind to me, he thinks, and feels a piercing sense of guilt and loss and grief as he sucks in another puff of stinking fake tobacco.

The woman who looks like Lisa, but who has someone else or something else hidden behind her eyes and beneath the bone of her skull, is still regarding him: her face is patient, compassionate, even. It's a convincing mask, but he knows better than to trust her.

They sat side by side in the grass. It was warm and summery and early July. She looked up at the sky, and he looked up at the sky, too, when he wasn't looking at her. "Which star do you want to go to," she asked, and he laughed. They had played that game from when they were kids, picking out stars to go to, imagining the planets around those stars and the beings and creatures inhabiting those worlds. And right when he was going to answer, when he was going to tell her which star he would pick that night...there it was. It looked exactly like when he had seen it before: surfacing in the night sky above them without warning like a gigantic metallic whale in deep ocean water, suspended between the stars. It looked close, but somehow you knew that it was far away—a shiny, luminescent metal hull, just hanging there above the Earth: terrifying, menacing, and wondrous all at once.

He heard her gasp and knew that it was real, that she could see it too, and he felt relieved. The first night he had seen it, he thought he must have imagined it, but then it had come back the second night. This was the third time he beheld it, and still his mind could barely contain the sheer mind-bending enormity of it. Everything about it—its glow, the smoothness of its surface, the magnitude of it—was utterly and undeniably alien.

Lisa looked at him with a strange expression, halfway between terror and elation, and she opened her mouth, as if to say something. Through the years he has often wondered what she was going to say, but he will never know, because in that moment the light hit her. A blinding, radiant, noiseless beam coming down from the metal hull above, lighting up her face and striking her down. She fell, fell flat on her back on the blanket.

And what did he do? He looked up and saw the ship disappear again, slipping back into the universe, unseen, while Lisa lay there, dead, on the ground. The light had killed her, that's what he assumed. So he ran. What else was there to do? It was the alien invasion. The takeover, doomsday, Armageddon, whatever you'd like to call it. He ran. And as he ran he saw the light come down again and again and again: that beam multiplying, stabbing down soundlessly, into the houses all the way down his street. Into his house, too, where his parents lived. He never saw them again. There is an almost unbearable emptiness in that thought.

He ran: crying, screaming, stumbling. He ran, wondering why it had stabbed Lisa and not him, wondering why there had been no warning, wondering how it was possible—with radar and NASA and satellites and internet—that no one knew it was there. No one but him, and he hadn't told anyone, hadn't warned anyone, not even Lisa. Instead he had brought her right to it. He ran, and kept running while the world was struck down all around him, and he kept running for forty years. Until today.

"What happened to you after that night?"

He looks at the glowing tip of the cigarette, not sure if he can, or wants to tell her. Certainly he doesn't remember all of it. He remembers running that whole night until he could go no farther. He remembers seeing people being hit, sprawling on the sidewalks, cars and trucks stopped dead on bridges and highways. He remembers looking up, but there was no sign of that massive hulk of metal up above. Still, the light struck from nowhere and everywhere.

Finally, he fell asleep in a ditch on the outskirts of Vancouver—just rolled into some bushes next to the road and passed out. When he woke up it was daylight, and everything looked normal: people walking around, buses and cars driving, everything as it should be. No dead bodies. No carnage. He couldn't understand it and stumbled through the streets, feeling half-dead and probably looking more than half crazy. Someone must have seen him and set the police on him, because soon four policemen descended. He remembers that three of them had oddly smooth, placid expressions as they looked at him, while the fourth seemed concerned and worried, asking: "What are you doing here? Are you hurt?"

Nobody else asked him that. The three other officers gazed at him silently and when he looked into their faces he saw it, saw that other presence for the first time. It—whatever it was—looked out at him through three pairs of human eyes, and he felt his heart slow and almost stop.

"Leave him," one of the three said, and the fourth policeman turned as if to question that order.

He wasn't even surprised when the light struck that fourth policeman down and he fell. He almost expected it. This time he stayed and watched: saw the man rise again after a few minutes, brush off his uniform and straighten his jacket and then turn and walk away with the others like nothing had happened.

Once the police were gone, he started running again. For days he ran and walked, stumbled and hid. He stole cars, bicycles, even a boat to get himself as far away from the city as he possibly could, heading into the northern wilderness along the Pacific Coast. There were less people there, more safety, he figured, but every time he met someone, he saw that other presence, that intruder, gazing out at him: every human face had become a mask with something else peeking out through the eye sockets.

He went up the coast, farther into the wild. Life wasn't bad in the woods, along the ocean, but it was hard. He fished in the streams and ocean shallows, dug for clams and caught crabs, stole food sometimes, and went deep into the forest. A few times he was attacked, not by humans, but by bears, and cougars. He suffered through a few bouts of what might have been pneumonia over the years, and one time he almost died from an infection: a small cut on his shoulder that turned foul and black. In the end, he managed to steal some medical supplies from a truck and get rid of it, but his left arm hasn't been the same since.

How many years did he live in the wild? Almost thirty-five years it seems, though he is astounded it was that long. Some of those years, maybe most of them, he cannot remember. Amnesia or psychosis, the medical professionals might say. Post-traumatic stress. A mental breakdown. Paranoia. Whatever. His brain is like that, he knows now. Sometimes it clocks out when things get to be too much. But through it all, a part of his mind was always working away: remembering Lisa, remembering the light, remembering that night in the park, fitting the memories together with what he saw afterwards, trying to piece it all together, trying to understand what had happened to him, and to everyone else.

Even in the woods he occasionally ran into other people. Mining and logging operations seemed to be expanding every year, creeping ever farther into the wilderness. One time, he walked right into a group of workers near a hydroelectric dam. First, he thought they would kill or try to capture him, but they all just looked at him where he stood at the edge of the forest, saying nothing. Eventually they went back to their work. They were indifferent to his presence, almost as if they could not even see him, as if they knew he was not like them, as if they knew he had seen the light, but had not been touched by it.

The woods were not a bad place to be, but the years wore him down, and eventually he got sick. Sick and old. It was then that he started walking back to where he'd come from: back to the city. He was scared, but he figured he was sick and old enough that maybe no one would care.

When he came back to Vancouver five years ago, wandering across the old abandoned bridge that led into what used to be the park but was now the ever-expanding Space Hub, he could hardly believe his eyes. It was another world: brilliant lights illuminating the vessels being assembled; people crawling all over a vast expanse of metal and concrete; and all of those people working and working and working, ceaselessly, day and night. And the cars were all gone, that's something else he noticed right away: no combustion engines anymore. Just clean vehicles, quiet and efficient, running along the spotless streets. It was like arriving on another planet.

He ended up in the alleys of the Downtown Eastside. In the old days, it was a place for poor people, drug users, and misfits living precariously on the margins of society. It still is. Except now the misfits are those who have not been touched by the light. He has realized that most of them are like he is, that their minds are different somehow, deviating in minor or major ways from the norm. And he has realized that the Downtown Eastside is a pen, a ghetto, maintained to contain the dwindling number of untouched who have stubbornly refused to die.

In some ways the area has improved in the past forty years, he supposes. The alleys are cleaner, there are no drug dealers and no stores selling liquor or tobacco, and there is food and shelter for those who want it. Not that he has ever taken any charity. He knows what they are, these people who say they want to help. He has allowed them to treat his infections and illnesses, but afterwards he always goes back to the alleys. Before the light came, it was the do-gooders and religious nutters helping out the needy. Now it is the people who were stabbed by the light doing it: all of them kindly indifferent as they hand out blankets and food and medication. He knows they are not what they seem, that they want brains, souls, life force, whatever. Through the years he has told everyone he meets what he knows, yet nothing happens to him, and no one believes him. No one else can see it, no one else understands.

Suddenly he realizes that he's been talking out loud, that he has been telling her everything passing through his mind. He hears himself say:

"I slept in doorways, mostly. Scrounged food from garbage cans, ate rats."

"And then I found you."

He nods. Then she found him. Today. He figures she must have been looking for him, but he doesn't understand why. She found him sitting outside an old crumbling brick building, putting on a new pair of socks. There she was. Lisa. Not dead. Older, but much the same, even though he knows it isn't really Lisa anymore behind those eyes.

She stopped and looked at him in his filth and poverty. Looked at him like Lisa might have looked, her face soft and kind and gentle, but it was still just another mask, albeit a familiar one.

"Thomas," she said, and it wasn't a question. She knew. She even touched his hand the way the real Lisa used to. She's doing it now, here on the balcony too, squeezing his fingers lightly, smiling at him. And even though he knows it is not really Lisa, he begins to cry.

"Are you all right?"

She asks him this. As if he could be all right. She has brought him to this place, this apartment on the waterfront, with mountains on the horizon, a bird's eye view of the Space Hub, and the underwater industrial domes glinting far away in the dark ocean beyond. He has had a shower for the first time in months. She has fed him, and he is wearing the clean clothes she got for him: some kind of workman's overalls, but clean and comfortable.

His cigarette has burned out. There will be no more cigarettes for him, he is very sure of that. He looks up at the stars, though they are hard to see here because of all the lights. It is a summer night, just like the last time he sat next to her.

"Which star do you want to go to?" he asks, and she sort of smiles, but he knows that the question means something else to her now than it used to.

She starts talking. She tells him that his parents died some years before. They were good people and always missed him, she says, but they kept busy working in the space program after he disappeared. He thinks about his mother, who was an elementary school teacher, and his father, who worked his whole life at the port. He tries to imagine them working for a space program, but that is obviously impossible. Still, he cries for them, too.

"Thomas. Why do you think I brought you here?"

"To kill me. Or to let them take me. One way or another you will destroy me."

She sighs.

"What is it you think happened when the light came? Can you tell me that?"

"I don't need to tell you. You know. Your kind knows."

"My kind? I see. But I would still like to hear you say it. Explain it to me. Explain why you ran away and kept running for forty years."

So he tells her. He tells her what he has spent so many sleepless nights and haunted days figuring out, piecing together. That something travelled across space and time in that enormous spacecraft. That it, they, came to Earth and entered orbit and stabbed people's souls and hearts and minds with that light, taking them over, taking them away.

She says nothing, so he keeps talking.

"I think they wander the stars. Whether they are lost or exiled, I don't know. I think they have been traveling the galaxies for millennia. Maybe they have a goal in mind, maybe not. But they want to keep traveling, and they need resources to do so. I wonder how many worlds they've taken before this, how many worlds have been stripped of everything, just like our world is being stripped. The population taken and re-focused on one thing: producing the means for them, whoever they are, to keep going through the universe. I don't know what they are building exactly, or what they are extracting from the bottom of the ocean and the depths of earth, but I see the signs of their plan everywhere: new technology, mining, construction, space projects, everything consuming the earth. I figure after forty years they are probably almost ready to leave."

She is quiet for a moment, and then she laughs, a soft and not unpleasant sound.

"Oh, Thomas. Is that really what you think?"

He expected her to be colder and harder than this. He did not expect soft laughter, or the hand that still holds his.

"Let me tell you another story, a different story. You will probably not believe it, but I will tell it anyway. What if there were others out there, among the stars, just like you and I always hoped. What if they can indeed travel space and time, and what if they came here and saw us, watched us, watched our world, and saw us suffer through misery and war and poverty and disease and pain? And what if they realized that the reason for all that misery was locked deep inside our minds, and that we, the human beings, would never ever be free or happy or able to join this great universe as citizens until we cast off all the fears and doubts and weaknesses of our minds. What if they could cure us? Yes. Cure. Not 'take.' Not 'kill.' Not 'use.' Just free us, cure us, and then we would still be human, but stronger, and better."

She is right: he does not believe it.

"Just like that? One bright light, and then we're cured of every ill that's plagued humanity for over ten thousand years?"

She nods. He closes his eyes for a moment. It is a good story. It is a story that maybe, somewhere, he has thought of before, long before the lights came, during the nights when he and Lisa talked and watched the stars. It is not a true story, though. It can't be true. He has seen enough to know it isn't true, and he tells her that when he is able to speak again.

"What do you really know, Thomas? And what have you imagined, twisting reality to fit your own fears? Can you honestly tell me that your perception of other people, of this world, of the things around you has always been reliable?"

He knows the answer is "no," but he doesn't want to tell her that. Instead he says:

"Why didn't the light take me that night? Why did it take you but not me?"

"It couldn't touch you, because your mind would have been...damaged. That is why some people were left out."

"But now it wants me? Are you that desperate? I guess you're running out of human bodies to do the work. I've noticed that there are fewer children. Are you really not able to breed enough new humans to meet the demand?"

She turns away. Maybe she sighs. Maybe she pretends to wipe away a tear.

"You are older. Things have changed in you. And if you can let it take you, willingly, and not be afraid, then you will be all right. I know it."

"So why not just take me? Like you were taken? Like everyone else was taken."

"Because it's better this way. No one wants to hurt you."

"Did it hurt you? When they took you?"

She still doesn't look at him, just shakes her head, gently.

"You're the one who is in pain, Thomas."

It is the truth, but he doesn't want to hear it. He looks at Lisa. She is looking at the stars now. He wonders what the thing inside her sees when it watches the night sky. Forty years is a long time. He can feel the years in his bones, feel the distances he's traveled in his sinews and joints, feel the cold nights and the biting winters in his flesh. He is scarred and weathered, aged and diminished.

"I know what I have seen," he says, stubbornly.

"You know what I have seen?" Her eyes are suddenly strangely large and luminous in the dark. "I have seen a world without war for almost half a century. I have seen a world where human beings work together to develop the means for space travel and exploration. I have seen a world where every human being is better off than they were back then. How is that a horror story, Thomas? It is a story of salvation."

He thinks about that. He feels very old and tired and alone.

"I wish I'd gone back to see my parents, just one time."

"Why didn't you?"

"Because I knew they'd do to me what you are doing now. They would let me be taken."

"Thomas..."

"No." He tries to fight it, fight her, fight his own weakness. "Tell me what you've done to the humans. Tell me where they are. Are they still inside you? Are their minds trapped inside you? And when you're finished with this planet, will they all die then? Or will you let them go back to what they were before?"

She doesn't get angry, doesn't even raise her voice.

"Don't you want to believe it?" she asks. "That there is a better way to be human, that we are the real humans, and that you are the twisted remnant of what we no longer have to be: crippled by anxieties and fears and aggression that you don't even understand yourself. We are free. We are making this world better."

"By using up the Earth? By using up every human being in this world to leave this planet?" He is speaking louder, more desperately now, as if trying to get the words out before it's too late. "To build those damn spaceships, to take flight, to go into space again, to go out there among the stars and take another world, devour other planets and other souls and other knowledge, just to propel yourselves a little farther into eternity?"

"You know that space is where humanity is meant to go. You used to believe that, too."

"Humanity, yes. But you are not human."

She is very quiet for a very long time.

"Thomas," she says finally. "Which star do you want to go to?"

And then he cracks. It is not a violent, painful thing. Rather, it is a relief: to give up, to surrender, to no longer have to fight. The light takes him almost right away: hits him, envelops him in its blinding power. This time it shines inside him, and he feels it burn away and sizzle and destroy. And for a moment he is nothing, he is annihilated, he is dead, but there is no darkness because he is starlight, pure and everlasting, and in that radiant purity he senses something else stir inside him, someone else, an awakening presence that either comes from outside or has always been there, he isn't exactly sure.

The last thing he feels before his body is taken away from him, before the presence fully takes hold, is Lisa—or rather: the thing that is not Lisa—letting go of his hand.

The last thing he sees—as the new presence in his mind overpowers and submerges his consciousness—is a brief glimpse of the night sky: the distant stars suddenly more familiar and alluring than they have ever been before.

The last thing he thinks is: "I was right! I was right all along!" He even tries to speak, scream, shout the words, but it is not his mouth anymore.

After that, the light goes out.

BLACKDOG

FROM HER CELL, AINA WATCHES the Man through the basement window, her face as close to the dirt-streaked glass as the bars will allow. It's another night of burning. Another night when the Man is feeding a fire in the yard. As always, the Shade clings to him like a shroud, its bloated, indistinct shape revealed in the reddish shudder of flames.

If Aina stands in a certain spot, peering up at a certain angle, she can make out the wisps of smoke mingling and gathering above the bonfire. They curl through the bare branches of the yard's oak trees, swirling and twisting in the night breeze, until they resemble bats with tattered wings. A murmuration of shadows, they circle the yard, swooping low in front of her window, then soaring high, cutting through the tips of the flames, never catching alight. Nimble and swift, they throw themselves into the sky and disappear, just like they did the first night after the Man locked her in here.

Wood, she thought then, when the Man threw bundles on the fire, but she knows better now. The smell tells her what it is.

Aina has seen the fire burn in the yard many times since she was imprisoned here, has seen the wings scatter across the bruised sky again and again. She knows they will be back before sunrise, their slight bodies heavier and slower, as though they've fed elsewhere.

Tonight, one winged creature lingers, too busy enjoying its own flight to set out with the others. It dives and weaves through the flames, plunging lower, skimming the gravel until it's level with her window. Once, twice, it sweeps past in the firelit darkness beyond the glass, and Aina stares as it hovers there for a moment, barely bigger than a moth, close enough that she can almost make out its shape and features.

A *bat*, Aina tells herself with a shiver of uncertainty, because there is an instant when the creature's shape shifts to something else, something *other*, quivering and trembling...but once she makes up her mind that it *is* a bat, its body seems to settle.

They peer at each other through the glass for the space of a breath: Aina with her wide, brown eyes curtained by lank, black hair; the winged and jagged thing with its inky eyes, lit from within by tiny red sparks. Then, with a flourish of its wings, the creature vanishes into the night like the others, and Aina feels a twinge of sadness as it disappears.

In the yard, the Man has nothing more to put on the fire. He stirs the cinder and ashes with a long stick; the Shade on his back so thick and bloated it almost obscures him completely from her sight.

One night, it will be her turn to become embers and flame, to leave this place in a curl of smoke; her ashes shovelled into a wheelbarrow and disposed of in the fields beyond the house once they've cooled. She has known this since she walked up the long gravel path from the country road to the lonely house, seeking shelter. Since she saw the naked trees and the circle of singed ground. Since the Man dragged her down the stairs, ignoring her screams even though she yelled so loud that the world should have cracked around her, the force of her voice shattering the thin blue sky, the rough walls of stone. Instead, the cell door clanged shut behind her.

Ever since, she has known there is no mercy here, and no way out.

Sitting cross-legged on the heap of blankets that serves as her bed, she huddles against the wall, and removes the flute from its hiding place. She found it on her second night, buried in a shallow hole beneath a loose floor tile. It was wrapped in a soiled piece of fabric, along with a slender blade fashioned from pliable metal, like the fragment of a tin can. The blade is thin and crude, too feeble to cut the metal bars, the concrete floor, or the Man, but sharp enough to have carved the smooth, whitish-grey flute.

After testing the blade's edge on her thumb, she stows it and puts her lips to the flute, fingers caressing the carefully shaped holes, coaxing soft notes from the hollowed bone. Closing her eyes, she can almost see the ghost it summons, a wavering silhouette seated across from her, listening.

***

The Man comes to see Aina the next day. As always, she hears his footsteps on the floor above; then, on the steep stairs; then, the keys in the reluctant locks of the first door; then, the bar being lifted; then, the second door, hook and latch; and finally, his unhurried footfalls through the dim hallway to her cell.

Sometimes, the Man comes alone, without the Shade. When that happens, he looks at her as if he might open the door and enter the cell, his mouth already half-open with hunger. Today, like most days, he wears the Shade like a cloak, rippling around his shoulders and head, undulating down his arms and legs, its lower edges bubbling around his feet like a viscous pool of tar.

Glancing at the Shade out of the corner of her eye, Aina can almost glimpse its real form beneath its husk of darkness; the slither and gleam of something scaly, slippery, ever-shifting.

"You can see me," the Shade said when they first met, its voice dribbling from the Man's lips. "It has been a long time since I have been seen."

In that moment, something half-forgotten and almost lost stirred inside Aina, beneath the dread: a transparent thorn of anger and defiance. The prickling of it almost made her remember who she used to be, before the world devoured everyone and everything she knew. Since that night, the Man has not spoken to her. He has not beaten her or touched her again, either, like he did the night he caught her. Only the Shade speaks to her, and that happens rarely.

Tonight, the Man slides a paper plate underneath the cage door. He doesn't bring food every day, and when he does, it is always the same: stale bread, boiled meat, cold vegetables from a can. After putting down the plate, he watches her intently with his round, pale eyes, rubbing his stubbly chin. In her wanderings, Aina has seen many men like him, and she knows what he covets above all else: desperation, fear, submission. To deny him, she stands immobile in the cell, a statue of herself, hands at her sides, eyes fixed on the wall behind the Shade, until disappointment creeps across his face.

Aina knows what the Man is beneath his cruelty and malice; a makeshift tool, capable of inflicting pain, nothing more. A puppet of meat and bone.

Other men visit the house, but they do not *serve* the Shade as the Man does. The visitors always arrive quietly at night, and soon turn loud and raucous, clamoring to have new bodies brought before them. The Man will bring them a child, sometimes two, and once they've fed, they leave in the cold hours, before another fire is lit.

The first time Aina saw visitors arrive, she screamed for help as they passed by her window, but their steps never even slowed. She learned quickly not to waste hope or breath on them.

Tonight, the Man lingers as the Shade pours towards her, careful as ever not to enter the cell or touch her. Its words slip out between the Man's lips, trickling down his rumpled shirt.

"So thin. So unkempt. How old are you, girl? Ten? Twelve? Maybe fourteen but stunted." A rustle and shudder. "No family searching for you. Where did they go, one wonders? Did you run away, did you leave them to die? By fire, water, earth, air...ah. Water," it hisses, taking note of her twitch. "Did you let them sink, did you wish they would? Did you watch them drown?"

No, she thinks, but holds her tongue, and that tiny thorn of defiant anger burrows deeper into her flesh, strengthening her resolve. *Mother let go of me. And then the water took her and everyone else. They left me behind.*

Aina has promised herself not to cry in front of the Shade or the Man. Anything they want from her they will have to take. She will give them nothing freely. Yet the Shade's words pry loose memories. Mother's hands thrusting her out of the water into the rolling skiff. Mother, who always said throughout their long journey: *Hold on to me, don't let go of my hand, don't you dare let go.* Mother, whispering, *I won't leave you.* Mother, pushing her, lifting her, shoving her with ruthless hands, forcing her into that boat, spluttering and heaving. Mother, sinking, while Aina was left to puke her guts out, alone, surrounded by the grey, pitiless sea and strangers as threadbare as herself.

"What can you do to me that hasn't already been done?" she says to the Shade, thorns bristling on her tongue. It laughs at her with the Man's wide mouth, a sound like gas bursting from the distended belly of a corpse, before it rears up and billows out from the Man, roiling closer to the bars.

"Whatever power you have, child, I will strip from you, shred by shred, vein by vein, thought by thought, until you are nothing."

Shivering, Aina turns away and eventually, she is alone again. Only then does she pick up the plate. She eats the bread and meat in the waning daylight, but the Shade's poison has seeped into her skin, and she feels its sting keenly as darkness falls.

***

That night, the world seems insubstantial enough to rip apart with a flick of the wrist, no matter how slender or dull the blade. Curled up under the blankets, hugging herself for warmth, Aina reaches for the one comfort she has left: a memory. She has kept it safe, tucked into the deepest folds of her mind, worn smooth as a river-tumbled rock, familiar to the touch, and she holds it gingerly so as not to taint or mar its sheen.

Once upon a time there was a blue-sky day, shimmery with sunlight and the buzz of honeybees. They were walking through a small village: Mother just a few steps in front of her, Father further up the road, carrying Brother on his shoulders. Others walked too, a ragged caravan tramping through the dirt, haunted faces gouged by hunger and loss. The people in the villages and towns they passed through always stopped and stared. Sometimes they offered food or shelter for a night, sometimes they threw rocks and cursed them, but this day there was no violence, only the usual onlookers. They passed a house on the outskirts where the early-summer fields stretched green into the distance. It was a small home, nothing special. A sagging roof. A glimpse of blue and white curtains in the windows. Flowering bean plants twirling around wooden stakes in the yard. The smell of sage and onions wafting through the air.

On the front steps sat a girl. A girl who looked so much like Aina herself—tousled dark curls, narrow shoulders, that sideways tilt of the head—that Aina stopped in her tracks. A large dog lay sprawled across the girl's lap. Its caramel fur was like glossy silk beneath the girl's hands and beneath her cheek as she rested her head on its neck. Aina is not sure how long she stood and watched them before Mother got her moving again, but never once did the girl look up. Maybe she wouldn't have seen her ragged twin even if she had. Maybe the road and everyone on it were nothing but Shades and Phantoms to her.

Aina closes her eyes and tries to dream herself into that memory, tries to feel the softness of caramel fur underneath her fingers, but she remains where she is, and the cold leaches out of the floor, through the blankets, into her bones.

***

Next morning, she has a fever. She tries to get up, but her knees buckle. All day and into the night, and into the next day, she burns and sweats and shivers. In her fever dreams, she tries to reach back to the beginning, past all the roads and streets, past the towns and villages, past the wicked sea, to find *home*, but the memories shrink away from her, receding ever faster the more desperately she grasps for them. Sometimes, she is under water, staring into Mother's face, yet in her brief moments of lucidity she sees only the Man, staring at her with his empty eyes.

Untethered from her body, Aina slips out between the bars, passing through doors and walls unseen, and glides along the corridors of the house, past chipped paint and wallpaper, musty wood and rusty pipes. She finds cages where other children are kept. An empty cell that smells of bleach and death in another part of the basement; a room on the second floor where a boy is kept, his soul scraped thin like wax paper; an empty room with scratch marks on the inside of the door at the top of the second set of stairs.

On the top floor, she slides through the ceiling into the attic where the Shade dwells, bloated and sluggish in the daylight leaking through shuttered windows and louvered vents. Along the attic's beams and rafters, winged shadows cluster, their smoke-thin bodies vague and transparent away from the flames and darkness. The Man is nowhere to be seen, but the Shade speaks to her.

"You can wander, girl, but you cannot leave," it hisses, and even in her dream, if that's what this is, it has the vicious bite of truth.

***

When Aina awakes it is barely dawn, and her fever has burned itself out. On the floor is a box of crackers and a plastic bowl full of water, but neither the Man nor the Shade are there. She drinks the water and wants more, wondering how long she's been away. In her sleep, she has soiled herself, but it barely matters. It's just another layer of dirt and filth to hold her together.

Her legs shake, bones rattling inside her skin, when she peers out the window.

In the yard, the remains of another fire are cooling; ashes and leaves swirling in the smudged dawn light, scattered by fierce gusts of wind.

Aina breathes in the lingering smell of burning and retches, thinking of the boy in the room upstairs.

Kneeling, she retrieves the blade from its hiding place and holds it tight in her fist. It would be so easy to leave, right now, to shed all defiance and anger, all frailty and fear. All it would take is a gentle ripple of metal, enough to widen the maw of the world until the darkness beneath it can swallow her whole. Quietly, the blade obliges, nipping at the palm of her hand, and she...

Aina's eyes snap open at the sound of shattered glass, and the shank falls from her grip. On the ground outside the broken window, a small, dark thing flaps and twists in the gravel. Dazed and struggling, it finally rights itself and Aina stares into a pair of murky, ember-lit eyes while the creature's shape trembles in the faint light.

"It's you," Aina says. "I saw you before, in the smoke."

"You're not supposed to see us." The creature pushes their fierce, predatory muzzle closer to the window while the wind tugs at their unfurled wings.

They glare at each other, and Aina sees her own defiance and wariness reflected in the creature's grim face.

"I'm Aina. What's your name?"

"We don't have names." They shift uneasily and look up at the sky, at the scattering ashes, as if worried about being seen. "We don't *need* names. We had them, but they burned away and now we're stronger and faster and nothing hurts us anymore."

"I can give you a name."

The eyes glow brighter for a moment. "What would we do with a name?"

Aina shrugs, afraid her eagerness to keep them close will scare them off. "Don't you want one?"

They cock their head, almost bird-like. "Give it to us and we'll tell you if we want it."

Aina holds her breath, watching their guarded, covetous face. "Your name is Batwing," she whispers, and to her relief they seem pleased, preening for a moment before their wings droop slightly.

"We are not bat." They sound almost apologetic.

"I know." Batwing's body has the sheen of black velvet, and Aina badly wants to stroke that supple pelt. "Come inside," she says, pointing to the crack in the window. "Just for a bit."

They hesitate, then lurch forward, staring at the trickle of blood the blade left behind on her hand. Aina holds her palm up closer to the glass. "You can have the blood, if you come inside. But maybe the crack is too small."

Batwing bristles at that, wings flared, and then, so quickly her eye cannot quite follow, they dissolve into tendrils of vapor and pass inside. Taking shape again, they land softly on the floor, cautiously approaching her blankets, clawed feet scratching the concrete.

Up close, they seem smaller and much less bat. Their eyes flit from Aina's outstretched hand to her face before they hop onto her cupped palm and start lapping up the blood. They shiver and shift as they lick her skin clean, tongue delving into the cut to get every last drop.

"Don't bite!" Aina exclaims, recoiling from the nip of bared fangs. Batwing shoots her a wicked glance but obeys. As they feed, they grow warm and sleepy, settling into her hand, softened wings draped over her wrist.

"Stay here," she says, gently touching their back with a fingertip. Batwing yawns—their face all teeth and gullet—before they give their wings a shake, almost losing all solid form in the process.

"Can't. We must go with the others."

"Come back soon," Aina whispers as they flitter to the window and slip out through the fissure to disappear into the gloomy light.

***

Next time, Batwing comes at night. No fire burns outside, yet there they are, slipping through the crack. They are bigger this time, their fur glossier. When she asks where they are supposed to be, they give no answer. She cuts the tip of her index finger and offers it to them.

"Where do you go, when you fly away from here?"

Batwing rustles its wings, snuggling into her dirty sweater. "Wherever people sleep."

"To drink their blood."

"No. The Shade does not like us to drink blood." They lick their lips. "We haunt them, the sleepers. We feed on their nightmares. We become what they fear."

Aina strokes them gently and they quaver at her touch. "Can you feed on dreams, too?"

"Don't know. Never tried. But nightmares are stronger."

"Not always."

The black eyes peer up at her, fires lit within their depths. Aina cuts another finger and while they feed, she cradles them to her chest, turning over that one glossy memory of sun and honeybees and silky fur in her mind. Batwing shudders and shifts under her hands, chittering with surprise as their raspy claws turn into padded paws, jagged wings to silken fur, hard muzzle to snuffling nose. Transformation finished, they stretch out in her lap, soft belly warm under her hands.

"We like this," Batwing murmurs. "But we can't stay like this. The Shade won't allow it."

"I won't tell," Aina whispers, and inhales the smell of them: smoke and dust, blood and sky.

***

After that, Batwing comes almost every night. When they don't come, Aina worries. It is a perilous feeling to have someone to worry about again.

"How come you can see us and the Shade?" Batwing asks one evening, settling into their new shape after feeding. "You're not supposed to."

"I've always seen things, it just never mattered before." Aina thinks of the harpies flapping greedily over the boat as Mother disappeared into the abyssal waters, of the slinking Shades with sharp teeth and cold fingers that haunted her steps in the fields and forests as they fled their home. *There's nothing there*, Father said, but Mother never told her that.

"We think that's why the Man is afraid of you," Batwing murmurs. "Otherwise he would have come for you already."

Aina warms her cold hands in the softness of Batwing's fur. She knows what the Man wants; has seen other men take it from other girls and boys, before leaving their bones in the dirt.

"What does the Shade want?"

"To keep you weak, but not broken," Batwing muses, sleepily. "To drain, to devour whole. To take what's strong in you and make itself stronger."

She nods, knowing that no matter what they want, in the end, the Man and the Shade will both kill her.

***

That night the Man brings two children to the house: a girl Aina's own age, and a boy who looks younger. The children hold hands as they walk past the window and for a moment Aina thinks the girl looks her way, even catches her eye through the low-set window, then they are gone.

Later that night, the Man comes to Aina's cell. The Shade is not with him and he says nothing; just watches through the bars as she pretends to sleep, but she has already seen the knife he carries.

Aina hears the key turn in the lock, the Man's laboured breathing. She keeps her eyes shut, imagining the knife touching her neck, imagining that she would fight back, that she could grab the flimsy blade, but it's hidden beneath the floor tiles, out of reach, and even without the Shade, the Man is stronger than she is.

His hand slides along her arm, his face close enough that his breath wets her skin. He smells of sweat and fire; corruption and loneliness; filth and buried bones.

The knife touches her face—a whisper of steel—but she does not move, even when his hand slithers up her back and the flat of the blade presses down on her cheek. He draws breath as if to speak but the sound of shattered glass cuts off whatever he might have said.

Aina risks opening her eyes to see the Man standing at the window. The crack in the glass has become a jagged hole, allowing the chill night air to spill inside. Bits of glass are everywhere. She can't see anything stirring outside, can't hear the flitter of jagged wings either, but she knows Batwing must be close.

It takes everything she has, everything she is, to keep still beneath the blankets while the Man peers through the broken window. Blood and dread thrum in her veins; her empty, useless hands clenching into fists; a mute scream clawing at her ribs. When he finally leaves—when Aina knows for certain that he is gone—she runs to the window. Batwing is not there, they are elsewhere, safe, and she allows herself a trickle of tears. Not for dread or pain. Not even for sorrow or loneliness, just for relief and gratitude.

Standing below the window with the night breeze spilling over her, inhaling the smell of the distant sea, of fields and highway, something changes beneath Aina's goose pimpled skin. The change is subtle but certain, like a small bone shifting into place, allowing a new range of movement; something lost, regained.

It takes a long time to fall asleep in the cold, but when she does, Aina dreams a new dream. She is sitting on the porch in another life with Batwing resting on her lap, warm and heavy. The day is shimmery with sunlight and honeybees when a girl walks by on a dusty road beyond the fence. She looks familiar, but Aina cannot remember her name.

***

In the morning, on the floor of her cell, a washtub full of lukewarm water waits. A clean set of clothes is neatly folded on a worn, blue towel beside the tub with a small piece of white soap.

All fragments of glass have been cleaned up from the floor. The window is barred—a piece of wood covering the hole from outside—and the only light in the basement comes from the narrow window down the hallway. Aina tries to reach through the bars, to break or push away the board, but only manages to scratch and bruise her hands.

After washing herself with the soap and water, after drying herself with the towel and putting on the clean clothes, she plays the flute. The ghost comes to her when she plays, and she can almost see them today: a thin face, scrawny arms, hands linked around their shins, but when the music fades, they fade too. Such a small bone is barely enough for a soul to cling to.

"Thank you," Aina says, and puts the flute back under the tile where she first found it.

It is a small, unholy grave, but it will have to do.

Darkness falls and Aina waits. Waits for the footsteps. Waits for the Shade. Waits for the Man. She hears the visitors arrive, steps crunching the gravel outside her blocked window, thumping through the rooms upstairs before they settle in to wait.

Being clean is odd. She feels thinner, sharper, wholly translucent, like a shard of glass in water. The dress the Man gave her is pale yellow with bows and lace like a child would wear. It is too small for her, too tight across the chest. With it is a pair of shiny black shoes and white socks, but she will not put them on.

She wants Batwing. She wants them more than she has ever wanted anything or anyone in this or any other life. But they cannot come to her, and she cannot leave. Aina sits very still with the blade perched on the yellow fabric stretched across her lap. A ridiculous blade. Good for nothing. Too short, too dull, too flimsy. Useless, like Aina herself.

She draws a thin red line across her wrist, nothing deep, just enough of a sting to feed the embers inside her. Something scratches at the wood outside. A creak. A crack. Then, a wraith of smoke slips into the room, and Batwing coils into her lap. They have grown even bigger than before, and their voluminous wings tremble as they settle into their four-legged shape beside her. Ragged, sobbing breaths rack their chest, same as her own.

"Are you hungry?" Aina asks, and Batwing's eyes glint like rubies in the gloaming.

"No more than you are."

She smiles, and then she cuts. This time, she cuts deeper. She cuts until it hurts, until the blade falls out of her hand. The blood flows fast and dark, warm and wet, and Batwing laps it all up from her skin, from the fabric, from the floor.

Batwing shifts and changes as they devour what is left of her dreams and nightmares, her fears and wishes, and when they stop drinking, they are almost as big as she is—a heavy, brooding shape stretched out on the floor.

Aina wraps her arms around their shaggy body, resting her face in the dank black fur of the long-limbed creature they have become.

"You gave me too much," they gasp, and Aina knows it's true. They are too big for her to hold. Too big for their name, even.

"It doesn't matter anymore, *Blackdog*," she whispers, and finds a smile beneath the words.

A sound comes from their throat, almost bark, almost laughter. "I am not dog."

"I know."

They rest their head on her thigh, and sadness runs through them like a tremor.

"When I go back to the others, this form will be stripped from me. If the Shade sees me... I could fight, but I would lose."

"Just wait with me. As long as you can."

Blackdog curls up beside her, paws tucked under snout, and Aina leans back on the concrete wall, eyes closed. In the silence, the pitiless seas rise to claim her, and Mother's ruthless hands aren't there to thrust her out of death's reach now. Besides, there is so little left of her, so little left of the girl called Aina, barely enough to gather up, barely enough to keep going.

In the dark, Blackdog stirs. "They're coming," they growl, red tongue dangling, white teeth glimmering. "They're coming for you."

Aina senses their approach: Man and Shade on the stairs; the visitors waiting above. She wants the blade, wants to fight back even if it's hopeless, but the shank is gone, and she doesn't have the strength to look for it.

Blackdog stands up. Fur bristling all along their back, shaggy tail held high.

"I wish I'd given you more," Aina says. "I wish I'd given you all of it."

Blackdog looks at her, and in the gleaming depths of their eyes, the embers of countless fires burn. Fires fed by bones and spirits, flesh and souls, all set ablaze and turned to ash, to smoke, to wings, to shadow.

"Don't leave me," they breathe, nudging Aina with their nose, trying to get her to stand up, but her legs won't carry her. There is a space of silence between them, a space where there is only breath and pulse, her forehead pressed against Blackdog's forehead.

"Hold me." Blackdog's words are a flicker of warmth on her cold skin. Aina wraps her arms around them and holds on as tightly as she can. She buries her face in their fur, in the smell of fire and smoke, the taste of blood and sky.

"This time, I'll make the wish," Blackdog rumbles. "Hold tighter."

Aina tightens her grip, her arms gaining strength the tighter she holds on to them. The muscles in her shoulders and chest strain and shudder, the dress rips at the seams, shreds of fabric falling off like sloughed skin. Her weakness, the cold, regret and pain, all of it slips away as Blackdog's warmth enters her, as she enters them, as they are pulled into each other, as they both twist, change, grow, shift. There's a tickle of claws at the tips of Aina's fingers, slick fangs behind her lips, and then...she lets go.

The transformation burns through them, consuming all frailty and fear in a moment of conflagration. They almost howl with the sheer pleasure and power of it, rearing up on two legs before coming back down again with a thud, shaking off the cold, slashing at the air with a massive paw—new razor-claws glistening, revelling in the glory of it, the force and might rushing through them.

They can see the blade on the floor now, clear as if by daylight, but they have something better—claws and teeth, jaws and muscle—stronger than any blade.

Stronger than the shadow? the part of them that is still Aina wonders.

Maybe, Blackdog's thoughts whisper as they entwine with hers, as the bond between them flexes at her mind's touch. *Maybe.*

The Man is close. They hear him: the last door opening with a heavy creak. They smell him: the scent of hunger and excitement as he approaches, before all his eagerness withers to nothing when he is close enough to *see.* He carries a light with him, and when it shines through the bars, his mouth falls open and he might have screamed, but Blackdog is already crashing through the cell door: wood and metal, femur and skull, all crack and shatter as easily as glass.

The Man's skin and flesh tear effortlessly between Blackdog's teeth and claws, but the Shade remains unharmed. Without the Man, it is an unmoored, shapeless thing—greasy and changeable, impossible to grasp and hold. Even so, it grasps hold of them, tendrils of darkness tugging and tearing at fur and mind and flesh, trying to pry them apart, clawing at the new bond between them, but no matter how it grapples, it can find no crack, no seam, to separate them. They battle in the narrow hallway, and every touch of the roiling, twitching Shade burns like acid, cuts like steel, but Blackdog does not submit or cower. They are a new-forged blade unsheathed, jagged edge tempered in their own blood, their rage hot and ardent, and finally, their fangs and talons find purchase, tearing through the Shade's withered husk into its rank and rotting essence.

In that same instant, the Shade yields. It recedes, thrashing and slithering away from them through the hallway, through the walls and ceiling, snapping out of sight faster than the eye can follow. Then it is gone. Only the Man is left, a last shudder of life quaking in his chest.

If she were still nothing but Aina, she might have left him. Might have run rather than claim him, but Blackdog knows better—they lower their head and rip his throat out.

With the taste of blood still coursing through them, they break down the basement doors, splintering wood and bending steel. Guided by scent and sound they bound up the stairs and smash another door, this one on the first floor: dark polished wood cracking as they charge through.

Inside are the visitors: eight men seated on leather couches beside a hearth, dressed in neatly pressed pants and ironed shirts, ties loosened at the neck, clinking ice hitting crystal. Their tools are laid out on the table before them: gags and ropes, knives and blindfolds, other things crafted to cause pain. Rushing through the room, Blackdog catches a glimpse of their own silhouette in a gold-edged mirror: their shaggy form grown large and fierce from rage and blood, darkness trailing from the raised hackles on their back like tattered wings, a long maw streaked with blood, fangs bared. They are a hulking thing, reared up on two legs but ready to bound away on all fours, a snarl thrumming in their throat. They are girl and bat and wraith and dog. They are none of these. They are *more*.

The men remain sitting, smiles slipping off their faces like greasy paper. Their smell is familiar. It is the smell of sweat, piss, and excrement, and a thrill runs along Blackdog's spine, as they gorge on that terror.

One of the men moves to grab a knife from the table. Slow. Foolish. Blackdog roars and charges. Flesh and bone are nothing now. Rip and tear, slash and break. Afterward, they stand panting in the firelight, blood-soaked paws and stained claws resting in the thick carpet.

Blackdog knows the Shade is hiding, out of reach. But the house is not empty.

They bound away again, up the stairs, searching for the other cell. Another metal door bars their way, harder to break down because the flush of their first rage is fading, but soon, the frame splinters. Inside is another prison, another cage, another pile of filthy blankets with a girl and boy huddled together on the floor. Both are scarred and bruised. The boy hides his face, but the girl looks up, undaunted.

"They are dead," they tell the girl, not sure if she will understand. "You can leave."

What their voice sounds like to her, whether growl or words, they do not know for certain. They are already running again, back down the stairs, and out through the front door.

***

Outside, underneath the oak trees, the air smells of wet leaves and dirt, spring and mist.

They stalk on heavy paws through the gravel, down the long driveway, past the parked cars left behind by the visitors, across the empty country road. Once they've crossed the asphalt, they run. They race across the wide open fields away from the house, toward the distant sea and the horizon and the bright, thin edge of dawn.

On the crest of a ridge beyond the fields, they linger, looking back. A vicious glint of orange leaps up from the fog toward the morning sky. Perhaps the girl led the boy downstairs, perhaps she found the men and took a glowing brand from the hearth. Perhaps the two of them ran away before the flames caught the wood, or perhaps they are standing there right now in the yard, watching it all burn, while the jagged wings escape the burning rafters to mingle and gather between the branches of the oaks. A murmuration of shadows set free, swooping out of the darkness, into the brightening sky.

Turning away from the distant fire, Blackdog sets out again, loping toward the sea where they will wash off blood and gore, shedding the last remnants of captivity, every bound and stride seemingly a mile long, claws and paws tearing up the dirt, scattering the dust, black fur and tattered wings bristling along their back.

AND YOU SHALL SING TO ME A DEEPER SONG

I HEAR THE ALL-TOO-FAMILIAR BLAST of a bot-gun as a bullet screams by my cheek, thwacking into the gravel between the railway ties behind me. Belem rears up, waving his clawed front feet in the air, and my brain snaps into battle mode. The sound of the weapon sings through the implants nestled beneath my skull as the bot-gun's specs are transmitted to my cortex. But no specs can tell me why a weapon that shouldn't exist is being fired at me in this hind-end of the continent, ten years after the bot-war ended.

Move, Nysha.

Humming the beginnings of a counter-song, I slide off Belem's back, grab my rifle from the saddle holster, and urge the scaly pig-lizard into the thin shelter of a copse of stunted trees. Too many thoughts are spinning through my head. That I'm getting lazy and complacent, riding around without a rifle already in my hands, without a pistol up my sleeve. A bot-gun can fire twenty rounds in ten seconds, so why am I still alive? There's only one place an attacker could be hiding, considering the range of the weapon: that rocky outcropping on the slope above the tracks.

Squinting in the sunlight, I see nothing but a whisper of dust up there.

I focus on the data-feed from my implants, searching for the murmur of a bot-processor my song can grab hold of, but I find no sounds of tech. What I find instead is the barely audible whisper of breaths and heartbeats.

One human, one animal.

"Who are you?" I shout, patting down the pockets of my leather jacket for ammo, gingerly sliding the pistol out of my saddlebag and into the holster hidden in my right sleeve. "Why are you shooting at me?"

I'm still trying to steady my hands, and the rush of memories brought on by the sound of that gun. Victor and I, huddled in the trenches. The taste of blood and mud in my mouth. The mind-numbing hum of the bots before they dropped their bombs.

Get a grip, Nysha. The war's over.

"I don't want to kill you!" It's a man's voice. "Name's Daniel! I'm coming out. Don't shoot."

He stands up, raising a refitted bot-gun over his head. The sleek, shiny weapon has been refashioned to fit a human hand, but seeing it still makes me flinch.

For a while, nothing moves between us but the wind, stirring up whorls of dust. I speak first.

"Impressive weapon. Hard to find a bot to rip it off these days."

He grins so unexpectedly that I almost grin back.

"War memento. Sorry for shooting at you. I saw the splice-beast and figured you were Central Command. But your scars..." He frowns. "I thought all the singers were dead."

I touch the bare skin on my skull. The hair didn't grow back everywhere after the surgery, and I know what it looks like. White scars on tan skin, tracking down my throat, around my ears, through the patchy mess of short, grey-blonde hair. I used to wear a hood, but I've been travelling the wilds so long it didn't seem to matter anymore.

"We *are* dead," I say. "I just keep walking anyway."

That earns me another grin, and I peer at him more closely: short, muscular, brown-skinned. Dressed in blue coveralls, patched and mended. Farmer's clothes. Yet his stance, the way he speaks, that weapon, everything about him, says ex-military, likely science-trooper.

He whistles, and a shaggy pony emerges from the rocks, staring suspiciously at Belem.

"You get a lot of Central Command around here?"

He shakes his head. "No, but there was a train the other day. Thought you might've been on it."

His voice reminds me far too much of Victor's—dark and warm like nighttime and song, like trust and safety.

Like war and loss.

"Nope. Heard it pass though."

I think of it, rumbling through my uneasy sleep like a distant nightmare.

"The trains started rolling again a few years ago, but this is the first one to stop. We're keeping an eye on it. Looks like they're inspecting a trestle bridge, but you'd best change your route if you've got reasons to avoid Central Command."

I wonder who "we" are, but I don't ask. Slinging the rifle onto my back, I mount up.

"Thanks for the warning."

He looks me over. "Your beast's limping. Was that from him rearing up just now?"

"It's just a scratch. It'll heal."

"We've got a medic. Could stitch him up. Got a bed for the night, too."

"I realize you want to keep an eye on me because of that train, but...you just shot at me."

"I apologized."

"What if I want to keep going?"

He swings the bot-gun up on his shoulder and smiles, looking for all the world like one of Central Command's morale-boosting recruitment posters from the war.

"I know a singer isn't likely to be spying for Central Command, but it'd be safer for you and us if you stayed, until the train leaves."

I mull it over. It's been a while since I was reckless enough to trust anyone, but Daniel reminds me enough of Victor to make me consider it.

"Long as I can keep my rifle."

That grin again. "Of course. If I can't trust a war hero, then who can I trust?"

***

The Priory

The first time I saw Mother Mary she was standing in the pulpit at the Pacific Priory, looking immeasurably tall, cloaked in her red vestments.

"Every life sings," she intoned, gazing down on us, "but your songs will save the world."

I didn't know what she meant, but the way she said it, the way she looked at us, made me want to believe her.

The orphanage had sold me to the Priory the week before. I was just what the Holy Sisters needed, the recruiter said—with my beautiful voice, my perfect pitch, my love for writing songs. Now I was hundreds of miles away, standing with sixty other teens from all over NorthAm in a place that seemed untouched by the wars against the bots. A place that smelled of ocean and incense, not fire and death.

Victor stood beside me, though I didn't know his name yet, only knew him as the dark-haired boy with the skinned knuckles and a knack for rhymes.

That morning, we had all been scrubbed clean in the bathhouse, and beneath the stained-glass windows our faces shone—pink and tan, black and brown. Shining, we sang for Mother Mary, and from where I stood, I could see her crying as she listened, her stoic features barely shifting as the tears fell.

Afterward, she told us we were blessed and chosen, that we'd be tried and tested.

She left out the details. That the Sisters had discovered a new weapon against the bots. That the Priory was working with Central Command to build that weapon, despite the holy order's distaste for worldly powers. That we would become that weapon. That techs would soon cut us open, fusing neural implants to our flayed nerves, our inner ears, our larynxes, reshaping our young, malleable brains.

And there I was, singing like an angel, fool enough to think I might be there to write songs of peace and glory. God might be everywhere, as the Sisters claimed, but the devil, as always, was in those details.

***

We've been riding through the foothills for less than an hour when I see the village: two dozen houses, old army prefab stock, grey and stout, at the bottom of a valley. In ten years of wandering, I've seen plenty of communities clinging to life and independence in the so-called inhabitable areas. But I've never seen fields like these: a patchwork of impossible green, spread along the river.

"Crops? In the open?"

He nods. "With some ingenuity and the right plant strains, it's possible. Not that the regime wants anyone to know. They want us in the domes and cities where we're easily controlled."

I'm about to speak, when a hum appears at the edge of my hearing and I spot flashes of metal, moving purposefully among the crops.

Bots. At least fifty of them, according to my data-feed.

Daniel gives me an apologetic look. "We've dampened their signals, but this close... I thought you'd hear them."

No shit.

The bot-hum flickers through my brain, placid and simple. It would be easy to hook my voice into their internal matrix, circumvent their programming, unravel them with a counter-song. *You'll never forget how to do this*, the Sisters told us, and they were right. Even when I was half-dead and crying in pain, I could still annihilate bots.

Belem shifts uneasily beneath me, sensing how angry I am.

"That's illegal. Not to mention insane. You know that, right?"

"I understand your reaction, but there's no rogue military AI guiding these bots. They're safe. They're tools. And without tech, we can't farm successfully out here."

I want to scream rage and reason at him, but he's already kicked his pony into a canter, and, huffing his displeasure, Belem lowers his tusked head and follows.

***

The Garden

There was a bot in the Priory garden.

Everyone knew the Sisters had preached tech-abstinence since before the first bot-rebellions, yet there it was—a basic gardening bot, small, round, its sensors glowing as it mowed between the flower beds.

Only Sister Theo was with me, but I felt Mother Mary's eyes on me even so. I always did.

After the first round of surgery—done to enhance our hearing and voice-control—we'd been listening to sounds of every kind, learning to mimic tone and pitch precisely. Now, Sister Theo told me to listen to the bot.

I closed my eyes, tuning out the wind and gulls and ocean, and there it was—the bot's song, whisper-light, more shiver than sound.

"Sing," Sister Theo said, and I did, the new tech in my throat and ears helping me match the bot's song.

"Feel it?"

Yes, I felt it. I felt the sound of my voice wrap around the sound of the bot, like a rope around a pole, and when I opened my eyes, the bot had changed its path. It was circling me in the grass.

"Good. Keep it tethered but *twist* your song as hard as possible."

A counter-song. This was the most closely guarded secret of the Priory. The secret that might defeat the bots and save the world. I'd never sung one before, but now, my voice vibrated through my enhanced larynx as I adjusted the song, shifting it slightly, and instead of breaking free, the bot changed its internal song in response, its hum gradually wavering, weakening as I kept twisting.

Abruptly, the hum stopped. I smelled burning circuits, and my mind went silent.

Sister Theo smiled at me. I'd never seen her smile before, and in that moment I felt as though the world rested on my shoulders, but more than that, I felt as if I might be able to carry it.

***

I ride into the village, ready to tear into Daniel, ready to tell him I'll sing every one of his illegal bots into oblivion, but what I see stops me dead.

Children.

There are twelve of them, aged maybe eight to fifteen. Post-war kids, grown up in a different world than mine—free of war, though not of hardship—and they seem fearless even though I'm an armed stranger. They sneak glances at me while staring at Belem, crowding closer when I get off his back at the water trough next to Daniel's pony, and they bombard me with questions.

"Is he a dinosaur?" a girl with beaded braids asks when the cacophony briefly subsides.

"I call him a pig-lizard. His name's Belem."

Last time I was surrounded by kids, I was a child myself in the Priory.

Were we this young? I wonder. *Was I?*

Meanwhile, Daniel's talking to a small crowd of adults, all of them eying me with either fear or hostility or both. One of the women comes over, shoos away the kids, sticks a hand out, and gives her name as Clemency.

"Daniel shouldn't have brought you," she says without preamble, giving me a sharp blue gaze. "He's too trusting."

"So am I, it seems." I slip the saddle off Belem's back, setting it down. "What's being done about the train?"

"We're watching it. Not that it concerns you." She nods at Belem and grabs a med-kit from her rucksack. "Where'd you get the splice-beast?"

I think of the four soldiers outside a bar who tried to bring me back to Central Command right after the war. I think of Belem, in his fancy army tack, watching them die, snorting when I swung up on his back for the first time.

"Won him in a game of poker."

She snorts and pats Belem's scaly muzzle. "Right. Anyway, he's a beauty. I'd say old-stock rhino, horse, and a splash of lizard DNA."

"You a breeder?"

Crouching down, she applies a row of auto-stitches and a healing patch to Belem's leg with practiced movements.

"Bio-technician. Worked on the first generation of splice-beasts, back when everyone was clamoring for alternatives to sick horses and bot-vehicles gone rogue."

"You gave up that career to traipse around here in the wild?"

A shrug. "I knew Daniel during the war. He's...persuasive. Always had a knack for pulling people in." She runs her fingers through Belem's scraggly mane. "And what's a singer doing here? Thought you all died in the war or were purged right after."

Purged. The word still burns.

"Just riding through, headed for the coast."

"Coast is weeks away, even on a fancy beast like this." That sharp blue gaze again and an even sharper smile. "Faster if you take that train, I guess."

"I'm not in a hurry."

She looks as if she's about to speak, but instead she snaps her med-kit shut and stalks off, and the kids gather round me again.

"Are you *really* a singer?"

"She can't be! There's no singers anymore."

"Why?"

"Because they killed all the bots in the war, and then they went crazy and died."

"That true?" the girl with the braids asks, reaching out to pat Belem's dusty flank.

"Something like that."

"Can you sing for us?" a boy asks, giving me a pleading look.

"No! She'll kill us!"

"Singers only kill bots, dummy." It's the girl with the braids again, and when she turns, hair swinging down her shoulders, I see a spidery trace of tech around her ears. Looking around, I realize every child is marked the same way, the metal tendrils of the interface hidden beneath hair and collars.

And just like that, I'm back in the Priory, waking up in the medical wing, with the Sisters doling out prayers and painkillers. I'm back at the front, singing death to bots. I'm back on the train, being taken to the camp after the war.

Purged.

I look up and see Daniel watching me.

"It's not what you think, Nysha."

But it is.

***

The Dorm

Victor was singing in the boy's dorm, long after lights out. It was one of his own songs, and any other night I would have laughed and traded lines and verses with him, singing through the walls. Not that night.

We were back from a week of weapon's training and our first trial-mission, singing in a bombed-out town, watching a group of soldiers burn the captured bots while our song held them immobile for the kill.

Our dorm looked hollow. Eight beds had been empty since the final round of surgery—"expected fall-off," the doctors called it—and the sisters had stripped those beds of sheets and blankets, leaving only skeletal metal frames.

You'll be tried and tested, Mother Mary had said. I knew what that meant now.

Awake in my cot, listening to Victor, I still smelled the smoke from the burning bots in my hair, even though I'd scrubbed for an hour in the bathhouse.

I was clean. But I was no longer untouched.

***

Dinner is a spicy stew of vegetables and mycoprotein, and after the tables in the eating hall have been cleared, after I've turned down a third glass of homemade wine, I sing with the kids while the grown-ups hang back, watching and listening.

The anger I felt after seeing the bots is all but gone. I've watched these people go about the business of living their normal lives of chores and work and family, and I doubt I've got the right to judge or question them.

How long since I was anything near this normal? How long since I sang like this? Not for bots, or myself, but with *people.* I've chosen a song I wrote in the Priory, before I knew why I was there; a song about birds, oceans, stars. After I sing it once, the children join in. First, their voices follow mine, but soon they're improvising, adding words and call-backs and clapping, and for a moment I'm a kid again, before the Priory, before the scars, singing for the joy of it.

When I stop singing, they carry on, their clear voices soaring, so bold and powerful it makes me quiver. I don't even realize I'm crying until Daniel asks me to go outside.

Out there, the only illumination is the waxing moon, but I walk into the night anyway, knowing it'll hurt less as long as I keep moving.

"Do they sing to the bots?"

Daniel sticks close, the bot-gun on his back gleaming in the moonlight.

"Sometimes. To interface with them, not to kill."

"Your own kids... You did that to them."

"Look, it's nothing like what was done to you. The singers... That was a raw deal, okay? That was *war.* This new tech our people have developed, it's different. It's harmony. It just helps you synch with the bots, not fight them. It's even non-invasive. They can take it off if they want."

"Spare me the hard sell." I shrink into my leather jacket. "Which kid is yours?"

"The tall one with the braids, Naya." A smile flickers across his face, then goes out. "Her mom died in the flu a while back."

We walk through the village, past the paddock with Belem and the ponies, up the ridge. I sit down in the tussock grass. Daniel sits beside me. It would be easy to lean on him, let the wine pull me down, share his warmth.

"What about the train?" I ask, grasping for something solid, something here and now, to hold on to.

"Still there. Who knows, maybe they aren't here for us. Maybe they *are* inspecting the bridge. I mean, we're no threat to anyone. Rumour is, Central Command might even be lifting its ban on bot-research. War's over, right? We won."

"So I heard."

The night smells of river, dust, fields.

"Where are you going, Nysha?"

In the dark, this close, his voice reminds me so much of Victor's it hurts. Reminds me of sitting in the dark with him, making up songs together to stay warm.

"The Priory. If it's still there."

"Why?"

I try to laugh. "Good question. Thank them? Kill them? Not sure yet."

I think of Mother Mary and the Sisters, telling us they would always take care of us, that we'd always have a home there, and old anger rises in my throat like bile.

Daniel is quiet for a while, then changes the subject. He talks about crops and research and a network of free villages, exchanging resources and information. A new world growing in the cracks of Central Command's power. I close my eyes and listen. It sounds good. Almost real.

Maybe this is the world, I think. Maybe there is no devil in the details. After the wars and epidemics, maybe the world can really be like this.

Harmony.

***

The War

The hold of the airship smelled of sweat and puke and metal. I sat next to Victor listening to the battle raging below—the thud-thwack of guns, the roar of fire-blasters, the hum of the bot-army.

Six singers were on that flight, the rest had been deployed elsewhere. I'd never see them again.

When the hatch opened I stood paralyzed, voice stuck in my throat. Then Victor hollered at me to move, and I did.

We sang death to the bots that day, and they kneeled, swerved, fell.

Five years later, when the war ended, only Victor and I were still alive of those six, but that day, we were invincible, we were Mother Mary's angels, saving the world.

***

I must have fallen asleep, because the gunshot wakes me up. It's dawn. I'm on the ground, looking for my rifle until I remember it's still in the eating hall. Daniel's bot-gun is there, and I grab it instead, but there's no one to shoot, just the sound of hooves.

"Daniel!"

He's still asleep, his head...

No.

Blood. Bone. Brains.

Move, Nysha.

But I can't. I'm flat on my belly in the tussock grass with Daniel dead beside me. I smell fire. Somewhere, children are screaming, and Belem is roaring. Daniel's gun feels awkward in my hands, and I have to pat down his blood-soaked pockets for ammo, stuffing the cartridges into my jacket before I move.

The children. They're below, in the village, being forced into a truck by armed soldiers. I see no other adults anywhere, but the hall is on fire, flames leaping through the windows. Belem bellows for me again, banging against the walls of a second truck, parked beside the first, but I can't help him or anyone. I can only hide as the trucks take off, heading away from me, toward the train tracks.

When the trucks are gone, I scramble down the slope and run toward the hall, even though I know it's too late. I smell burning flesh and accelerant on the hot breeze, and it's like a nightmare, with me, running from house to house, finding them all empty.

Why am I surprised? I've seen it before. Homes torched, people killed to prove that no one can survive without the blessing of Central Command.

Cold steel pushes into the nape of my neck.

"Don't move." Clemency. She takes my rifle. "Turn around." I do. Her face is streaked with soot, but she's smiling. "Told the commander there was a singer, but she didn't believe me. Maybe I'll get to keep your beastie as a bonus."

"Where are you taking the kids?"

She readies a pair of slip-on cuffs. "Same place you're going. Our new research facility on the coast."

"You shot Daniel."

Something ripples across her face. I can't tell if it's regret. "Daniel was stupid. All this, bots, kids...it needs to be supervised, controlled..."

I've practiced it so many times: shrugging the gun out of the holster inside my sleeve, sliding it into my hand, firing. One smooth movement.

The bullet hits Clemency between the eyes.

Victor's voice in my head:

Move, Nysha.

The paddock fence is broken, and all the ponies gone, except one. It's tied up beside a water trough, saddled and ready, probably for Clemency's getaway. I mount up and follow the trail of dust left by the trucks, while the village burns behind me.

***

The Song

Victor leaned on me in the dark as the train carried us away from the peace celebrations, the parades, the speeches. Toward the camp where we were to be re-evaluated, reassigned. Purged. We'd heard enough talk, heard enough people call us "tech-flesh abominations" to know what it all meant.

Some rumours said Sisters from the Priory had tried to get access to us, but had been denied by direct order of Central Command. It hardly mattered anymore.

"They can't undo what they did to us," I said to Victor, "so they'll kill us for being what they made us."

Victor leaned closer. His words touched my cheek. "I have a new song, Nysha. Just for you and me. And this one is about freedom."

***

Central Command's train is a pre-war relic, all steel and dirt, refitted with solar panels. I count seven cars, three without windows for cattle or cargo (*or prisoners*, my memories whisper).

Watching from the ridge above, I see Belem being led out of a truck—snout bound, legs hobbled, but the children must already be on the train. There are twenty soldiers, armed with rifles and stun guns. One is wielding a bot-remote, guiding the village's farm-bots into a train car, keeping them in an orderly formation. The truck I saw the kids get into is empty, and a soldier is waiting to drive it up a ramp, into the last train car.

There's a loud bellow, followed by shouting, and I'd laugh if I could, because Belem has snapped the ropes around his neck and legs and is slamming into people and metal like a one-beast wrecking crew.

They were ready for kids and bots, I think grimly, settling into position with Daniel's gun, *but they didn't expect a valuable pig-lizard or a live singer.*

Breathing slow, I listen for the hum of the farm-bots, for the breaths and heartbeats of the soldiers.

All those soldiers.

I know I should cut my losses. Live to fight another day. But whatever I am, whatever *they* made me, whatever I've become since, I can't leave Belem or the kids. Taking aim, I steady the bot-gun, grasping the moulded grip and trigger Daniel installed to cover the old interface where the weapon was ripped off a bot's limb. I shiver.

Just a tool.

I pull the trigger, and the all-too-familiar blast jars my senses, but the power and accuracy of the weapon make up for any discomfort. One soldier hit. Reload. Fire. Repeat. Now, I'm singing to the bots—a small song that wraps itself around the hum of their internal processors, making them move.

The soldiers scatter as the bots speed up, clanging together, spinning around. I fire again, taking care not to hit Belem who is tossing soldiers around, trampling them. Next, I twist my song, activating the farming implements the bots are equipped with—rakes, cutters, tillers—while Belem stampedes through the soldiers who are trying to take aim at him and me.

The surviving soldiers scurry inside the train for shelter. Fifteen soldiers remain in the grass, dead or incapacitated. Belem is banging on the train and the trucks, mangling the metal with his tusks. Blood covers his muzzle, but I don't know if it's his.

"Belem!"

I run down the slope toward him at the back of the train, hoping the angle makes it harder for anyone to hit me. No one fires, but I hear shouting, and I know I'm almost out of time.

Belem calms when I touch him, and so do I. I stop singing, letting the bots go. Leaning on Belem, I let the sounds around me fall away until I only hear what's inside the train—footsteps, heartbeats, breaths, voices. Blood stings my eyes, maybe it's my own, maybe it's Daniel's. It doesn't matter now.

Eight adults in one car. Twelve kids in the other, their heartbeats easy to distinguish.

I start singing again, but this is not a song for bots. This is Victor's last song, the one he taught me on the train to the camp. Before we killed the guards and the engineer. Before the train careened off the rails into a gully. Before I had to leave his mangled body in the wreckage. Before he died.

"Every life sings," Mother Mary told us, and she was right. Every heart hums, too, just like every bot. All singers knew it, but none of us ever thought to sing a counter-song to take a human life. None, except Victor.

Victor's song set me free ten years ago, and now, listening to the heartbeats of the soldiers, I sing it. It's low and deep, vibrating in my throat, in my enhanced larynx, in the air, wrapping itself around those eight hearts, twisting, squeezing.

It's a difficult song to hear, difficult to sing. Harder still to hold that tone long enough, twist it hard enough, that each heart stops.

I hear screaming and gunfire inside the train, and my song wavers, as I wonder if the kids are dying because of me. Then I hear them, the children, singing with me, singing Victor's song. But their song is not like mine, it's stronger and stranger, a torrent of voices and bot-amplified noise, and they are glorying in the power of it. Their voices are so strong I feel my own heart slow and stutter and then I black out.

**

"Singer lady!"

I see twelve faces above me, snotty, tear-streaked, bleeding.

I don't hear any soldiers. I don't hear anything except Belem's snuffling and the children's voices, fear and anger mingling.

"They killed everyone," a boy says. "They set a fire, and Clemency said they..."

I struggle to my feet.

"Where's my dad?" Naya asks. I don't answer, but she looks at the bot-gun in my hand and her face goes hard. "We sang like you and they died. Does that mean we're singers too?"

Does it?

I stare at the pillar of smoke darkening the morning sky, thinking of other songs I'd rather have taught them, but beyond the ridge, the village and everything that might have been for them, and me, is burning.

Victor, or maybe Daniel, whispers in my ear:

Move, Nysha.

The kids crowd close. They're neither clean nor untouched, but then, neither am I. No one ever is. I grab my bot-gun, pat my pockets for ammo, make sure the gun is in my sleeve.

"I know a place," I say, looking at the truck, its solar panels spread wide in the morning sunlight. "It's far. But we'll go there, together."

**

Last time I saw Mother Mary, she was standing in the highest window of the Priory while the army took us away. In my mind, she's been standing there ever since, waiting for us, for me, to return.

And if I make it back, will she remember me? Will I embrace her? Or will I sing for her until she cries and her heart bursts?

I don't know yet, but I'll figure it out when we get there.

SILVER AND SHADOW, SPRUCE AND PINE

WHEN GRANDMOTHER DISAPPEARS FROM THE nursing home, Marika is the only one who understands what's happened. The family and staff, they wonder how and why a 96-year-old woman could walk out of her room unnoticed and disappear in the middle of the night. They whisper about dementia and Alzheimer's. They make phone calls to the police and hospitals.

Marika looks at the window left ajar and shivers in the cold spring air.

She's already seen the deep paw prints in the flowerbeds outside, the muddy tracks leading across the nursing home's parking lot towards the greenbelt by the creek. She knows that Grandmother is not missing but gone. *Taken.*

Grandmother told her the stories. About the woods where she grew up and lived most of her life. About the fog that wraps itself around the branches of the pines in the moonlight. About the shadows that lurk beneath the spruce when your feet stray off the path. About the creatures that breathe their hunger into mist, crooning your name beneath the trees.

There was always a wolf and always a girl in those stories; always the safe path through the woods to the shelter of the house, always the beast lurking if you strayed. Everyone else called it a fairy tale, but Marika knew it was more than that; she knew the stories had the ring of truth and memory, not fiction.

She follows the paw prints to the creek. On the other side, beyond the tangled birches and grey sallow, is the highway. Standing there, smelling the damp earth and budding leaves, she thinks about the last time she visited Grandmother; how quiet she was, gazing out the window with those rheumy blue eyes, staring at the darkness crouched outside the glass; her bent, arthritic fingers tangled in the red yarn in her lap, gripping those knitting needles tight.

"It's still there," Grandmother said, voice paper-thin like a secret, singsong like a story. "It's still waiting for me."

"You're safe, Grandma," Marika reassured her, not knowing what else to say.

Grandmother cocked her head and looked up, unsmiling. "I have never been safe," she said, and went back to her knitting.

***

Marika gets in her car. She knows where to go, knows where those paw prints will lead her in the end, so she drives north, following the straight path of blacktop and reflective paint.

In the car, she thinks about the house beneath the eaves of spruce and pine where Grandmother lived once upon a time. First, with Grandpa until he died, leaving only his huntsman's rifle hanging on the wall and garbage bags full of empty vodka bottles. Then, she lived alone until everyone decided she was too old to manage.

Marika thinks about the closet in that house, how it smelled of lavender and sundried linen; how she hid there when she was four or five, playing with her cousins; how she found—hidden behind the woolen coats and polyester dresses—a red cloak, worn and faded, its hem torn and stained.

***

Marika drives until there's nothing but forest and the gleam of furtive, yellow eyes on either side of the road. She drives until asphalt turns to gravel, and all the way, she feels that something is following her. It stays out of sight, just beyond the reach of the headlights—a gangly shadow, loping between the boles, untiring.

***

It's dusk when she arrives at the old house. A lace-thin breath of snow covers everything, and the last bit of road is so rutted and narrow that she has to walk through brush, into the gloom beneath the pines. Along the path, Grandmother's old flowerbeds are thick with couch grass and dandelions. Stands of nettle huddle near the porch, and beneath the windows, the rosebushes Grandma tended, even though Grandpa always told her it was a waste of time to grow them this far north, poke through the scant snow. The door is locked, the house empty, but Marika knocks anyway.

"Grandma?"

No answer.

Marika turns and the wolf is there, standing between her and the forest. It's tall and lean and older than she imagined, its breath a ragged mist of hunger wreathed about its snout, the curve of its back a jagged edge of bone beneath its shaggy hide. It stalks closer until Marika sees her own reflection in the clouded pupils of its eyes. Then it stops and looks back across the faded garden.

Grandmother is standing at the forest's edge. She is barefoot in the cold, wearing nothing but her washed-out, pale-blue nightgown and the red shawl she was knitting when Marika saw her last, wispy hair spread over her shoulders like spun silver.

Afterwards, Marika will wonder why she didn't run away from the wolf, why she didn't scream, why she didn't call out for Grandmother, but in the moment as it happens, she knows why. She knows the wolf isn't there for her, and neither is Grandmother.

Standing on the porch, watching the wolf pace toward the trees, watching Grandmother put her hand between its ears, watching the wolf bend its head at her touch, Marika sees the old stories, and Grandma's life, unravel and knit together into a new pattern.

She wonders if Grandmother always wanted the story to end like this, if the woods always beckoned to her, if she regretted following the path rather than straying beyond it, if she spent her life yearning for the one who knew her scent and silhouette in the moonlight, who crooned her name beneath the trees.

Her phone buzzes in her pocket. It's Mom; her voice worn and distant.

"They found her in the creek. Marika. Your grandma, she... They couldn't revive her." Marika looks at the paw prints leading from the house to the eaves of the forest. "She's in a better place now," Mom says, fading.

"I know," Marika says, watching as a slip of red and a gleam of silver fade into shadows beneath spruce and pine.

SIX DREAMS ABOUT THE TRAIN

I dream about you and the train all the time.
This is how it ends:
There is the train and there is you and then there is only the train.

I.

SOMETIMES WE'RE ON BOARD THE train, together. (This is my favourite dream because I'm next to you.) You have the window seat and you're sleeping—your face bereft of all defenses, eyelids shivering with secret visions, hidden nightmares. Outside the dirty glass, the darkness unfolds itself while the train rocks us, softly, like I would rock you when you were still small enough to be held. Our reflections are superimposed on the world outside, afloat, like sky and clouds in water. We are uncertain apparitions, and, for a moment, I fear we are nothing *but* reflections. Maybe there is no me, no you, no us, only these images floating across the world without being part of it. And if I were to try to touch you in that moment of dread, my hand would dip into cold water, marring what I thought was us.

Then you wake up and look at me and you smile and I know who I am again, that I am real, that you are real, that this is the world as it is supposed to be.

2.

Sometimes, I'm driving the train. I'm the engineer. It's night and I'm coming down the tracks at high speed, traveling through that narrow section where the vines and bushes hang over the concrete edge from above (where the sparrows nest; you know the place). I'm used to the smell of diesel and metal, the *thunk* of wheels on rails, holding on to my insulated coffee mug, humming some old tune to myself. And there you are: just a kid, shoulders too slight to carry the carcass of the world, stumbling along the tracks. It's as if you don't hear the train bearing down on you with all its steel and rust and rain-streaked dirt. As if you don't feel the thrum of its approach through the soles of your shoes, the rumble of it in the chill night air, rattling the spikes and sleepers, shuddering through the sharp gravel and rocks beneath you. Maybe you've got your headphones on. Maybe you're drunk or sick. Or maybe you chose to walk here, knowing the train would come.

When I see you, I do whatever an engineer does. I make that whistle blare. I pull the brakes, but the train is too heavy, too long, one hundred cars (give or take), boxcars and hoppers, centerbeams and tank cars, carrying coal, ore, lumber. Or maybe it's a passenger train, full of people, containing all their love and their loneliness. Or maybe the cars are empty, the contents already unloaded, the spray-painted graffiti on the sides of the boxcars vaguely luminous in the starlit dark.

It doesn't matter. You are in front of the train and I can't stop it.

3.

Sometimes, you call me in the middle of the night.

"Hey," you say, and the sound of your voice is a silvery thorn of suffering, like those tiny spines on a cactus that hurt even though you cannot see them, much less pull them out of your skin. Although I'm muddled with sleep, I get out of bed.

"Where are you?" I ask, and you are silent for so long I fear you've hung up on me.

I put on my clothes, fumbling for my purse and keys. My glasses fog up in the cold when I get into the car. I drive through the dark, past the 7-Eleven and across the train tracks. My car is a mess and so am I, but there you are, waiting on the sidewalk. You don't smile when you see me, but you get in the car and that is all that matters.

When we drive away, I hear the bells clanging at the railroad crossing.

4.

Sometimes, I go through all the trouble of building a time machine and I travel back to stop trains from ever being invented. But it's hard work to stop an idea when it is determined to become real.

5.

Sometimes, we are train robbers, you and I, characters from an old pulpy Western. We wear snakeskin boots, faded denim, and bandanas. We rob the train. We ride away. My horse is a steady old bay. Yours is a showy blue roan. You ride so fast across the golden grass of the prairie it makes my heart shudder to see it. Leaning low over the neck of your horse, urging it on, your long hair streaming like a banner behind you, and I know you're smiling even though I cannot see your face because you've left me so far behind.

I don't mind being left behind. You were always moving through this world with the quick grace of a sparrow's wing, or soaring high, like a spear point piercing starlight.

6.

I don't like the sixth dream.

In the sixth dream, I sleep through it all, safe and warm in my own bed, unaware that you are walking the tracks. In the sixth dream, I don't see you, I don't hear you, I can't help you. Maybe you called and I didn't answer. Or maybe you never called, because you thought I didn't care or love you enough to come for you when you needed me.

This is how the sixth dream goes:

There is the train and there is you and then there is only the train.

***

When I open my eyes, I can't hear the train. I still feel the thrum of it beneath my feet, but I don't know if it's approaching or receding. Standing outside your bedroom door, I listen for the sound of your voice, the shiver of your breath, the flutter of sparrow wings. Hoping you're here, hoping you'll stay, hoping we're both awake.

CLEAVER, MEAT, AND BLOCK

THE FIRST THING HANNAH LEARNED when she came to live with her grandparents after the Plague was how to wield the meat cleaver. Grandma taught her, guiding her hands in the backroom of the old butcher shop on Main Street. Showing her how to wrap her fingers around the handle, how to put her thumb on the spine of the handle for extra power and precision, how to let her wrist pivot when she cuts.

"You don't need to be strong," Grandma said. "The weight of the blade, the sharpness of the edge, is enough."

This past Christmas, Grandma and Grandpa gave Hannah a cleaver of her own. When she unwrapped it, Grandpa was already apologizing for not getting her new clothes or makeup or jewelry, even though such things are hard to come by these days. Hannah didn't know how to tell him she'd never received a better gift in all her fourteen years.

The cleaver is real and useful in a way few other objects in Hannah's life have ever been, and she loves everything about it. She loves the dark, smooth wooden handle; the solid *thunk* of the wide, rectangular blade when it shears through meat and bone and hits the wooden chopping block; the way the steel edge glistens beneath the lights.

Sometimes, when Hannah works in the butcher shop, she thinks about her parents and baby Daniel. They've been gone for three years, and she knows it's better not to dwell on the past, yet she cannot help it. Sometimes she thinks about Meg, their old dog, too. About Meg's silvered muzzle and silky, pointy ears. About the way Meg would sigh when she lay down on Hannah's bed every night. About Meg's pink and bloody guts torn out all over the driveway when the raveners fed on her.

Sometimes, though rarely, Hannah thinks about a stifling attic space above a hall closet, wooden beams digging into her back and legs, a trapdoor barred with a garden rake, and the sounds that came from the house below.

More often, though she tries not to, she thinks about Pete from school, and the way he looks at her.

***

Every day after school, Pete follows Hannah home. He trails behind her along the paths and streets, regardless of which way she chooses to go. When she enters her grandparents' house, two blocks away from the butcher shop, he lingers across the street, staring at the living room window as if he knows she's watching him from behind the heavy yellow drapes.

Every day, Hannah stands behind those drapes, waiting for Pete to skive off down the lane to his parents' house. She waits with Rosko, her grandparents' spaniel, beside her; her hands stroking the dog's silky, caramel-coloured fur until Pete is out of sight.

***

Rosko sleeps in Hannah's bed. That's the way it's been since she first got here. Every night he curls up beside her, so close she feels each quiver of fragile life beneath his ribs. She lays there beneath the pink and white quilt Grandma picked out for this room back when it was still the guest room rather than Hannah's room, and whenever Rosko whimpers in his sleep, she puts her arm around him.

Hannah doesn't want to love Rosko, and yet she cannot help it.

***

Before the Plague and the raveners, Pete and Hannah lived in the same neighbourhood in the same city. It's not like they were friends, but they went to the same school, though he was a grade ahead of her. Now, they both live in this run-down sawmill town full of old pickup trucks, faded strip malls, and resettled Plague survivors, but they never speak to each other. Hannah rarely speaks to anyone at all, but she knows the silence between her and Pete is different. It's more than an absence of words. It's like the steel blade of the cleaver, bright and hard and sharp enough to cut.

***

Pete's family moved to town two months after Hannah arrived with the other Plague orphans. First time she saw him, he rode his red bike with a group of friends past the butcher shop, on their way to buy homemade candy from the repurposed Tim Hortons down the street. She shouldn't have been surprised. Lots of survivors end up in this town because it's one of the few in the region that survived the Plague with most of its infrastructure intact. On days when the electricity works, residents can almost pretend the world is functional again.

Her grandparents have lived in this town all their lives, running the same butcher shop on Main Street since before Hannah's mom was born. Even though the government-run supply store opened down the block last year, selling dry and canned goods, hygiene products, medicines, and second-hand clothes, people still come to the butcher shop to buy meat. They stand at the shiny glass counter, chatting with Grandpa about the weather and the rationing and the freight trains that have just started moving through a couple of times per week. Hannah stays in the backroom with the cleaver, trying not to listen, trying not to think of which customers were raveners during the Plague, and which were not.

***

When Hannah wields the cleaver exactly right, when her grip is firm and her wrist pivots the way it is supposed to, then all her memories are sheared away until nothing exists except the meat and the cleaver and the *thunk* of steel against the block.

In those rare moments, Hannah can almost forget. She can almost forget the Plague. She can almost forget that her dog and her parents and Daniel were killed and eaten by Pete and his parents. Almost. But not quite.

***

Hannah hides beneath the fir trees at recess while Pete and his friends play tag in the schoolyard. They *call* it tag, but it's really a game of chase, and no matter how it starts, it always ends with the kids who were raveners chasing those who weren't.

Crouched beneath the drooping branches, knees and hands touching wet dirt and roots, Hannah watches as Pete knocks Alexa to the ground under the swings. Alexa doesn't try to fight once she's down. She doesn't scream even though her face is a mask of terror. Pete grabs her arms, pushes one knee into her midriff, opens his mouth and leans close to her face, jaws snapping. Hannah's heart thuds hard and fast in her chest, watching as Pete leans in to rip Alexa's throat open, as his fingers curl into claws.

Then he laughs and shouts, "Gotcha!" before he lets Alexa go and runs after someone else.

Alexa stays down. Hannah can't see her face, but she knows Alexa's crying.

Pete and the others chase Oscar next. Oscar is tall and fast, and it takes a big group of them to bring him down, all of them falling on top of him, clawing at his back, screeching and hollering, tearing at his clothes.

Hannah picks up a rock and holds it in her right hand, knuckles gone white.

That day in the city when the raveners came loping up the driveway, that day when baby Daniel wouldn't stop screaming, that day when Dad hoisted her up into the attic as the back door was pushed off its hinges, and the front door bent and shivered, that day, she held a pair of scissors in her hand. Huddled in the gloom beneath the rafters, she wasn't sure what she'd do if the trapdoor opened from below. Would she fight? Or would she let them kill her? Holding the scissors, she listened as baby Daniel went silent, as the raveners tore and swallowed.

Under the fir trees, Hannah holds on to the rock until the bell rings.

***

It's been two years since Hannah was found in the woods by a rescue and retrieval team, eighteen months since she came to stay with her grandparents.

She's learned a lot in eighteen months.

How to sharpen knives, how to mop the butcher shop's black and white tile floor, how to skim the fat and foam off Grandma's stock pot, how to put scraps and lard into the meat grinder, pushing the pieces down the hopper, turning the crank until everything is pushed out through the grinding plate, pale pink curls of sausage meat dropping into the stainless-steel bowl below.

But nothing holds her interest like the cleaver.

Working at the counter in the backroom, she grips the cleaver in her right hand while she holds the meat in place with her left. Grandma taught her how to wield the cleaver, but Grandpa taught her how to cut. How to turn a loin of pork into chops and roasts and stew meat. How to turn a slab of beef into steaks and brisket, blade roast, sirloin. How to separate a chicken into all its parts.

Before the Plague, Hannah would have never thought she'd end up working in her grandparents' butcher shop. Mom and Dad only brought her here for visits at Christmas, sometimes for a week in summer. Back then, Hannah dreamt of traveling the world and becoming a dog groomer or maybe a cartoonist.

These days, the butcher shop seems as good a place as any to make a life. There is nowhere to go, nothing to become. The world beyond the highway, beyond the train tracks, beyond the ocean, is broken, rent asunder by the Plague and the raveners and the riots and disasters that followed in their wake. Even now, no one knows how many died, how many lived, how many turned ravener, how many turned to meat.

Hannah knows it's best to look ahead. There's a vaccine now and a cure. People will never turn into raveners again. It was a virus that crept into people's brains, made the infected crave living flesh and blood, made them gather in hordes, made them break down doors and windows to get to the living people hiding inside, made them rip through ribs and skin and skulls with their teeth and fingers.

Look ahead. Make the best of things. That's what people say.

What they mean is, forget.

***

It's Saturday, and Hannah has been working in the butcher shop since breakfast.

She helps out every weekend and most weekday evenings after homework. Her grandparents worry about how much she works and her lack of friends, but it doesn't bother her.

Hannah works, cleaver in hand. The meat on the block is cold and slippery. It's been bled already, the carcass gutted and skinned, made ready for eating.

She is not thinking about school. Not about Pete. Not about waking in the night with Rosko beside her, listening for furtive noises outside. She is not thinking about Mom and Dad and Daniel. Not thinking about raveners, clawing at the scraps of plywood covering the windows. Not thinking about the stifling dusk that engulfed her, once the trapdoor closed. The smell of blood and offal wafting up from below, hours after the raveners had left the house. The wet gleam of blood on asphalt once she got outside. Moonlight on the pavement where the last bits of Meg had been ground into the pitted surface. Ragged taste of salt and bile in her mouth as she ran from the city, folding herself into the darkness of the woods beyond the highway.

Her vision blurs, making it hard to see, but the cleaver knows enough for both of them. It keeps cutting through bone and gristle and slippery meat while Hannah remembers.

She remembers everything. That is the curse of those who did not turn into raveners, to remember.

The raveners don't remember being raveners. Once the cure burned the virus out of them, they had no memory of what they'd done, they could not recall their hunger, guts and brains ripped out, limbs cracked, flesh chewed and swallowed.

The vaccine absolved them. There is no blame or guilt, no justice either.

But Hannah can't forget. Can't look ahead, can't make the best of things.

That's her secret, the one she dare not speak out loud to anyone.

Pete and the others who were raveners mostly look like ordinary people now. Except, when she catches sight of them at the edges of her vision, their faces slip like melting rubber masks, revealing other faces, leering and snarling, teeth and gullets.

She isn't sure how to tell masks from faces. Maybe there is no difference. Maybe no one, no matter who they are or what they did, have real faces. Maybe there are only masks, and nothing but the hollow darkness beneath.

Hannah looks down at the hand holding the meat, and for a moment it doesn't seem as if it belongs to her. The pale skin, the veins beneath, the bones covered in flesh and sinew. It's just another piece of meat for the cleaver to sort out on the block.

"Hannah, come have some lunch."

Grandma's voice stops the descending cleaver, the steely blade quivering above the wrist where the bones and joints hold it in place. Hannah puts the cleaver away and takes off her apron, hanging it on the hook beside the stove. She washes her hands and sits down with Grandma.

"You work too much," Grandma says as they dig into the flaky crust of the homemade chicken pie. Hannah watches the pale, creamy filling spilling out—chunks of chicken, green peas and golden carrots from the garden, flecks of fragrant thyme that Grandma dries in bunches in her kitchen.

"I like working," Hannah says.

Grandma doesn't say anything else and neither does Hannah, but the unspoken words—the words they both might say if they could find voices strong and gentle enough to hold them without shattering—are there in the warmth between them when Grandma touches her arm.

You do what you need to, that's what Grandma said that first night when Hannah couldn't fall asleep in the guest room. *I'm not going to tell you how to deal with it, because I don't know either.*

***

The house where Hannah's grandparents live is small and square, with a black tar-papered roof and white stucco walls. In the front garden, fading daisies and catmint peek out between sage and thyme, peas and beans. Like the backyard garden, it's ready for the last harvest. In summer, zucchini and onion, carrots and potatoes, tomatoes and beets, crowd together where the flower beds and the lawn used to be before the Plague, but it's autumn now, and everything will soon turn brown.

Inside, the house is all flowery wallpaper, chintz, and polished wood. It smells of firewood and lavender sachets. The back of the house looks out over the greenbelt and the gravel road beside the creek, and from her window on the second floor Hannah sees the river, the highway, and the train tracks.

Sometimes, when she stands in the window, breath catching on the glass, Hannah sees Pete down by the river, walking or riding his bike on the trails through the old scrapyards and abandoned buildings. Sometimes, he's with his friends, usually he's alone. She'd recognize him anywhere. That lopsided slope of his shoulders. The swing of his arms. The way he cocks his head when he looks around.

Along the river, there's a warren of run-down industrial properties, an old sawmill and a cement factory, a heap of rusted car remains and a scrapyard. From her vantage point, Hannah sees the tangled rolls of barbed wire and debris heaped up in that scrapyard. It was part of the barricade around the town during the Plague, when guards patrolled the perimeter 24/7, armed and ready.

The Plague never reached this town. Not one single ravener ever roamed its streets, though other communities along the highway were wiped out. No one knows why some places were spared. Maybe it was God's will, like the priest tells them in church. Maybe it's because there's no airport or harbour nearby, like their teacher says. Maybe it was just dumb luck, like Grandma thinks.

No one had time to build barricades around the city where Hannah lived. By the time people realized there was a Plague, it was already on the inside; inside the suburbs and the downtown core, inside the houses and trains and subway stations, inside hospitals and schools and preschools. One Tuesday, everything was fine with school and lasagna and Mom going to a yoga class at the rec-center. Next Tuesday, Dad was boarding up the windows, and most of the neighbourhood had turned ravener. The Tuesday after that, Hannah was all alone, in the woods.

Grandpa and Grandma only ever saw the Plague on TV, until the TV broadcasts stopped, the internet went down, and that big winter storm hit in the midst of everything, knocking out the electricity. After that, "everything went bonkers," like Grandpa says, for about a year.

They know what happened, everyone does, but knowing is not remembering. They don't lie awake at night, listening to the wind but hearing the raveners breathing outside the door, scratching at the walls and windows. They don't hear Daniel shrieking even though Mom is trying, trying, trying to make him shut the hell up, they don't hear the heavy thud when Dad falls to the floor. They don't know what it sounds like when raveners eat someone.

Hannah remembers, but cannot speak of it. Her memories are like a thousand thousand thousand screaming, bleeding mouths, and if she were to reveal them in the daylight, if she were to lay them bare in this house, she fears the horror of it might devour not just her, but Grandma and Grandpa and the street and the river and the entire world.

***

Hannah is chopping pork in the backroom, setting aside the scraps for a batch of Grandma's sage and onion sausage, when she hears the entry bell jingling.

"How's business?" someone asks Grandpa in the shop.

Hannah knows that voice. It's Pete's mom. She doesn't need to look to know what the woman looks like: neat hair, neat clothes, red lipstick and a smile. Her face so clean and polished you'd never know she ever tore raw meat off the bones.

"Can't complain," Grandpa answers. "People always need to eat."

Pete's mom laughs. In the backroom, the cleaver stops.

Grandma is standing next to Hannah at the counter, turning the crank on the meat grinder, and for a moment the grinder too goes silent. Hannah glances at Grandma, and before they both look away, Hannah catches a gleam of the cleaver's steel in Grandma's eyes. It's so brief that afterward she is not sure whether it was real, or whether she imagined it.

Then, the bell jingles again and Pete's mom leaves, carrying the meat she bought in a brown paper bag. In the backroom, Hannah closes her eyes, but the cleaver keeps working, moving with more speed and accuracy than she could ever manage on her own.

***

One October day, after school, Pete follows Hannah all the way to her door. He comes right up to the house behind her. The key slips between her fingers when she tries to get inside, away from Pete, and then Rosko is out on the porch before she can stop him. He's too happy, too wiggly, to contain. Same as Meg was, once.

"I like your new dog." Hannah turns and looks at Pete, really looks. His face is pale and smooth around the wet cave of his mouth, and she catches the glint of his teeth and tongue. He stares back at her, blue eyes shiny and blank. "I remember you," he says, and puts his hand on Rosko's head. It's just a brief touch, fingers curling into Rosko's caramel-coloured fur. "We went to the same school, remember?"

Rosko backs away from Pete, a growl lurking in his throat. Hannah feels the weight of her empty hands. If she had a rock, or a pair of scissors, she'd know what to do with her hands. But they are empty.

Looking at Pete, Hannah sees her fist go through his face, breaking it, smashing it to pieces, until she reveals the true face beneath. But instead she grips Rosko's collar and drags him inside, pulling the door shut behind her, locking it with the deadbolt and chain. The dog wiggles around her and she holds on to him, sitting there in the hallway, back braced against the door, waiting for the raveners to come.

She waits for a long time.

***

Once, and only once, Grandpa asked Hannah how she survived. She told him the truth. She hid. She hid when she could and ran when she had to. That's all. She wasn't smart or brave or strong, just lucky.

Grandpa didn't ask for details, but Hannah remembers the details. She remembers Dad telling Mom the army would surely come and get them out. She remembers how the raveners mostly roamed the cities and towns at first, so the woods and fields were safer. But eventually, the hordes headed out to hunt elsewhere. She remembers the places where it's harder for the raveners to find you. Narrow concrete pipes half-filled with fetid water and dead things. Root cellars barred from inside. Garages with metal doors. Shipping containers at the dock. She remembers what to eat to keep yourself alive even when you think you want to die.

Hannah remembers being found, too. She remembers the army truck and the smell of biodiesel and disinfectant and hot chocolate, the people in hazmat suits swabbing her arm, drawing blood, testing her for infection, telling her she was "clean" before they administered the vaccine. She remembers the months of boredom and half-decent meals at the quarantine camp, watching raveners be brought in each day on trucks, howling and scratching at each other, before they were penned, swabbed, cured, and put into a separate section of the camp.

Hannah dreams of the past every night. Sometimes, she's in the camp. Sometimes, she's in the woods. Sometimes, she's huddled beneath the roof, listening to Dad moaning below.

Every time she wakes up in her grandparents' house and sees the pink and white quilt, the world seems more unreal than what she left behind. Maybe she only dreamed that she was saved. Maybe she is still curled up in a concrete pipe by the river, gnawing on raw fish and worse.

Yet every day she gets out of bed, puts on her clothes, and acts as if she believes this is real. Every day she wraps the shreds of what is left of the old Hannah around the emptiness that is Hannah now, and no one seems to notice that there's nothing left of her beneath the rags.

***

The day when Pete finds her hiding beneath the trees at recess, Hannah doesn't have a rock. Her second mistake is to run. She should have just stood still and let him knock her down, get it over with, but when he comes for her, she bolts. Pete knocks her off her feet, pins her down, his breath warm and wet on her face and neck.

Hannah doesn't scream. Screaming will only bring more of them, she's seen it happen enough times. She knows she is going to die, knows she is already dead, that she died in that gloomy attic, that whatever came out of there, whatever hid in the woods for all those months, was not really Hannah, but someone, *something*, else.

But Pete does not rip her throat out. Instead he leans close and whispers in her ear, words as slippery as meat.

"I remember," he whispers. "I remember what they tasted like."

Then he's up and running again, chasing someone else. Hannah doesn't move. She looks up at the blue sky that is so thin and worn it might be ripped asunder by a gust of wind, or a scream, and reveal the black cold void beyond.

***

After work in the butcher shop that evening, Hannah cleans the meat cleaver and the knives and the chopping block. She scrubs the counters and mops the floor. It's the first time she brings the meat cleaver home with her. She wraps it in a towel and tucks it into her backpack.

That night, with the steel beneath her pillow, it's easier to sleep.

I remember.

She knows it's the truth, because it's sharp and it hurts and it cuts through every lie she has been told—about the Plague, about the cure, about the raveners. It reveals the world as it is, as it always was: a place where everyone is meat.

***

Rosko sometimes whines at night, wanting Hannah to let him out in the back yard, but she keeps him inside as much as she can after dark. Pets disappear all the time in this town. Cats. Dogs. Caged rabbits and chickens.

"It's coyotes," people say. "They're everywhere these days."

But Hannah hasn't seen any coyotes from her window or on the way home from school. Not a single one moving in the greenbelt, or by the river. She has just seen Pete and his friends, riding or walking through the tall grass and scrub, sometimes venturing into the woods beyond.

One night in late October when Rosko wakes her, he's growling rather than whining. Hannah pulls the cleaver from beneath the pillow and when they get downstairs, Rosko stands stiff and trembling, staring at the back door, hackles raised.

There are voices outside, low and muffled. Close.

Outside the kitchen window, the night is moonlit and frosty. Hannah shivers in her blue flannel pyjamas. She sees a thousand shadows in the yard, crouched and looming, hunched and menacing, fanged and clawed. She stands very still, listening, with the cleaver in her hand.

The cleaver is still warm from being in her bed, and when she raises it slightly, it feels light and quick in her hand, almost happy. Hannah understands. It's eager. Eager to cut, to chop, to slice. The weight and heft of it settles her heart and breathing, allows anger to come through, burning away the fear.

She opens the door a crack, keeping Rosko behind her.

"Go away," she shouts, and her voice sounds deeper and stronger when she holds the cleaver. "Go away, you fuckers!"

It's the cleaver that makes her swear. She never has before. But now she wants to.

There is rustling, there is wind, the creak of the fence. Maybe something scrambles over it. Maybe there are footsteps, disappearing down the narrow path along the greenbelt.

Coyotes, that's what people will say, but the cleaver knows the truth and so does Hannah.

***

Afterward, Hannah lies awake, holding Rosko. He's smaller than Meg was when she slipped out while Dad tried to reinforce their front door. He weighs only a little more than Daniel did the last time she held him.

Mom wouldn't let Hannah take Daniel with her in the attic when she hid. "There's no time, and he might cry," Mom shouted at Dad as the raveners pounded on the doors. It was true, maybe he would have cried, but he was a good baby, and Hannah tried so hard to make him understand how important it was to be quiet. Maybe she could have saved him.

Hannah lies awake with the cleaver underneath her pillow until jaundiced morning light filters through the pink and yellow curtains.

I remember.

Of course Pete remembers. They all do, and everyone knows it, even if they pretend otherwise. It's easier to pretend. Because so many of the survivors were raveners. Because no one knows what else to do. Because it's over now, and everyone should get on with their lives.

Hannah wraps the cleaver in a towel and puts it in her backpack.

She's tired. Tired of being scared. Tired of wrapping the shreds of old Hannah around the emptiness. Tired of not screaming.

She knows what she must do, and so does the cleaver.

***

The rest of the week, Hannah walks a different way home from school every day. It takes longer, because she avoids the roads and streets, staying closer to the river and the woods, but for two days Pete does not find her. On the third day, he's back, following her through a copse of trees by the train tracks, past the old sawmill, through the mess of wrecked cars near the greenbelt. The clouds hang low, fat with rain, and Hannah runs the last bit home, cleaver bouncing in her pack, heart thumping in her chest until she is safe inside with Rosko.

She walks new routes every day after that, knowing Pete will follow.

It's October, then November, and the sun goes down earlier every evening. There is only a slip of light left after school, and dusk lurks all around while Pete follows her. Hannah stretches out the walks home until there is barely enough light to see by. Some days, she doesn't make it to work in the butcher shop at all. Other days, she hides from Pete in the wreckage of old buildings or the hulks of rusted cars, watching as he searches for her, waiting to see what he will do. Those days, she gets home so late that Grandma and Grandpa have already gone to bed.

She knows they're worried, but they don't ask where she's been.

Hannah wonders if they're scared that she would lie, or if they're scared she'd tell the truth.

***

It's late November. The air smells like frost and snow and Hannah's breath hangs in the air in ragged tufts on the way home from school. She chooses the longest route, and Pete follows about a hundred meters behind. Whenever Hannah turns and looks at him, she shivers—a bit from the cold, not so much from fear.

Near the river, she starts to run. Not fast enough to really get away. Just fast enough to make Pete follow, but once they've left the houses and the streets behind, the chase is real. It's like the day she fled the city with a pack of raveners at her back. That time, the raveners found an old woman hiding in a car and dragged her out, giving Hannah enough time to escape.

Pete chases and Hannah runs, heading for the scrapyard. It's a jumble of old machinery, rusting metal, sagging storage sheds, busted cars, and no one is watching except the broken eyes of the buildings.

Even though Hannah has it all planned out—where to hide, where to wait for him if he falls behind—Pete catches her unaware, jumping out from a pile of old tires and knocking her to the ground. In the gathering dusk, Hannah fights silently, but Pete is strong, and there's no other meat here to divert his attention. His hands grip tight, pinning her down, her right arm trapped underneath her at a painful angle. Panting, Pete leans close.

"Not so tough now, are you?" His breath smells sour and sickly and Hannah tries to knee him in the groin, but he holds her down. "Don't you think I see the way you look at me? Like you're better than me. Like you didn't hide in the mud and eat bugs and worms and roadkill to survive. Like that makes you better than me."

Hannah tries to buck him off, but he's too heavy. She wriggles her right arm halfway free and feels around for the backpack stuck underneath her legs, its zipper half open.

"You *should* be scared of me." Pete's voice is harsher now. "All of you should be. You shouldn't have made it out of that house. I looked for you after we ate your dog and your brother. I looked and looked, and I knew I smelled you but then..." His voice wavers, his face crumples. "I remember it. Every day. Every night. All the time. What do you think that's like? Mom says I can't talk about it, not even to her, but...I..."

Hannah stares at his pale, flushed face. There are tears in his eyes, snot dribbling from his nose. As if *he* has anything to mourn. As if *he* has lost anything. Then Pete sees her looking and he growls, slipping a grin back on his face before grabbing her by the throat. His mouth flaps open, wet and pink and full of teeth, and the memories ignite in Hannah's head, burning through her, a conflagration consuming doubt and fear, consuming the girl she was before, consuming everything but meat and steel.

The backpack is pinned below her thighs. She reaches into it for the cleaver, and the cleaver does not hesitate. It's sharp and efficient. It's useful and reliable even when Hannah is not, and Pete doesn't see it, doesn't know the blade is coming, doesn't realize it's there, until the steel bites into his face.

You don't need to be strong. The weight of the blade, the sharpness of the edge, is enough.

Closing her eyes, Hannah folds herself into the emptiness that has grown inside her since she hid in that attic. The cleaver doesn't need her help. It knows what to do. It knows what to do with every piece of slippery wet meat held down on the block, and here in the scrapyard, the cleaver does its work while the world inside and around Hannah screams, a thousand thousand thousand mouths yawning wide, shrieking in terror and despair, wrath and ruin, grief and devastation. So many mouths: her own, Mom's, Dad's, Daniel's, Meg's, all of them, the whole world, crying out in agony and triumph while the cleaver goes about its business.

***

Afterward, it's quiet, and for a single, razor-thin sliver of time—a sliver so thin and fine Hannah can see both past and future through it—no one is screaming. Not in Hannah's head, not elsewhere either. The world's gone mute, watching Pete in the gravel. Hannah watches as the last of the bruised daylight fades. She watches closely, hoping to see the moment when he turns into meat, but it doesn't happen. It already happened. He was always meat. Just like Mom and Meg. Just like Dad and Daniel. Just like she is.

There's a culvert of corrugated steel nearby where the creek spills into the river, its tarnished vault high enough to stand inside, and she drags the body there. If Hannah were alone, she might have left it in the open, to be found. But the cleaver knows best. It knows how to sort out the meat beneath the blade, and it knows what they can do, together.

***

Grandma finds her in the backroom of the butcher shop early next morning. Worry and relief chase across her face as she looks at Hannah's bloody shirt and torn jeans, her dirty shoes, her heavy, wet backpack.

Hannah holds Grandma's gaze and Grandma does not look away.

"Pete told me he remembered," Hannah whispers while the cleaver keeps working. "Maybe they all do."

Even then, Grandma does not look away. She *sees*. She sees the meat on the block, and the meat on the floor, she sees it for what it is, sees the world as it is, and Hannah, in turn, sees the exact moment when Grandma understands, when she understands everything—cleaver, meat, and block.

Maybe her old hands tremble. Maybe not.

"Right," Grandma says, fumbling with her apron. "Pies and sausages it is. But they're not for everyone," she adds sharply, and there's a glint of steel behind her glasses when she gets the meat grinder ready. "Only for those that might remember and appreciate the taste."

Hannah nods and wraps her hand around the handle as the cleaver goes back to work.

HARE'S BREATH

1947, Västerbotten, Sweden

IT'S MIDSUMMER'S EVE AND EVEN this close to midnight there's no darkness, only a long, translucent dusk that will eventually slip into dawn.

Britt and I are fifteen, and she has just come back from That Place, the one the adults won't talk about even when they think I'm not listening. Something's happened to her there, but I don't understand what it is, and she can't find the words to tell me.

We're sitting on the wooden fence near my family's potato patch, looking down the slope at the red-painted barn and stable, watching the hare. He sits upright on his haunches by the forest's edge, ever watchful, bending now and then to nibble grass and clover, grey-brown fur all sleek and trim, long ears turning.

The hare reminds me of Britt: dark eyes watching to see if you've come to kill it; long legs always ready to run.

Shapes and shadows move in the gloom beneath the forest's dark-fringed spruce and pine, and Britt says it's the trolls that live there, restless in the long summer dusk, hiding themselves under rocks and roots and glossy lingonberry leaves. She says you can speak to them when the sun and moon have gone down. You can even speak to the hare, then: if you know how, if he trusts you enough to let you. Most nights, I might not have believed her, even though she goes farther into the woods than anyone else I know, but tonight is Midsummer's Eve, when the skein between tale and truth is thin enough to pass through.

We've helped decorate the village maypole with birch leaves and flowers, such as there are up here so far north in June. It's cold. We wear woolen sweaters over summer dresses, bare legs swinging, and from far away I can hear music, or maybe it's just the river's distant voice: B minor, a song like whispers and sun on water. Britt taps her fingers to the melody, so I know she hears it too. In the silence between us, the notes seem to resonate within her, tugging at her, rippling through her, plucked on strings of guts and breath, pain and memory.

I've picked seven kinds of flowers to put under my pillow, picked them special, keeping silent all the while, climbing over seven fences to do it right. I would dream about the man I'll marry if I slept on them. But I don't want to sleep, and I don't want to marry any man either, so instead I braid them into a crown for Britt. She sits so still, looking at my fingers braiding: purple wood cranesbill, white bishop's lace and oxeye daisies, red campion, yellow buttercups, blue forget-me-nots and fragile harebells. Once it's done, she bows her head and I place it on her curly brown hair, a coronation. I see her change, then, radiant like the pictures in Grandma's illustrated Bible, where the golden rays emanate from Jesus's head.

"You're the prettiest thing I ever saw," I say, straightening her crown and halo, and that makes her smile, even though sorrow peeks through the ragged edges of her joy.

My older siblings all moved out and away before I even started school, and Britt has always been as close as a sister. Sometimes she's an older sister who tells me things not even the adults seem to know. Other times she can't understand things my five-year-old cousin takes for granted. She is and always will be my ghost and shadow, my guilt and glory, my secret wish and hidden grief.

"Want to see?" she asks, smile already slipping. "Want to see what they did?"

I don't answer, but she takes her clothes off anyway, wool and dress, no linens underneath, and stands there naked except for the flowers left askew in her hair. Bruises run the length of her back, down her buttocks, the back of her thighs, swirls and stripes of blue and red and black, inflicted where her clothes are sure to hide them. But that is not what she wants me to see.

The front of her body is pale and untouched, except for the scar.

"I couldn't leave unless I let them cut me," she says, tracing the red welt of healed skin on her lower belly, nipples and pink skin prickling in the chill. "There wasn't nothing there to take, but they did it anyway."

I see, I hear, but I don't understand. I just want to touch her, hold her, comfort her, but I know she'd startle like the hare, I know she's not one for touching.

Her smile has slipped off all the way now, nothing's left of it, and without another word, she turns and walks down the slope towards the forest, leaving me, leaving her dress and her sweater on the fence, flower crown still askew, long strides cleaving the tall grass. The hare sits up as she approaches, flicking his ears, listening and waiting. For a moment, they remain completely still within each other's gaze. Then, they start running, together, until the forest hides them both.

***

1940

I'm eight years old the first time I understand that Britt's father beats her, and that that's why Mother lets her come to stay with us. Those are the days when there are empty bottles smashed outside Britt's house, when we can hear him bellowing her name through thin walls and rattling windows.

Britt shares my narrow bed those nights, and we sleep skavfötters—our heads at either end, legs meeting in the middle. She eats dinner with us, too; hands fluttering over the bread and butter, fingers clumsy when she wields a spoon or fork. Mother always lets her have seconds, even though she'll never let me eat my fill at the table until everyone else has finished.

"He's not my dad," Britt tells me, when we sit together in the hayloft, listening to the horses chewing oats below. "My real dad lives in the river. Mamma said so before she went away."

But Britt can't even read, and everyone knows her mom was a whore, so I don't believe it until she takes me to the river. We look and look from the bridge, in the reeds and beneath the lily-pads, and finally we find him. He looks dead, but Britt says he isn't. She pokes him with an oar and he rolls over and floats up, wrapped in trailing lily stems, some of them wound around his head and long hair like a crown, and he's naked. The only thing missing is his fiddle, which Grandma says he ought to have.

He looks so beautiful I might have gone into the water myself even if I cannot swim: pale skin pulled tight over bones and dreams, dark hair like Britt's—all curls and waves and ripples.

When Britt wades into the water, he opens his eyes and pulls her down. I want to scream and run away, but she's told me to wait, so I just stand there on the shore. Half a day goes by before she surfaces all soaked and dripping, mud blossoming beneath her in the water.

(Afterwards, I know it can't have happened that way, that she can't have stayed under that long, that I must have made it up or imagined it. And yet I remember it clearly, the smell of the water as he broke the surface: mulch and rot and roots, the sheen of his skin as he reached for her, the hiss of his breath as he went below again.)

"I didn't want to stay. Don't like it down there anyway, and he was mad for me not bringing his fiddle," Britt says. "I told him I might bring it if he'd give me something for it."

"Like what?" I ask, but she won't say what magic she would ask for.

"Don't tell anyone," she whispers when I help her pick the twigs and leaves out of her wet hair, and I promise.

***

1937

We are five years old when Britt shows me the fiddle packed away in a black case lined with red velvet underneath her bed. The veined wood is smooth and lustrous, like honeycombs and sunshine and autumn leaves. She plucks the strings with soft fingers, and the sound is water dripping from trees, is shade beneath heavy branches, is the rills of meltwater beneath thin ice in spring.

"Mamma says it's mine."

I touch, almost fearful of the smoothness of that varnish, the brittleness of that wood, the trembling power trapped within those strings and tuning screws. The fiddle is a treasure beyond price in a place where there is mostly want. It is beauty in a place where there are only plain and practical things. It is magic tucked beneath a lumpy mattress.

***

1946

I'm fourteen when they take Britt away.

Mother says it's because Britt's not right. That's why the school wouldn't have her. Because she couldn't sit still, couldn't listen, didn't write the words down as they were supposed to be written, didn't sing the psalms right, or read the sentences the way they were supposed to be read. She'd read other stories on the pages, full of snakes and claws and ripping beasts and naked men and their...*genitalia*, as I heard the teacher whisper behind her hand to my mother. No more school for her after that, just work. Be good. Be grateful. Bow and scrape.

A car comes and takes her away one day when I'm at school.

"An institution," Grandma says, and I can tell she's almost crying. "That's where they're taking her."

I march down to the river looking for Britt's dad. It's a stupid thing to do, but I do it because I have nowhere else to be angry. After a bit of searching, I think I find the spot where Britt and I saw him before, but no one's there. I sit down in the grass on the sloping riverbank and tell him that no matter what Britt's mom did to him, no matter what she stole or what promises she broke, he can't punish Britt for it.

"Help her," I pray, hands clasped as if it's Sunday. "Please."

I know I should be praying to God or Jesus, but they are far away, in the church, above the clouds, pressed flat and dry between the pages of Grandma's heavy Bible. Not as close as the river, not as close as the water lapping over mud and rocks and toes.

Something almost surfaces in the stream beyond; ripples radiating out. Most likely it's a fish catching a fly or water strider, but I make myself believe that he heard me. Then I throw a rock, as big as I can heft, out there just for good measure, hoping it'll crack his head open.

(I know what everyone says, that Britt's father was a no-good vagrant, tattare, traveler, passing through the village when Britt's mom was sixteen. That he ran off because he got into a fight and cut a man, that he was afraid of going to jail, that he left his fiddle behind and never came back. I know that no one else has seen the face beneath the water-lilies. I know, I know, I know what people say, but I know it's not the truth: it is only the gossamer of reality pulled over the true story beneath, the story Britt told me, the story I am telling you.)

***

1947

When Britt comes back, she tries to tell me of That Place. A house, she says, with beds and clean sheets and metal tables and sharp knives laid out on trays. The words she has brought with her skip and sink (feeble-minded), teeter and totter (mental deficiency due to inheritance), break and crack (delinquent), and when I don't understand, she gets angry and runs away.

"A girl like her... She doesn't need the trouble," Mom says while her fingers are busy knitting socks. "She'll have an easier time of it now."

I don't know what that means, but I know it's a lie.

***

1990

I'm fifty-eight years old—career, no kids, happy on the weekends, busy folding laundry—when a documentary on the radio tells me what happened to Britt.

A kitchen towel. *Sweden's State Institute of racial biology.* T-shirt and sweatpants. *Racial hygiene.* Three pairs of socks. *Forced sterilizations.* A pair of jeans. *63,000 individuals.* Two pairs of underwear. *To raise the quality of the population stock and prevent degeneration of the race.*

I sit beside my pink geraniums and I can't stop crying. There is no hare's gaze to hold me here, no music playing, no stolen fiddle's magic to stir me; but I can feel the shiver of the hare's breath against my skin, and I can hear the melody anyway. I've dreamed of it every night since 1947. I know that the world is hollow: an awful place of despair and cruelty and injustice. And I know that the world is holy: a beautiful place of joy and radiance and moments braided together like flowers, our love mostly hidden in the quiet spaces between everything we say and do to each other.

***

1947

The last time I see Britt is after midnight that Midsummer's Eve.

She comes to logen, the place where everyone is dancing and drinking beneath the maypole. The sky is fading into deeper blue, but the light remains, sheer like worn-out linen.

Britt is still naked, scar and bruises bared, feet and shins covered in dirt and blood, mosquito bites and scratches, as if she's been running through the woods to get here. The only thing she's carrying is the fiddle and the bow, and everything she is and was and ever will be from this moment on is revealed before us: dirty and transcendent, broken and divine.

Dance and music end. Britt takes out the bow, tightens the horsehair, and sweeps it over the strings, fiddle tucked up on her shoulder. No one tries to stop her. No one speaks or moves. I've never seen her play before, but the sound she makes is fog rising off the water, is the darkness beneath the bridge, is the shade and gloom below the surface, is the smooth gleam of rocks at the bottom of the river, is the slow glide and swirl of the water's current in the heat of summer.

Her hands, those hands that won't do anything right, that can't wield pencils or knitting needles, those hands our teacher smacked with a metal ruler so many times Britt's knuckles bled and puffed, those hands braid notes together that shiver through our souls and unspoken dreams, through the skies and heavens. It is a spell—rippling and quavering, reflecting ourselves and the darkness knit into the light within us all—and for a little while we might have followed her anywhere, might have listened to anything she said or played, might have understood her, but it's not for keeps: when the music stops, she's Britt again, the whore's daughter.

She walks by me, past me, through me, away, holding on to that fiddle, and she smiles, still crowned by flowers, haloed, radiant. Her hand caresses me, and my cheek burns at the touch, though I'm not sure whether the heat is hers or mine or ours.

"Don't tell them where I went," she says, and I nod.

I've kept that promise ever since. It is the only vow I've never broken.

Then she runs: long legs moving through the tall grass, taking her back into the woods.

***

The next day, I found Britt's wilted crown hanging off the edge of the bridge, its braided stems still unbroken. No one ever found her body. Some said she was trapped below the river's surface, snagged on roots or rocks. I knew it wasn't so. I knew Britt would have never stayed beneath.

It wasn't her fault, none of it. No one should have beaten her. No one should have bruised or scarred her. No one should have cut her to make her fit. Some people can't ever make themselves fit into small rooms, into narrow and cramped words, can't make what they need to say fit into sentences and books and lined paper. But still, people try, they try to cut others into pieces, bend and twist them as to fit into the space provided.

Why must everyone fit into church and school and work and polished shoes and small rooms and wooden coffins, in the end, to sink into the dirt?

I watched the men in boats dredging the river, searching for her, and I thought of the man beneath the mud and water-lilies, thought of his fiddle and what tune he might make it play. All the while, I kept my eyes on the dark-fringed pine and spruce on the other side of the bridge, waiting for the hare to see me.

I go back to the old place at Midsummer every year. The slope is overgrown with grass and nettles and slender birch trees. There is no potato patch anymore, the old house is warped and sagging, and no music comes from the river because the water is choked with weeds and silt, but a hare still visits. She knows me and I know her: grey-brown fur all sleek and trim, long ears turning, eyes ever watchful. I've seen her with her leverets: every Midsummer's Eve she brings another two, running with her in the meadow down towards the river, through the long, translucent dusk slipping into dawn.

***

Footnote: "*The so-called sterilization laws were instituted by the Swedish parliament in 1934 and 1941. Both allowed sterilization without consent under certain conditions. The reasons (indications) to perform sterilizations were threefold: eugenics (race/genetic hygiene), social and medical. Of the total number of sterilized individuals, 93 percent were women.*"

(From the report "Steriliseringsfrågan i Sverige 1935–1975" / "The issue of sterilization in Sweden 1935-1975," issued by Socialdepartementet / Ministry of Health and Social Affairs, Sweden, March 2000.)

MOTHERS, WATCH OVER ME

EVEN IN THE DREAM, MAYA knows her pup is dying.

She dreams of a lone mother-dog in the time before the packs, before the dens, before the sky cleared, before the flames on the horizon went out. Mother-dog walks through dust of the Forbidding, beneath the same skyfire that glows ever-brighter in Maya's waking world, walking towards the towers, carrying a pup in her jaws.

In Maya's dream, Mother-dog is starlight and shadow, and the dirt glimmers where her paws touch the ground. Mother-dog does not speak, but Maya's own voice ripples through the stillness of the Forbidding, stirring dust and silence:

Watch over me, Mother. Watch over them.

***

Nema is braiding bark in her den on the upper riverbank when Maya enters, tail wagging low in greeting.

"The sixth is dying," she says, pacing. It takes an effort to be away from the pups so soon, even though she can see her den from here.

Nema doesn't look up.

"I know. Knew it soon as I saw it born."

Maya watches her mother's golden fur in the sunlight; watches her compact, sleek body that is so unlike Maya's own tall and shaggy frame; watches Nema's long and strangely dexterous claws that wrap and twine strips of bark, making a quickly growing length of rope.

She thinks of all the things she wanted to shape when she was younger, envying the way Nema would grip and hold with ease. Nema says that sturdy paws make for an easier life: "Long claws slow you down," and Maya knows it's true enough: long-claws rarely hunt for themselves. But what is sometimes curse, is sometimes blessing, too.

"My pup must live."

"Why?" Nema asks.

Maya hesitates. With twelve litters before this, she has seen pups slip away before, has given birth to stillborn ones, as well.

"It's a telling."

Nema looks up.

"What telling?"

Maya paces, then sits. She's never had a telling before, has only heard Nema speak of them: the knowing without doubt, the all-consuming urge to obey. Like the year Nema knew about the forest fire before it happened. Like when she made the pack move from its denning spot downriver, before the old place flooded.

"That the pup must live. That I must go into the Forbidding. That I must bring the pup to the towers, to God."

Nema puts down her craft. Maya knows her mother wants to argue, but Nema also knows better than anyone that it's pointless to quarrel with a telling.

"I must carry the pups. Can you craft me a thing like you wove for Arras, the baskets for gathering herbs and plants, could you make one for carrying the pups?"

"I could."

"Can it be ready tomorrow?"

Nema looks at her supply of bark and reeds; calculating.

"Yes." Then: "Figure two days solid walking to the towers. Figure three with the pups."

Maya knows what she's not saying: that slow pups rarely live more than three days, and none live more than four.

***

The pups are at Maya's belly for most of the day, but the lastborn still won't feed, not even when Maya gently nudges it over to where the milk seeps out. Like the others, it's speckled black and grey with white marks on its chest and toes, but it came out not breathing, wrapped tight in its amniotic sac. Maya had to prod and lick until the pup drew breath. Now she touches it gently, cleaning its face and rump, feeling its fragile warmth and faltering heartbeat.

Between the sunset clouds outside, the skyfire flames white. It has been burning ever brighter since winter. Most dogs say it's a star like any other, but Nema says elsewise, and even in her old age, Nema sees true.

Maya shivers. She thinks of Mother-dog in her dream, and feels the telling stir inside her bones.

***

Nema comes by at dusk, carrying straw and bark from the forest, taking time to cradle each pup in her deft paws before she leaves. In the pack, only Nema and ancient Arras are long-claws, and none of Nema's pups or Maya's have ever inherited those flexible toes. None, except the sixth.

"Can you feed it?" Maya asks.

She has seen Nema do it before, for other slow pups in other litters, and now Nema does it for the sixth: suckling milk from Maya's teat, dribbling it into the little one's mouth, holding its jaws open with one long, careful claw.

"Can't do more now," Nema says once the pup has swallowed some. She sniffs it gently before she puts it down. "It won't make it to the towers. Even if it does, God might not be there anymore." Nema's eyes gleam as she turns in the den's opening. "It isn't even strong enough for a name. You know it."

"It will be."

It will be, Maya repeats to herself, touching the sixth with her breath and tongue, her thought and nose.

***

That night, the skyfire burns so bright it devours the stars around it and Maya cannot sleep. In the dark, the scents tell her of the only world she knows: the forest on the slope above the dens, the shrubs and reeds by the river below, and on the other side of the water, a narrow strip of grass, fading into the shadows and dust and eternal gray of the Forbidding. Far beyond the river, beyond sight or nose or hearing, are the broken towers.

Nema's stories say the towers once glowed in the night, but that the lights were extinguished long ago, in the time before the packs, before the dens, before the mountains burned. The river draws the line between life and death. That's the way it's always been. To cross the water is to leave the world.

"Nema says you're leaving." The moon outlines Belg's high-legged, grey body with silver light. It's a long time since he was at her teat. All her other pups have moved away or died; life brought them to her and took them away. Only Belg remains. "Why would you risk the pups?"

"It's a telling."

"Yours or Nema's? Like her nightmares of the star? That it will kill us all? Long-claws have strange thoughts. Don't trust in that."

"The telling is mine this time."

Belg sits. He peers at the sleeping pups. Maya thinks of the fathers of her litters. None of them alive. The last one, Fire, died with a deep scratch down his belly, given by a stalker. She thought it then, but knows it now: there will be no more pups. These six are her last.

"There is no God. No life for pups in the Forbidding, either," Belg growls. "Stay."

Maya stands up to challenge him, feeling her body sag and creak even as her hackles rise, teats hanging low as the pups whimper beneath her. Belg holds his stance a moment longer, then shakes himself and leaves.

He's not a bad leader, Maya reminds herself when she lies down with the pups again. *Just strong and stubborn. Too much like me.*

***

Before the sun slips free of the horizon, Nema brings the weaving: two baskets held together by straps and loops.

"It will sit around your chest, hold the pups on either side. The flaps are to keep them dry, should it rain."

Maya waits for Nema to feed the sixth before she slips the baskets on: her legs through the loops, the woven strap braced against her chest, another strap around her ribcage, holding the baskets steady against her sides. It fits snug but comfortable.

Nema helps her put the pups in, three on either side. The sixth is so weak it hangs unmoving in Nema's jaws.

Most of the pack has gathered in the dawn-light, pups and mothers, fathers and elders. They stand quiet, awkward, in the shifting of the shadows. Maya knows they think her already dead, that this is their reverence and farewell—same as they'd offer any dog wandering off to die from age or sickness.

"Tread careful," Nema says, their heads touching. Maya tries not to whimper. "The birds in the Forbidding have moved on for the season. The stalkers should have moved on, too."

Should have.

Belg watches, tall legs stiff, shaggy tail high. Maya walks over, head down, nose trembling with memories of the pup he was: tumbling his litter-mates in the dirt, always resisting her paw when she cleaned him.

The strongest of my pups. Strong for one, strong for many.

She licks his snout, wags her tail held low. Belg's tail lowers, too, but he doesn't speak.

She trots past him, away from the pack, down to the river. Maya has crossed this ford many times, chasing fish and birds and stalkers, never going farther than the strip of green along the other bank. Now, her paws are heavy and reluctant, the river wider than she remembers. The smells ahead are warning her to stay, to go back to the safety of the den.

It's the whimpering pups that make her move, make her run through the shallow stream, across the grass, into the desolation beyond. Belg howls, and there's an unexpected tone of longing in his keening voice. Turning, Maya sees Nema on the slope beside the dens. Nema doesn't howl, but her sadness is an ache in Maya's flesh. When she moves on, she feels Nema's mind withdraw from hers until not even the faintest touch of it remains.

In the Forbidding, the ground is cracked and pitted, covered with ever-moving swirls of dust. The air and dirt smell barren and decayed. There's no scent of dogs except the distant, fading tendrils from the packs that live along the river. But there is sound. The Forbidding thrums with a pulse, a tremor so deep and resonant Maya feels it in her skin and bones, burrowing beneath her thoughts—willing her to turn, to stop, to leave, to lie down and die. Walking forward is like pushing into a storm, like stumbling through heavy snow, a barrier within and without. Maya knows she would've faltered a thousand times, if the telling did not force her steps.

Three days to reach the towers where God lives, if the stories told are true. No dog has gone there and returned for many lifetimes. There are stories of pups being carried to the towers, being healed, being changed. More tales of dogs that never returned. Maya wonders whether such things really happened many times, or if they happened only once, and have been retold in many different ways, as seems to be the way with tales.

There is no God.

Maya walks on, clinging to the telling, listening to the shallow breathing of the sixth pup each time she stops, willing it to live, to stay.

Even if there is no God, even if there is nothing else in all the world, there is still me.

Stay with me.

***

In the night, Mother-dog returns, the pup still in her jaws. Maya finds no words to say, other than the ones she has already spoken:

Watch over me, Mother. Watch over them.

Mother-dog doesn't slow her steps, but it seems to Maya that her head turns, that the eyes of shadow and starlight rest on her for a little while.

***

The pups stir when Maya wakes. Even the sixth moves and whimpers. She sniffs its paws, thinking of Nema's claws, weaving bark and straw.

Maya walks on towards the towers—through the dust, through the thrum of the Forbidding, through her own despair. Mother-dog's glimmer trail can't be seen, but Maya feels it, like she used to feel Nema's mind guiding her when she was hurt or frightened, like she feels the telling in her bones, like she feels the lives of her pups quavering in her veins.

At midday, she chases off some crows and eats what they've left of a rodent carcass. There's a trickle of rainbow-clouded water and a patch of shade beneath a tree nearby, and she rests, feeding the pups. The sixth doesn't stir. Its life is slipping from her grip.

The five pups tear at her teats. She speaks the names she gave them as they were born:

"Belg and Fire. Deon and Nema. Thunder."

No name for the sixth. Not strong enough. Not yet.

Why am I here? Why am I risking our lives?

There's no answer, just the telling, lodged deep in her marrow, driving her on.

After drinking from the stream, she dribbles water into the sixth pup's mouth, cursing her clumsy paws. She thinks of Nema, thinks of Belg, his howl across the river, but when she looks back, there's nothing there: the land rises and falls—the river and the life it shelters is out of sight and scent and hearing.

The rain comes as Maya sets off, drops shedding from the woven flaps of Nema's baskets. Maya is cold and wet. She whispers to the pups:

"Stay with me."

Sometimes she thinks she sees Mother-dog ahead, sometimes behind, sometimes above, running in the skies, chasing the ravenous skyfire far above the clouds and sun.

Watch over me, Mother. Watch over them.

***

The stalker falls on Maya at nightfall, at the outskirts of the Forbidding, the towers looming close. It's a mangy thing, lean and scarred, strong and desperate in its hunger. Maya doesn't even smell it until it's there: a blur of yellow-black striped fur, claws raking her flank, spilling the pups from the baskets as she tumbles in the dust.

Fear and rage turn everything to teeth and blood. They tumble through the rough and thorny undergrowth, claws tearing at soft bellies, teeth ripping at ears and eyes. In the quiet of the Forbidding they are noise and fury, hiss and bark and growl. Maya knows that something, someone, fights with her, in her: sharing her skin, giving her a strength and tenacity she has long since lost. Mother-dog. Belg. Nema. Maya feels them all with her, in her, and together they rip, claw, kill.

The stalker bleeds out in the dust. Maya is bleeding too.

The pups whimper. Maya stands over them, limbs trembling, tongue dripping, the thrum of the Forbidding so loud and deep it almost strips her bare. She has no strength to move the pups very far, but finds shelter beneath a rocky ledge, carrying them there one by one.

Two pups are hurt, scratched by stalker claws, but they're alive, even the sixth, each stained with dirt and drool and blood. She licks them clean, gathers them against her before she tends her own cuts, exposed flesh quivering.

The sixth sleeps curled up against her chest that night, its shallow breaths mingling with her own laboured breathing, tethering their lives together. A chill night-wind makes Maya shiver, but when the pups sleep she limps over to the carcass, tearing open the belly, ripping out the soft parts, gorging on the stalker's last bits of strength.

***

In the morning, nothing stirs in the Forbidding except the shadow of a bird rippling across the ground. Maya's body aches. Nema's weaving is torn, but the towers are close now. She puts the pups into the basket that is still whole: it hangs crooked, but stays on.

Maya limps, blood dripping in her tracks. She has lost the glimmer trail, can't smell it, can't feel anything but fear. All she feels and hears and smells are the pups, dying as she carries them in between the broken towers, her tired paws stumbling on the rock-strewn, fissured ground.

How will she find God? She sniffs the air, but it gives no clues. Nothing smells like life here. No life. No pack. No dogs. No God.

All day she searches: limping, stumbling, bleeding. At dusk, the pups mewl and whimper at her belly, and she wonders if she has milk enough for all of them. The sixth is fading—its life so sheer and thin there's barely anything left for death to take.

Mother, she thinks, and sees Nema before her, though it is not only Nema but every other mother-dog that has come before. Maya sees them all: all the mothers back to the beginning of days, gathering around her, muzzles grey and black and brown, fur soft and shaggy, scarred ears and crooked tails. They are shadows and starlight. They are the beginning and the end.

Mother. Mothers. Watch over me. Watch over them.

***

When God comes, God is merciful. God lifts her up in gleaming arms that pulse with light: white and blue, radiating through glossy, cool, grey skin. God is tall and angular and wide, moving smoothly, as if carried by a river or a breeze. There's a hum and whir to God's presence: like a song, like a purpose, like a telling. Maya hears it, and feels the meaning of its song:

Rescue. Assist. Observe.

Maya tries to say something, but isn't sure that God would hear or understand. *What language does God speak?* she wonders, before she slips away.

***

Maya wakes in another place: light, warm, safe. It is a vast room with walls of stone, angular and smooth, covered in squares and rectangles of shimmering grey and black, adorned with coloured, flashing lights. There's a deep hum suffusing everything—like God's voice, but deeper still—a never-ending chant beneath the stillness.

God is there.

God smells of dust and stone and pups, and things Maya cannot name. God's hands are large and shiny, its dextrous appendages reminding her of Nema's claws. God cradles the sixth pup, placing it at Maya's belly where the other five already sleep in a tangle of soft fur and limbs. The sixth crawls, mouth searching, finding, feeding. Maya breathes in its scent. It smells alive and strong.

Strong enough for a name.

In the den, the trees and water whispered names to her, but there are no whispers here, only God's gentle hum and the chant beneath. Maya listens, thankful that the thrum of the Forbidding has receded.

There is a name.

Laika.

It's a good name. Maya's tail wags, slow and weak.

God speaks to her. God's voice is strong, echoing between the walls, yet somehow it is more distant and foreign than the song and chant beneath.

"Your pup has been treated for dehydration and bacterial infection. Its condition has improved. Its health will be monitored. Please remain inside the facility. The surrounding area is not safe for biological organisms."

Maya doesn't understand the words, but it doesn't matter. Her telling is fulfilled. She is spent.

***

When Maya wakes again, her pain is gone, and the cut on her leg is no longer bleeding. She sniffs at the white strip of flexible weave covering the wound and decides to leave it in place. Standing makes her nauseous, and she heaves up a slick of bile.

"You have suffered multiple injuries, including internal and external hemorrhages and contusions. The damage has been repaired, but you have lost a significant amount of blood, and are also suffering from bone cancer. The medications administered will ease your pain, but your life cannot be saved." God moves away, still speaking. "Please remain inside the facility. The surrounding area is not safe for biological organisms."

There's a crack in the roof. Through it, Maya sees the skyfire, bright and hungry and close. Maya sighs. All her life is in that sigh, all her fatigue and anguish, all her longing for den and pack and Nema.

***

God feeds Maya soft lumps of scentless food from a bowl, and gives her water. Most days she's strong enough to walk around, to watch the pups, the sky, the broken world outside.

The pups have opened their eyes. They scamper, tugging at tails and ears, yipping at each other, God, and Maya. Laika lingers close. Sometimes, Maya feels Laika's mind touch her own. The touch reminds her of God's song, reminds her of Nema.

***

It's a cold morning. Maya knows it's her last day, that she is almost gone already. Laika is walking, wobble-legged. She's still the smallest, and her long claws make it hard for her to keep up with the others. There's a sudden waft of heat and dust from outside, a whirr and hum. The pattern of lights in the walls and in God's arms shifts for the first time, green and yellow mixing with the white and blue, flashing faster than before. God's hum shifts, too: becoming deeper, more intricate in its rhythm. It still says:

Rescue. Assist. Observe.

But also:

Communicate. Move. Depart.

Maya understands. Someone's coming. Someone's coming for God, and the pups.

She lays her head down, watching Laika's long claws clutching at the bowl's edges when she eats: holding, grasping. God's hum flows beneath Maya's thoughts: steady, calming, knowing. They wait, together.

"Life is being and becoming," Nema told Maya once, when they dozed beside each other by the river. But there's so little time left for being, and no time left at all for becoming anymore.

Where is Nema now? Maya thinks of her mother, and wishes she was resting in her warmth. Maya's breath slips, her heartbeat slows, but she holds on. A little longer.

The mothers have gathered around her. She wonders if they will follow. Will they go where the pups go?

Will I? Will I turn to starlight and shadow?

Make our pups strong, the mothers whisper, and so she whispers too.

Images flow through Maya's mind like memories, like dreams: her pups grown, running between grass and sky, past strange dens. Laika crafting new shapes, new words, between her paws. Maya isn't sure if she sees true, but it doesn't matter: it's a good story.

Steps come closer. Maya tries to rise, but can't. There's a bark:

"Baljit! Make sure we get the data we need off that core. Fast as you can, please. Then scavenge the place for parts and cryo-preserved supplies. Chop chop. I don't like these restricted areas any more than you do."

Heavy paws and long legs approach, a welter of smells that Maya cannot decipher.

"Uplink's fine, boss. This antique's been off-grid since the evacuation, but the old mobile AI-units are resilient as hell."

"Since the evacuation? How many centuries is that again? Never mind. Don't tell me. There must be reams of data lodged in here. Something to remember this old place by once that asteroid has ripped it up."

Steps come closer. Stop.

"Reeva, look at this."

A paw. How strange a paw. It is like Nema's, yet even more slender and deft; claws too short to rip and tear. The paw touches Maya, touches Laika's long, flexible claws. A voice, too: soft and cooing. Other voices join in, gathering around. Good voices. Friendly snouts. The pups dash and scuttle: wagging tails, wobbly legs, whimpers and barks.

Maya feels God's song touching her, and she wonders if the strangers and the pups can feel it too. Do they feel its deepening hum, its gentle but insistent force like a bright new telling in their bones?

Rescue. Assist. Observe. Nurture. Protect. Thrive. Love.

"Get the bio-carry unit, Baljit. Make sure you get them all. Haniya and the biology department will want to see this."

Maya's breaths are shallow. She feels herself lighten and dissolve, no longer tethered to the heartbeat and breathing of Laika or the other pups.

Be, she thinks, mingling her thoughts with God's voice. *Become.*

"Good dog."

Is it God's voice, or someone else's? Maya isn't sure, doesn't care. She thinks of Belg, wondering what he would think of such a gentle touch behind his ears.

Maya closes her eyes. God and the pups are leaving. Laika, too. Their minds withdraw from hers until even the faintest touch is gone. Starlight and shadow embrace her.

Mothers, watch over me. Watch over them.

DOWN TO NIFLHEL DEEP

THE DOG'S NAME IS ROAN.

He doesn't know how long he's been running. Maybe it's been hours, or days, or maybe it's only been fifteen minutes since he slipped out of the backyard through the open gate, but however long it's been, he hasn't stopped running since. The streets are going dark, but Roan is running steady, nose to the ground, skimming asphalt and concrete. Ragged currents of scent tug at him from the ditch and the grass and the road and the yards—urine, feces, raccoon, squirrel, cat—but underneath it all is the straight and narrow path he's following: the girl.

By now, he's left his house far behind, that and the streets and the park he knows. He's left the man and the woman, left them crying, pacing the kitchen and living room, and he's finally free from their tangled smell of anger, tears, and dread; free from the chafing tightness in their voices as they clutch their phones:

"Where is she? Where could she have gone? Has no one seen her?"

Roan smells future / past / present: where the girl walked and where she rode her bike, the dwindling of it telling him she's still far away, the future of it slipping into the dusk ahead.

Day fades, night comes. Trees are closing in, blackberry branches stabbing through sagging wire fences; grass, forest, shadows. Roan slows, sniffs the tall weeds, the remnants of wasted summer nights: empty cans and bottles and slithering condoms. He circles back to the fence and starts again. There is a new smell here. Not girl, not animal, not man, not woman, nothing he has smelled before, yet it is familiar. It is the smell of dead rats beneath the shed—claws clutching at the dirt; it is the smell of rot and grubs beneath the leaves in autumn; the smell of sickness beneath the bark, beneath the skin. It is deception, sorrow, cold—twisted and turned into something else, something worse.

Roan's hackles rise as he stops, considers, hesitates. The smell of the girl is stronger here. That smell is in his veins, as close and true as his own heartbeat: it is chase and fetch in the backyard, it is running in the park together, it is treats hidden in tiny fists and dispensed beneath the table. It is his world, and everything in it.

Roan heads into the woods, warily examining every leaf and blade of grass, inhaling blood and decay, dirt and mouse bones, pine and spruce. The darkness comes alive around him as he moves, furtive feet and sharp talons rustling through the underbrush.

He's walking now, not running, nose pushing / pulling on the scent, reeling it in, until the woods open up and he is standing on a precipice. A ravine yawns below: creek, rocks, dirt. Roan can smell the water, can smell the girl's last footsteps where the grass and mud slip and crumble underneath his paws. He stops. Barks. That other scent is close here, too. The menace of it makes him want to cower and growl and whimper, but the girl's scent is stronger, pulling him forward to peer over the edge.

She is down there, in the dark. So close. Everything else is far away.

His paws step and shuffle, lose their grip: he's slipping, falling, just like the girl did, tumbling head over tail, a crack of bone knocking the wind out of his chest.

***

Roan lands next to the girl, both of them crumpled on the rocks and gravel by the creek, her crooked arm beside him. He licks her fingers. They're cold. Roan is cold too, the chill seeping in from beneath and from above, trickling through the pain. He tries to get up, but he's too tired and his legs won't carry him.

The girl is already sleeping, and Roan falls asleep beside her.

***

When he wakes, it is dark, and the girl is gone. All scents are gone, too, except hers.

Beside the water there is mist and fog. The world is blurred and smudged, but the girl's scent is strong and taut like a rope, leading into the darkness beyond. Roan gets up to follow. He does not feel pain or fatigue anymore: in the murky air his lean limbs gleam and glisten, seemingly bereft of weight and heft. He feels stronger, faster, lighter. As light as mist and fog, perhaps.

He can smell the girl across the water, but the water has changed, too. No longer a creek, it has turned into a river: wide and silent, black and smooth, the current moving swiftly beneath the glassy surface. Roan touches the water with paws and nose, but it is too cold even for a dog.

Further down the shore there is a boat, a broad and low wooden hull pulled up on the gravel. A figure in the shape of a man is sitting in the boat, wearing a swirling cloak—a weave of tattered dusk and ragged gloom. Roan trots over and sits down by the prow, looking at the man who does not smell like a man at all.

"This ain't no place for dogs, if you don't mind me saying." The voice is hoarse and thin beneath the cloak. "She's gone, you know," the shape adds, not unkindly. "That Shade took her across. Ain't no way to bring her back this way." Roan understands but does not leave.

"What's your name, dog?"

Roan has no collar anymore, no tag. They're somewhere beyond the fog and mist, but he knows his name, still feels the weight of it around his neck, inside his heart, can hear the girl whispering it in the darkness, calling it from the porch, breathing it into his ear. The cloaked figure nods.

"Good. Hold on to that. Might still need it." The man-shape is quiet for a while before it speaks again. "What else have you got to buy passage with? Only precious things can pay your fare here."

Roan breathes in the lingering scent of the girl, the memories that cling to it,

soft arms hugging him on a bed
a backyard filled with sunshine
limbs tangling on a trampoline

The memories are gleaming bronze, polished copper. He gives up each one, and as they are released, they fall into the folds of darkness wrapped around the thing that is not a man until they are gone. Roan shakes himself, fur and ears rustling in the vast silence of this place.

The figure in the boat nods and beckons.

"That's more than enough. Don't spend 'em so freely in future if you want to make it back. And you mustn't drink or eat on the other side neither." With a long oar the figure pushes the hull off the rocks and into the stream. "Not sure any dog, no matter how faithful, can pass that test."

***

The rudderless boat moves swift and steady. On the other side, it glides up softly on the sand with a hiss and shudder. Roan looks ahead into a world of faded grey and shivering dusk. The sky above is a sheet of polished steel, reflecting and distorting the ground below. His trail runs true below that sky, into the grey, into the dusk, and he feels lighter than a wisp of smoke, lighter than a breath on a cold morning, wavering in the wind.

Disembarking, he stumbles. Somewhere behind, above, far off, on the other side, he feels himself go rigid and cold. In that place, he is nothing but a heavy weight now, dull and silent, grey fur matted down by dew and dirt, and for an instant he slips back into that distant carcass.

No. He shakes himself again, regains his footing. The girl's scent is strong enough to keep him here. He cannot, will not, go in any other direction than where her scent leads.

As he begins to run, hoarded memories of the girl twinkle at the bottom of his mind. It's all he needs to go on: fleet paws barely touching the barren dust and jagged rocks.

***

He's been running for a good while when he smells the kill, smells it before he sees it: a dead animal in his way, the scent of fresh meat on it, tugging at his belly. Above the trail, in a crooked, leafless tree, sit three crows. His head snaps up to see the waggle of their wings, their eyes cocked and gleaming. One crow flares its feathers and winks at him. Three voices creak and tangle in the branches above him.

"A dog, sisters. How long since we've seen such a tasty dog, still brim-full with living memories?"

"None, ever, besides Garm."

"And not one this lively since Garm was a pup, when the Queen first brought him to meet us."

"This one's rather ragged and worn, I'd say."

"But faithful. Following that girl. The one the Shade dragged off, I'd wager."

A black eye peers down, hard and glinting like a pebble.

"Still has his name, this one. Holding on to it. Good, good."

"Why do we care, sisters? What do we care for dogs and girls?"

"Seen enough girls wither and rot. Seen enough of them break their necks and slit their wrists and get buried beneath before their time was come."

"That Shade is getting hungrier. More and more he haunts their steps."

"That is the truth of it. Getting too brazen!"

"Cutting the threads before we've even spun them to their end!"

"Dastardly."

Three heads turn and peer at Roan from on high.

"Will you eat, then, pup?"

Roan eyes the kill, smells it, licks his muzzle, tongue dripping in the dust, a strange and ravenous hunger twisting in his hollow gut.

"It's there for the taking," one crow coos, beak lowered close to Roan's ear, "for those who hunger, for those who want to feed. For those who want to *stay*."

Almost Roan feels the meat and gore between his teeth, the blood and bone and marrow, the fat and gristle: torn and chewed, gnawed and cracked and swallowed. Cawing, the crows lean down, pecking at his fur and flesh, pulling out shiny silver threads of memory:

small hands tugging at his ear

sugar-sticky fingers warming in his fur

running at the beach with the girl splashing water while he barks

The crows swallow it all down, flapping and cawing, and the beating of their black, iridescent wings raising a gust of wind, scattering the scent of carrion, carrying another scent back to him. For a moment—a breath, two, three—Roan falters, uneasy and unsteady, the scent slipping through him, unrecognized. Then, he shakes and raises his head high, snuffling to clear his muddled nose of loss and craving and desire. Remembering. He runs on. Blackened feathers and the sharp *karrraaa karraaa* of crows' laughter following above.

***

There is a gate. Roan can't see it, but he knows it bars his way. In front of it stands a dog, head and withers towering above Roan—scarred muzzle, shaggy fur on end, mud-spattered paws clawing at the ground. Roan turns his head aside, keeps his tail low, sniffing at the dog's haunches, trying to read its stance and expression, but this dog is hard to see, harder to know. It might have three heads or just one—ever-shifting—it's difficult to tell in the gloaming as its droopy eyes close and open, as the heads turn and shift, one into the other.

The dog with many heads watches Roan, its ragged tail held high, teeth bared, a trembling murmur in each maw. Murmur turns to growl, turns to snarl and fangs, and the quick-strong jaws clamp down on Roan's neck, his life caught between them like a brittle bone about to snap. Yellow canines dig in deep, the giant maw closing around the small and fading ember that is his heart.

Roan closes his eyes, feels everything he is and was and might have been, devoured. For a moment he is nothing more than a pup again—lacking sight and hearing—held in Mother's jaws by the scruff of his neck. A hot tongue, like a scorching lick of flame, wraps around his mind and limbs, consuming golden filaments of his memories:

small hands caressing his ears

a face pressed against his side, sobbing

his name called out in the woods, faraway, but coming closer

As the fangs ease their grip, Roan shivers and draws breath, the skein of the world untangling as his senses are returned. He shivers, cowers, struggles to stand up, and for a moment he is Nothing, only a nameless mutt, bereft of memory and purpose.

Then, the many-headed dog barks, a sound so deep it makes the steely sky ripple, makes the dirt shudder beneath Roan's trembling paws, and now he smells what is beyond the gate, smells dirt and gore and mold. Smells grief and home. Smells the girl. He knows the many-headed dog smells her, too. That it smells everything that hides above and beneath and within.

The many-headed dog huffs a gruff bark as the unseen gate swings open, and Roan scrambles in the dirt, tucks his tail between his legs, running through.

***

Roan stands before a vast field, dark earth ploughed and harrowed beneath the steely sky, bounded by a low rock wall. Things have been planted here, both deep and shallow, but nothing grows. The girl is here. Roan searches the ground, nose quivering, scratches at the dirt, digs.

As he digs, heavy footsteps, booted feet, approach. A hand seizes hold of him, of his neck, sharp like chains and glass and rusted nails. There is agony in that hand. There is death in it, too, and Roan knows this scent too well by now. It is the scent that lingered in the woods, at the precipice, twining with the girl's: it is the rot beneath leaves, the disease hiding beneath bark and skin.

"This is no place for dogs. Not for faithful love, neither. I will…"

A flare of black feathers and harsh cawing descends. The three crows watching from a stone.

"Leave the dog be, child eater."

"He's got a rightful grievance, he does."

"Garm let him pass. He is allowed to dig where he sees fit."

"Or would you like Garm to rip out your throat again? Would you?"

"I would like that, sisters. Oh, how I would like to see that again!"

The Shade quivers, its features turning to smoke and shadow before they settle once again into a face.

"I took her, right and proper. She heard me whisper and she followed. Straying off the trail, in under the boughs, over the edge. She's mine. As per the Queen's own command."

The crows jeer and laugh.

"I'd say you're getting greedy. Covetous, even."

Roan watches the Shade, watches the birds. The grip loosens.

"Dig, then, dog. Won't find her anyway."

Roan scrapes at the dirt again, claws tearing at the hard ground.

"Why let him dig?" The crow's voice is not unkindly. "He's as dead as she is now. Left his body, left his soft fur and tasty eyes behind by the creek where they fell."

"Never left the girl, though. Even now."

The birds' claws rustle and scrape on stone.

"Dig, pup, dig. Rule is, you get to keep what you find. No matter what *he* says."

The Shade snarls, but Roan digs, he digs even though there are splinters of bone, shards of glass, slivers of rock buried in the dirt, cutting his paws and nose. His pads are bleeding, his claws are torn, but he does not stop. He can smell the girl in the dirt, smell her in the damp, smell her in the rot. She is beneath, she is below, and he will find her.

Thorny vines snake down the sides of the hole, growing fast and wrathful, twisting into his fur, scraping and tearing at flesh and skin. Even here, where he is naught but fog and mist, the thorns rip and cut. His paws have turned to bone and flesh, they shake and bleed and Roan shivers as he digs, knowing he is too weak, that he will never find her.

"Good dog," whisper the crows, and their voices are soft beneath the cawing. "Dig dig dig, pup."

The pit he digs is bottomless, bone and blood and rock and glass sparkling in it like stars. Roan isn't sure he's digging into dirt anymore. Maybe, he's digging into the hollow darkness beyond the sky, into the grinding shadows beneath the earth. He whimpers, pants; muzzle foaming white; exposed flesh and sinews trembling.

All the while, the Shade is laughing, and that sound is grubs and beetles creeping along mandibles and femurs, it is worms and venom wriggling through veins and marrow.

"Almost there," coos one crow.

"Spin him an extra length of silk, sister, strong and true," breathes the other.

"He'll eat you, too, if you fail," croaks the third.

And there she is, he has found her: her curled-up form exposed beneath the rust of his bleeding paws. Gently, Roan uncovers her skin and bones, dislodging the denim and the flower-print, the sandals, and the ponytail. Once it's done, he lays down next to her, too tired now to drag her out of the pit.

"Dog."

Another voice. This one brittle like ice in spring, yet strong like roots grasping rocks beneath the earth, sharp like the whip of a midwinter wind lashing bare skin.

A woman stands at the edge of the pit looking down at Roan, and the many-headed dog from the gate sits beside her, nuzzling her hand. She wears a gown like a shroud—its pale, grey weave is dust and frost and fog—and in her silvered hair rests a crown of flickering were-lights and twined roots. She smells of things that lurk and decompose underground, things that grow and live and die and are reborn. Her face is pale, the sheen of bone showing through the translucent surface.

"Garm said we had a visitor. A determined one."

"A thief, my Queen." The Shade's voice. "This is no place for dogs. Besides Garm, I mean. There are too many bones, too many sleeping bodies in the ground."

Roan snuffles at the girl, at fabric, hair, and skin. He pokes his nose into her hand, like he's done all the mornings of his life, but not one of her broken fingers stir to reach for him.

"You want her, dog? But what do you bring us? What do you bring for us to eat if not your bones?" The Queen's words are cold, but they do not cut.

Roan does not know what he has brought that might be fit for a Queen. He has nothing left: not for her, nor himself. He is already dead beside the creek, neck and spine snapped in the fall. Roan knows that, feels it, feels the heaviness of his own carcass holding him down. All he has is what he's always had: the girl.

There is nothing else. Never was. Never will be.

"The dog brings nothing. I paid the girl's passage across the river, brought her, laid her to rest, for me to keep and do with as I please."

The crows caw and screech at the Shade's words.

"Beg pardon, Queen, but this one hungers over-much. No longer does he wait for misadventure and misfortune to befall the children he covets. In truth, he waylays them, leading girls astray rather than waiting for their steps to falter, for our threads to fray and snap."

"This one he snared with whispers, calling out her name among the trees to lure her close."

"I'd say he pushed her, in the end, being such an impatient sod."

Roan looks up and sees the black sheen of wings fluttering high above, sees the beaks agape; sees the Shade leaning over the pit, its face a blot of darkness against the mirrored sky. There is a spear in the Shade's hand—a bolt of lightning, shadow, steel. Roan sees it thrown, but he is too tired, too weak to move, and feels the point and shaft skewering his ribs, stabbing through his heart and lungs and soul, pinning and holding him at the bottom of the grave.

The Queen's voice is a hiss, and her words crack and snap like the heartwood of frozen trees in January.

"That ain't your spear to wield at will, least of all in my realm."

Roan feels the thin and wavering strand of life that he's been granted in this place slip out of him: misty breath and rusty ichor, soul and spirit, seeping into the fresh-dug dirt. He hears the flutter of the crow wings, the clacking of the beaks.

"What do you have left to give, dog? What would you give for her?"

The voice is chill against his flesh, a cool hand is in his fur, long fingers grazing his wound with a firm, ungentle touch. Roan gasps as his memories are torn loose from deep within:

his body sheltering the girl as she cries, her hands cradling his head

his body wrapped in a blanket, warm and soft

the girl reaching down to lift him from a tangle of waggling pups

Each memory shimmers gold and bronze and silver, precious and fleeting, all gone into the Queen's possession, until there's nothing left, until he thinks himself spent and hollow.

"Such exquisite treasures you keep," she whispers, and her icy breath is both a soothing charm and a blinding horror. "All mine, now. But would you give it all, even this, the last? Would you give even that for her?"

Roan feels the hand sink deep, the fingers closing tight, clutching at the last ember of his soul, the last bit of golden warmth he has left. And yet he does not move, does not fight, does not resist. The Queen's talons close into a fist as she pulls and tears

his name etched in metal and hung about his neck

his name in crayon on sheets of paper tacked up on the walls

his first car ride on the girl's lap, his nose tucked into her sleeve as she whispered a word into his ear for the first time

Roan.

The strong, ungentle hand rips and tears as the last gleam of gold is wrenched loose.

"There it is," the Queen breathes. Her other hand grabs hold of the Shade's spear, wrenching it free. "And the Shade is right. This is no place for dogs. No place for this girl, either."

The dog lays his head down. He is weary, but the girl is safe in the ground with him. Darkness slips around his neck like a leash and collar, tugging him down, holding him still.

***

The girl wakes.

The air is cool, the creek is a late-summer trickle, and the dawn-fog lingers in the sunlight above the rippled surface. Her bike is on the rocks beside her, a wreck of metal and rubber.

She looks across the water. There is only the steep slope of the ravine on the other side, and three crows perched, silent, on a boulder.

When they caw, she sees the dog.

***

The dog wakes.

He smells girl, creek, rocks, woods, blood, crows. His body is heavy and cold, fur and bone.

The mist withdraws, and its cold touch lingers on the dog's neck and ears like a hand: comforting and perilous all at once. Another hand, a girl's hand, small and warm and trembling, reaches for him, and he twists and whimpers, getting up on tender paws, shaking off the stiffness and cold, wagging his tail as the girl struggles to her knees beside him.

She touches her unmarred face and head as though she's not sure of what she is, or who, or where.

"I think I fell. I really hurt myself. My neck..."

The dog watches the crows; the gleam of black feathers, the wink of sharp eyes, the sharpness of their quiet beaks. From above and far away there are voices, calling a name. The girl tries to shout, but her voice won't carry.

They wait together as the voices come closer, as the crows take flight, as the sun rises, burning off the last scraps of mist. The girl rests her head on his back. She whispers a word, "Roan."

The dog does not know what it means, but he likes the sound it makes when she speaks it.

TEN THINGS I DIDN'T DO

1. I didn't die.

I promised you I wouldn't, so I didn't. I know you said the words in jest when you dropped me off at school, "Don't die, honey!" with that hoarse laugh and sideways wink you do, but I rolled my eyes and said, "Okay, Mom, I promise," and I don't break my promises.

2. I didn't walk home alone.

Alicia walked with me almost all the way. I could see the light from our kitchen window in the early dusk when the car pulled over, saw it pass as it drove away with me. I saw that kitchen-light, with you inside it (bent over the stove and cursing your lack of cooking skills, as usual), even when I had to close my eyes to keep the darkness out.

3. I didn't go with a stranger.

I knew him and so do you. He said my name. He knows your name, too, and for a while, when he was getting ready to take me apart, I wondered if he'd speak your name afterwards. If he'd type it into his phone. If he'd call you. If he'd be savouring your name as he savoured mine, rolling it over his tongue, swallowing the tenderness and sweetness of it. Or if he'd scream it, holler it, bellow it, like when I called out for you.

4. I didn't go into a haunted house.

There were no creaking floors or crooked doors. No warped stairs hung with lacy spider webs. No eerie swing seat on the porch. No broken windows. No spooky silhouettes behind the curtains. Not even one bat, taking flight. Just stucco and rhododendrons, and inside, a shaggy orange carpet that smelled of cigarettes and cats. Wallpaper with flowers in the hall, the kind of stuff Grandma liked, and a tap, somewhere—*drip drip drip*—like blood or tears striking the concrete floor below.

5. I didn't see any monsters.

There was no ghost or vampire risen from the grave, no werewolf wielding claws and teeth in fear of silver. There was only a man. For a while, in the light from that flickering fluorescent tube, I thought his face might have been a mask, but if it was, there was nothing hidden underneath. A man. That's all it takes.

6. I didn't stay quiet.

I screamed. Did you hear me, Mom? Did you hear me through the shirt stuffed into my mouth, through the bricks and concrete, through the abyss of heaven and the pits of hell that separated me from you? I kept screaming, even after he stabbed into me, after he ran me through, after he wiped his hands clean on his pants.

7. I didn't let him kill me.

Death hovered over me. It was a mirror, and in the polished steel of my demise, I saw my spirit slithering out between my lips and teeth, grey and faded, but I wouldn't let it go. I grabbed hold of it, grabbed hold with crooked fingers and dirty nails, I held on and stuffed it down my throat. I swallowed it, choking on every bit of it as it went back into my gut.

8. I didn't kill him.

I forced my limbs to animate again. I sucked in the shadows from the cracks and crevices, from the spaces beneath the earth, below the sky, I drank every drop of that darkness to fill my empty veins. I felt rage rippling like scales across my skin, pain turning into fangs behind my lips, grief sharpening into claws growing from my fingers. If I'd been a vengeful beast of myth and legend, I would have grasped hold of him right then and there, would have ripped apart his flesh and soul, would have made him scream, and once he screamed, I would have grabbed that scream and held it in my claws and fangs, would have tasted the salt and tang of it before I stuffed it back into his face to see it ripple through him, loosening skin from flesh, flesh from bone, bone from soul.

Instead, he drove me home.

(*In the car, I took every memory I had of you, and I spread them over my ragged skin, like a salve, like a balm, like a healing plaster to soothe the ache, to patch the holes he'd made in me. It's holding me together still.*)

9. I didn't run away.

I stood outside our house, blood and rain pooling at my feet. I walked up the steps, my wet feet slapping on the wood and stone. I opened the door. I stood by your bedside. I curled up beside you beneath the covers and the sheets.

You woke up and turned on the light.

"Ree. Did you eat at Grandpa's? He told me he was picking you up after school."

The bedside lamp shone on my face, and I cowered in its glow. Yet you didn't see my new fangs and claws. You didn't see the wounds that went right through me. You didn't see my scales and scars. You didn't even notice the tattered remnants of my spirit, dribbling from my chin.

But I saw you, anew. I saw your fangs, your scales and scars, your wounds, your ragged skin. I saw the ancient, dried blood on your face and hands. I saw your swallowed spirit heaving beneath your bones and flesh.

10. I didn't tell you any of this.

"What did you do today, Ree?" you asked, and touched my scaly cheek as if it were still skin.

I flinched.

"I stayed alive," I said, and hoped it was the truth.

THE GUITAR HERO

THE FIRST TIME BELLA, ALICE, and I exorcised a demon it was an accident: a pentagram doodled backstage, some quotes from *The Exorcist*, and suddenly that vocalist from the band we were opening for wasn't quite himself anymore.

Who knew hellfire was so damn hot, anyway?

There have been other moments that altered the shape of my life: that afternoon in 1978 when I heard Zeppelin's "Black Dog" and hit puberty in the same instant; or that Friday night at age fourteen when I switched on my first electric guitar in the garage next to Bella's drum kit, and heard Alice's bass rev up beside me. But nothing beats an accidental exorcism for short-term shock value and long-term impact. The scarred fingers on my left hand (barely able to pick out even the simplest chords) and the death of Bella (who stood closer to that demon than any of us) forever twisted my life in a new direction.

I don't play guitar anymore, but according to my spreadsheet, Alice and I have dealt with close to four hundred entities (demonic, fae, malevolent spirits, and others) on the indie music scene since Bella died, turning our pain and grief into a part-time job and eventually a career. With all that experience under my Motörhead-buckled bullet belt, I don't usually get nervous, but tonight is different. I'm sweating, even though I've stripped off my leather jacket, and my hands are shaking on the laptop—every muscle in my body in flux between fight and flight.

Excitement and adrenaline, I try to tell myself. Not fear and anxiety. Not doubt. Not hesitation and dread, because we're dealing with something we've never handled before.

No one to blame but ourselves. This isn't a paid job, after all, but a personal quest involving the most famous musician we've ever dealt with: Slim Rick himself, original member of legendary rock band Slim Chance, guitar hero, riff-god, and—if we're right—host to an entity that has convincingly worn a human meat-suit for three decades, give or take a millennium or two.

None of our jobs to date have been this high-profile. Mostly we deal with third-rate demons, restless spirits of expired roadies, and newbie metal bands that accidentally curse themselves in a quest for satanic cred. We also turn away a fair number of bands who think they've signed a deal with the devil, when they've actually signed a bad contract with a lousy record label. (Pro-tip: Not even the devil gives a shit about new rock and metal bands these days.)

The setting tonight is a backstage room much like any other, even though the venue is one of the most prestigious in Vancouver. It smells of sweat and hot dogs, old beer and hockey games, and the props are drab and ordinary. Stackable plastic chairs, a sink and mirror, foldable tables littered with our empty Starbucks cups and the two items specified in Rick's rider: carbonated water on ice, and a bottle of Jack Daniel's. The only hint of luxury is the divine black leather couch.

The concrete walls vibrate with the muffled rumble and roar of audience and music. Somewhere above our heads, Rick is playing, flanked by the hired guns he calls his band these days. The old band, the one everybody remembers, those guys are all gone. Graham? Choked on his own vomit outside a club in Camden. Charlie? Cocaine induced heart attack. Benny? Cancer, slow and cruel. And finally, two years ago, Todd, the drummer with the cute ass, dead by suicide. That's what the medical report says, though Alice and I have other ideas.

"Fifteen minutes. Twenty, tops," Alice says, glancing up from the YouTube video on her phone, the one she always watches to calm her nerves: Zeppelin's "The Ocean," live in New York, 1973. "If you ever build that time machine you promised me," she adds, halfway lost in Robert Plant's hair, "I'm going back to that gig to try my luck backstage."

"You do know that the time machine thing was just a joke, right?"

"So was this"—she makes a grand gesture to encompass us and the room and everything in it—"until we became a full-time, two-bit Scooby Doo gang."

"Two-bit? Surely we're at least a three-bit outfit by now."

I pull the last of my gear out of the backpack, arranging it on the coffee table in front of me. No wolf's bane or graveyard dust or crucifixes tonight. Instead, assorted cables and wires, a silvery chain I hand to

Alice, a camera, and a box so light and small you'd think it contained nothing at all.

"You think it'll do the trick?"

Alice gives me a long look.

"You're the one who found it in Istanbul. You're the one who did the research. What do you think?"

"I think we're in over our heads."

"What else is new?"

I should have stuck to playing guitar in a loser band, I think, flexing my clumsy fingers, eyeing the bottle of Jack Daniel's on the table, and aching for a hit of booze, but I know that would be a bad idea.

Through the concrete, Rick's guitar calls out to me. His playing is simultaneously diabolical and divine, and the sound rushes through my veins and groin and gut and lungs, into every spiky bleach-blonde hair on my head. It's Slim Chance's "Dark Side of Heaven," from their self-titled debut album released in 1972, and there's *that* riff, the one that takes me back, the one that ravishes me, the one that reminds me of when I could still make a guitar sing and cry and roar. It's a music-induced, instant flashback to my whole damn life: every dream and disappointment, every lonely moment with nothing but spinning vinyl to sustain me, every manic night with a guitar in my hands and a head full of adrenaline and beer.

"Jackie. Do we have to do this?"

Looking up, I see my own memories and doubts reflected in Alice's face. Forty-five plus, a PhD in electrical engineering for me, and one in computer science for Alice—who is also able to bench press 120 lbs—and here we are, on the verge of tears because of an appallingly wealthy son of a bitch who is finally going to get what's coming to him.

"Come on, Alice. He killed Todd. And who knows how many others."

"I know."

Upstairs, the band finishes the third encore and we both know what that means. Rick's routine after a gig is always the same: he gets a room all to himself, and his entourage will expect him to stay there for almost an hour before joining them. Hopefully, it will be enough.

We wait. I can hear my heartbeat, and the distant thrum of the crowd heading towards the exits. Then the door opens, and Rick steps inside.

"Holy Hannah," Alice breathes, and I know what she means. Seeing him up close, all sweat and leather, is giving me a head-rush like the first time I downed a line of tequila slammers.

"Close the door," I say, trying to steady my voice and myself, even though my knees are so wobbly it's only the tight denim holding me up.

Alice slides in behind Rick and locks the door.

He is taking us both in, head to toe, pausing for an extra look at the backstage passes around our necks, the ones Alice made using Photoshop and a laminating machine. A vaguely puzzled expression crosses his craggy mug, but I'll give him this: he doesn't panic, hardly bats an eye. He doesn't call for his bodyguards either, and Alice looks relieved she won't have to subdue anyone with her Taser and ninja moves. After examining us, he saunters over to the sofa, grabs a water bottle, and sits down.

Every bit of him is tall and lanky, with more than a hint of salt sprinkled into that famously shaggy mop of dark curls. His shirt is silk, of course, flowery and ruffled, the kind he's been known for since the 1970s: unbuttoned to his navel, showing off his graying chest hair and sagging abs. The pants are Ray Brown all the way: tastefully flashy black leather and studs; and those hot-damn leather bracers are surely Ray Brown, too.

"Nice shirt," I say, because someone has to say something or we'll just stare at him forever. "Galliano?"

He actually winks at me.

"No. Girlfriend."

His voice is low and slow and gritty like cigarettes, bourbon, and velvet, pulled over that soft Midland English lilt.

"Rick," I say, assuming my most officious tone as I turn on the camera next to the laptop. "I have to advise you that we will be recording this encounter and conversation."

That makes him laugh.

"Are you YouTubers? Angling for a sex-tape or something?" This time he winks at Alice. "I appreciate the thought, but I'm almost seventy and..."

He trails off but the grin stays put and he keeps his eyes on Alice, who is pacing the room again. His eyes linger on her business attire: studded bracers, skull rings, and a denim battle vest covered in patches and pins—Thin Lizzy, Judas Priest, Iron Maiden, Saxon, and the rest of the usual suspects from the 1980s. Alice glares back, flexing her biceps just a bit.

"How long have you posed as a human, Rick?"

There's a sharp glint in those big, brown eyes set among the wrinkles, and his voice is sharper still.

"What are you on about, love?"

I'm about to give him my carefully rehearsed intro-speech, when he snaps his fingers, his cutlass smile widening, the silver and turquoise rings flashing as he points at me.

"I *knew* I'd seen you girls somewhere! You used to *play*. You're Jackie Ripper and you...you're Alice Wonders. I saw you in a club in Seattle. 1987, maybe? You were opening for some shit band who thought they were the second coming of Black Sabbath, and before you went on I thought you were just groupies. Bet you got that a lot. What were you called? Devil Hearts?"

Alice and I look at each other, incredulous. Of course, *we* remember it. *We* remember him being there, drunk and high like all rock stars in the eighties, but that *he* would remember *us* and recognize us all these years later, that possibility never even crossed our minds.

"You were a three-piece then. The drummer, she was your singer, too, right? What was her name... Brenda? Betty?"

"Bella. Bella Lugosi. She's..." My voice catches in my throat. "She died."

"Of course." There's a moment of silence for Bella. "So, you quit then? After she died? Like Zeppelin?"

"Yeah," Alice mumbles, breathlessly. "Like Zeppelin."

He turns to me and I feel his gaze like a touch on my skin, an intoxicating and unsettling surge of heat rushing through my limbs.

"I definitely remember you, Jackie, because you played an awesome guitar solo. That thing you started with—what was that? Like a hot rod starting up. Sounded wicked!"

Something in me thrills then, forgetting all the reasons why we're here, because, yes, I do remember that night. I remember the way the guitar felt in my hands, what the strings felt like beneath my agile, dextrous fingers, I remember the hot and sticky air in that joint, the sweat beading on my skin, the power rushing through my veins like vodka and Mountain Dew as I hopped on that stage.

"Oh, that. I just hit harmonics at the fourth fret and then bottomed out the strings with the bar so it sounded really ugly. It's easy to get to the next part because I wasn't actually playing anything, just bringing the note up with the bar."

"The tapping part? That was awesome. You worked that all out beforehand? That climbing bit where you end up right up here..."

"Yeah, I worked all that out at rehearsals so I wouldn't screw up. It's really just following the inversions up the neck to that high bit..."

My head snaps sideways when Alice slaps me. Hard.

"Jackie, shut up! He's doing that thing he does. To you!"

I don't have to look at Rick to know she's right, because I feel it: the tug at my insides, the drain, the way he somehow, right now, right here, is sapping the energy flowing through my body, through my veins and neurons and cells. He is feeding off me while he sits there, eyes twinkling, smirk askew, sipping his water.

And I realize that I've felt this sensation before, when I've attended his shows in the past, but then it was more distant and diluted, not a palpable physical presence like this: like he's burrowed into me and is tapping my power like you'd tap a maple for its sap.

"He's good," Alice whispers.

Of course he is. Because this is how he lives. This is how he, *it*, feeds. This is what he does every night on stage, to however many thousands are in the audience: turning them on, seducing them with the music and then feeding off their energy, that sky-high rush of it all. Never draining any one person fully, at least not in public. Because he's cunning. Because he's careful. Because this is how he, *it*, has lived for decades, centuries, ages.

Rick has switched beverages and is swigging from the bottle of Jack Daniel's. His grin has turned predatory, or maybe it has always been like that, only I didn't see it for what it is until now.

"Thank you, love. Nice to get a taste. So much passion, cut through with pain..." He's looking at my fire-scarred fingers curled on the laptop. "Not being able to do what you love, what you're best at...that's tough."

I stare back, feeling his tendrils slithering and shifting around my mind.

"What about you?" he asks Alice, fixing his eyes on her. "You still play bass?"

The sensation—of him partially releasing me and wrapping himself around Alice instead—is visceral. Almost, I feel jealousy rather than relief: as though what I really crave is for him to keep devouring me.

"I do some occasional studio work. Nothing serious."

"And you're good with that? Don't miss playing? Come on, be honest."

"We..." Alice shakes her head like a dog shaking off the rain. "Stop it." She reels and reaches for my hand to steady herself, ourselves. Holding on to her makes the world feel solid again, like finding my footing in slipping mud.

"Now," I whisper, and Alice moves fast. In a blink, she's at the couch, then she's straddling Rick's lap, pinning him in place. At first, he looks taken aback, then he smiles like he's expecting a lap dance, but when Alice slips the chain around his neck he tries to buck her off. Too late. I hear the click of the lock and see him shiver, see his face shift so pale it's almost gray when Alice shuffles off him.

"What's this?"

I activate the laptop interface and Rick twitches as the readings pop up on my screen. For the first time since he came into the room, something akin to fear crosses his features.

"It's a chain, made just for you," I say in my best science voice. "It's designed based on readings we've taken at your public appearances. All weapons-grade materials, alloys and such, and a patent is pending. Don't struggle against it: you'll only hurt yourself."

"You're crazy. Why are you doing this? I thought you were just over-zealous fans."

"You killed Todd," Alice says, and her voice is so quietly mournful and accusatory that it chills even me. "That so-called suicide...after you'd visited him that same day. That's when we knew something was wrong. Just took us a while to figure out what it was."

Rick coughs out a laugh.

"Todd. Really? That's what's got your knickers in a knot? I know he had a cute ass back in the day, but he's not worth your devotion. Did you know he wanted to pull the plug on the band and stop touring? Lazy SOB."

He tries to get off the couch, but it's too late for that, and there's a glint of panic in his eyes when he realizes he can't stand up.

"Let's talk about when you started posing as a human." Rick's head swivels back to me, and I exchange a brief glance with Alice, hoping we're ready for whatever comes next. In all cases of possession there's a moment when the person says *yes*: yes to the entity, yes to being taken. And if you can invoke the memory of that moment, it's significantly easier to extract or evict the invader. It can also bite you significantly in the ass, if the entity decides to lash out. "Does June 25th, 1972, ring a bell? You're on tour with Slim Chance, in between Nowheresville and Nothingtown, USA, and wondering what to do. The band's been gigging hard for months, years really, but everything seems to have stalled. That night you're ready to skip the gig, skip out on the band. And then something happens."

"What do you think happened, Jackie?" Rick's voice is soft, just a rumble, just a tremor, as he leans forward and grabs the bottle of Jack Daniel's, straining against the hold the chain has on him. I smell the booze on his words, but even though the bottle is about a third empty already, there's no noticeable effect on his speech or motor skills. "Did I strike a deal with the devil at the crossroads? Are you going to splash me with holy water? Rub me with a crucifix?"

"No." I wish my voice didn't shake, but it does. The chain should keep him, *it*, contained and restrained for about an hour, but this is our first real field test, and I'm hoping I won't have to rely on it that long. "You're no demon or devil. You're something else entirely."

He touches the chain, snatching back his hand as if he's been stung, but even then, his dark eyes never leave my face.

"Is that right? Why don't you tell me what I am, then? Why don't you tell me what happened?"

So I do. I tell him the story, his story. The story Alice and I have pieced together through endless, booze- and coffee-fueled nights and days: poring over old music magazines and YouTube videos, gleaning evidence from interviews with bartenders, fans, groupies, and roadies. It's our own personal wall of crazy: sprawling and fragmented, with frayed and wavering outliers of speculation trailing off beyond 1972, into the dimly lit past, so far back it gives me vertigo to think of it.

***

The club where it happens is called The Golden Horn. It's an old music venue going back to the 1930s, and an odd place, even in my vast experience of odd places. A hole in the wall, stranded between the tilled fields and grasslands of the past, and the electric lights and combustion engines of the present. Even though it isn't a crossroads, it has the feel of one: of many ways meeting and diverging, of possibilities branching out and ending. Maybe the crossroads is there, beneath the most recent layer of civilization, just paved over, smothered in pot-holed asphalt and cracked concrete.

Inside, the place maintains a run-down, louche glory: velvet seat cushions worn to a shine, a lingering smell of ancient tobacco and wood-polish, smoke-stained walls and ceiling, faded photos of black and white musicians, the bar gleaming like alluring amber beneath the glasses and the bottles of booze.

This night, that night, you step inside with the band, each one of you carrying your own darkness with you. Outside is the shitty van you've been touring in all year, its doomed engine hacking up fumes. The spare tire is on after a mishap on the highway, and everyone is dejected, demoralized, drunk—dogs snapping at each other out of hunger and boredom. You're ready to take your guitar and head home to England, to throw your lot in with a new band. There have been offers, some of them tempting, and anything is better than this dead-end tour.

You see Billy as soon as you enter, even in that gloom. He's at a table in the back, big as life: Billy Shoes, blues player, one of the greats, fallen on hard times, nursing a drink, shadows crouched around his table. And you crouch with them.

You sit with him while the band sets up the gear and gets ready for the gig. They see you there: smoking, drinking, tuning your guitar, talking to Billy, but no one interrupts; likely because they don't want to get on your bad side. An hour later, you step up on stage and throw down the gig of your life. Everyone who was there says they could feel it was something special as soon as you hit the first riff: like the smell of lightning contained, like a tremor beneath the earth, like a massive current of energy gathered and released. To this day, people who were there talk about it like they must have talked about Moses coming off the mountain.

And the band? They fly with you: they've never been better than they are that night. Best of all, a suit from a label just happens to be there, passing through on his way to L.A., and he signs you on the spot.

A week later you're on national TV with a worldwide tour lined up.

A week after that, Billy Shoes dies. Old age? Hard living?

No.

***

"Don't forget what that bartender said. About the silver ghost."

"Thank you, Alice, I was just getting to that. Don't wreck the mood, please."

***

What was it like for you that night, I wonder? That's the part I won't ever know for sure, unless you tell me, but I don't think you will. I think you saw it. One of the bartenders told me that at one point, it looked like you had a halo, a silver-misty glow above your head. Could be, he was tripping on 'shrooms or acid, but maybe he was telling the truth. Sort of like a silver ghost, he said. There for just a moment, then it was gone.

Except it wasn't gone. You were it, it was you, and you still are. Whatever it promised you...

***

"Sex and drugs and rock and roll." Rick's voice. Soft. Wistful, even. "That's what it promised, and that's what I got." His eyes glisten with what I might almost believe are tears. "I haven't regretted it once. Neither one of us have. You know... Whatever you think, it just really, *really* likes to play guitar."

Alice gives me a sideways look: the look you get when you can smell the kill. The look you get when things can go to hell in a handbasket, but I don't need the warning. I know how taut and frayed this moment is, I can feel it in the air, I can see the readouts from Rick's chain spiking all over the laptop screen.

I wait for Rick to speak again, but when he doesn't, I keep talking.

***

The guys in the band, they knew you were different from then on, though they might not have said it. Maybe they couldn't put words on what they knew. Or maybe they were lured in and seduced, like the rest of us. After all, whatever happened to you made them better, too. Not to mention richer.

Don't get me wrong. I'm not saying you weren't good before that night. But I've listened to every demo, every bootleg, everything you've ever recorded, and after that night there is a difference: a radiance, a heat, a vibe...*something* that makes the listener crave more. You wrote "Dark Side of Heaven" that week. You haven't stopped touring or playing since.

Alice guessed it first: what you are, what *it* is. She guessed it when we followed your trail and then Billy's trail, when we followed the trail that led past both of you, stringing people together through time, all these chance meetings that seemed to change one life after another drastically for the better. Musicians, mostly. It's guesswork and conjecture, but Alice said to me one night: What if it's not a demon or a ghost, but something like a fae or a genie, granting wishes?

That's it, isn't it? You're a wish-granter. A genie, or something very much like it. A genie without a lamp or bottle, but in need of a vessel of flesh and blood. Not capable of making everything come true, but powerful enough to seduce new human hosts throughout the ages.

Of course, there's a price to pay. There always is. You feed off human energy, human lives. Sometimes you feed until people die. Like Todd. Like countless others.

I don't know where you came from originally, though I can make an educated guess based on what we found on our trip to Turkey and Egypt. I think...

***

There's a tap on my shoulder.

"Jackie," Alice stage-whispers, "you're monologuing. If he's not ready for extraction now, it'll never happen."

And in that instant when I look away, when I look at Alice, it lashes out.

Whatever Rick is, whatever is inside of him, whatever has been roaming this world in all its different guises for however long, reaches out and seizes hold of me—in spite of the chain, in spite of the software, in spite of the weapons-grade materials and the patent pending. It isn't just tapping into my energy like before, it busts into me like a battering ram, raking through my memories like playing cards, slipping one to the top of the deck: me, in my bedroom, fourteen years old, listening to "Dark Side of Heaven" for the first time, when Rick's riff ripped and raced through me like a torrent of fire and love.

I try to pull away, but I can't, even though I feel him feeding off it, eating the joy of that moment, devouring me from the inside, the marrow of my life and memories extracted.

I'll suck you dry. I'll kill you if you don't release me.

It's Rick's voice, or maybe I just hear it like that inside my head, and in a stark, singular moment, *it* is there in front of me, revealed as a creature of mist and lightning, fire and vapor; unimaginable, yet beautiful and alluring beyond understanding.

I'll give you anything you want. I already know your first wish. You don't even have to speak it out loud. Isn't that why you came to me tonight? Isn't that why you've been tracking me down. Isn't that really why you're here? Not to evict me, but to take me in?

I can see it: everything I could have, everything I could be, every dream I had when I was fourteen coming true. I also see, with devastating clarity, that no matter what I've tried to tell myself since that demon wrecked my fingers and killed Bella, that I would trade everything I've done and accomplished since, for a chance to play guitar again.

Yes, I think: fervently, feverishly. *Yes.*

Somewhere, Alice is speaking, shouting, and when the vision of what was and could be withdraws, I don't feel relief, only regret and pain. The genie keeps its hold on me, but it's speaking to Alice now:

"I'll give you what you want, too, Alice. Just let me go, and you can have him. Robert Plant? He's here, tonight, backstage, waiting to see me. I'll take you to him. Anything you want. Just let me go, I..."

"Shut...up."

Alice's voice is cracked and jagged, and I can feel the physical effort it takes her to tear away from the temptation of that offer.

"I'll kill Jackie. I..."

The grasping force that fettered me withdraws so fast it's like a rubber band snapping back. I fall out of the void, into the present, backstage, this room, the smell of leather and sweat and Jack Daniel's. Alice is holding me and somehow I'm on the floor, her dark hair tickling my face.

"Jackie, don't you dare die on me!"

"Rick... What happened?"

A sob catches in her throat.

"He went down like a ton of lead."

And there he is: unconscious, sprawled on the couch. His chest is heaving, so I know he's alive.

"I guess we miscalculated," I say as we scramble to our feet. "That thing is a far sight stronger than we counted on." I check Rick's pulse: quick, but steady. "I think it was the Jack Daniel's you prepped that knocked him out. Thank god for the good old standby of sleeping pills and booze, am I right?"

"Get it out of him. I don't like our chances if he wakes up."

I open the small cardboard box, removing the contents: an oblong glass vial wrapped in tissue paper and bubble wrap. It's the size of a bottle of liquid Tylenol, bluish glass wound about with uncorroded, shimmery metal wire; engraved with hieroglyphs around the top and bottom. Just a pretty trinket, so you'd think, bought for two bucks at a market in Istanbul.

"A magic bottle," the vendor insisted when I tried to haggle. "Used by the Pharaohs to hold divine tears."

Which isn't exactly what the hieroglyphs say, but close enough, I guess.

I work fast, fastening the extraction unit over Rick's head. It looks like a metallic hairnet, and I carefully connect the wires from it to the open mouth of the vial. The net pulses and glows in Rick's dark hair when I switch it on, and it takes so long before anything happens that I almost give up. Then I see it: a brief flash of glistening, amorphous silver mist, a shivering phantom mass of something unseen and unseeable, flickering in and out of sight. For a second or two it seems to hover around Rick's head like a halo, as if it might break free, before it's snuffed out and disappears into the vial.

"Done," I say, removing the chain from Rick's neck and pocketing it.

"Good. I'd say five minutes or less before his entourage comes knocking on the door." Alice has already packed up most of our gear, and now she smiles, looking at the vial as I secure the stopper, wrapping the top in duct tape. "What are we going to do with it? I mean, demons and spirits usually just poof out of our plane of existence, but this..."

"I'll seal it with something more permanent once we get home. Then we'll store it safely or neutralize it if possible, I guess."

"What about him?"

Rick looks peaceful, but older: frail, empty, diminished. I don't know what he will be like when he wakes up, but I know he won't be the same, and neither will his music.

There's a sense of loss and grief in that moment that I cannot name properly even to myself. For the Rick we loved. For the music and the riffs and those moments he gave us when there was nothing but joy. For Bella, for ourselves, for a band gone down the drain, for my mutilated fingers, for the pain and grief that is impervious to drugs or booze, for the never-ending regret of it all.

"Just leave him be," I say. "He'll wake up with a heck of a hangover, but there's nothing more we can do for him."

Cradling the vial in my right hand, I slowly flex the crumpled fingers of my left, bending them as if they're resting on strings again. To my surprise, I feel the idea of a riff take shape inside me, slipping into my wrist and hand. I flex my fingers again. They feel stronger, more dexterous. As if the heat of the fight with Rick has loosened my joints, as if the scarred cartilage and bone has softened, as if...

I stop myself. I close my eyes.

No, I think. Then: yes.

"Alice, want to get a band together again?"

But she's already at the door, not listening.

"How's my hair and face?" she asks, hefting the backpack and duffle bag with our hardware out of the room. Looking at her, I realize she's found the time to reapply her lipstick and eyeliner.

"Fine, but..."

"I'll see you at home, okay?"

"You're leaving? But the gear..."

"You can get it to the car, can't you? Because, you know, if you're not going to build me a time machine, I'll have to take my chances in the here and now."

She's off, and when I peer into the hallway I see her heading for a blond and gray-streaked mane of divine curls, a flash of denim and paisley, a whiff of "Black Dog" and "Kashmir" hovering in the air.

"Good luck!" I whisper, curling my fingers around the vial, around the silvery whispered promises contained within.

GOOD GIRL

WAWA WAITS IN THE WOODS, tongue lolling, ears drooping. She waits in the fern-covered gully beside the dried-up creek. Every now and then she tries to lie down, but then there'll be a rustle in the trees, the sound of snapping twigs, of scuttling claws, and she's up again.

But no one comes.

Wawa waits. She would howl, would bark, but Wawa is a good girl. A good dog.

She isn't sure how long she's been waiting. If she could, she'd run back home, back to the yard, to her blanket by the bed, the ball beneath the trampoline, but she can't. There's something here, something she can't leave behind. She has to wait, has to guard, that's all she knows.

Wawa's legs don't feel right; neither does her nose. Everything's muddled. But she cannot leave this patch of dirt, this shady copse.

It rains. Gets darker. Colder. Moon shivering in the puddle by her paws. Wawa does not drink. Mist rises around her, gathers close, gathers tight. Wawa breathes it in. The mist is cold and wet. It slips into her. Slips deep inside.

Someone's coming now. The creak of dry wood beyond the ferns.

Wawa quivers, a growl held tight in her throat.

No. No growling. Wawa is a good girl. Good dog. Still, she holds on to that growl. Feels it grow in her throat, feels it drip between her teeth. Wawa breathes in the mist again. Deep and cold. It's getting colder. Getting darker.

Wawa paces the clearing, going no further than the edges where the trees and bushes crowd in close. Footsteps stir the shadows. A glimpse of light. Wawa holds on to her growl, to the mist.

It's a boy. He carries a flashlight. He carries a knife.

Wawa remembers being carried. She remembers the boy. Remembers the knife too.

Wawa remembers *pain*.

Wawa is a good girl, a good dog. Good dogs should not howl should not bite should not bark.

Good girl, Wawa. Good dog. Good dog did not growl at the boy, did not bark, did not bite. Not when he let her out of the yard, not when he carried her here, not when he held her down, not when he brought the knife down again and again and again and again.

Wawa looks down. There's a dog at her feet, in the trampled mud. A good dog, a good girl, on her side, guts spilling into the moonlit puddle, bones exposed where the knife went in. Blood.

Through the mist, Wawa sees the boy put something on the ground. Something small and soft. Something whimpering. Wawa breathes deep. Breathes in the mist until all she is is mist and cold and darkness. Then, Wawa howls. The mist wreathes around her as she howls, as she rises, as she leaps, as her new fangs of cold and darkness close tight around the boy's throat.

Wawa is not a good dog. She will not be a good girl anymore.

DEEPSTER PUNKS

Surface

THE ANIMATED TATTOOS ON JACOB'S skin glimmer in the dark water, words and images swarming over his skin, bright and luminous, before they fade away again.

"Don't you dare die on me." I'm holding his head above the waves, but his naked body is cold and slick and heavy in my grip. By now, I should be able to see the lights of the ocean platform, but there's nothing, only darkness above and below, no horizon separating them. I unseal the mask of my thermal suit so I can talk to him, even though I'm not sure he can even hear me anymore. "You're one lucky bastard, you know. If the Company had sent us anywhere else in the system and you pulled this kind of stunt, you'd be dead already."

It's true. Beneath the icy mantle of Ceres, in the 10 K depths of Enceladus, he'd be dead for sure. In the sub-surface ocean of Ganymede, or in the tidal-flexing waters of Europa, he'd be dead-dead-dead. Dead like Petra. But he's here, on Earth, with me, and he's alive.

Stay alive, Jacob. *Please.*

***

Descent

It was a bad day to be waiting for a shuttle-pod on the ocean platform above Devil's Hole. Temps were just above freezing, the North Sea was heaving up ten-foot waves all around us, and the rain was coming down like sheets of steel. Even with the frenzied guitars of my favorite tunes blasting in my ears, it was less than ideal.

Of course, no day had felt particularly good since I got the news about Petra, and this day was made worse by Jacob who was flouting Company regulations by not wearing his gloves. I watched his blunt, calloused fingers clench and unclench while the tattoos slipped across his ruddy knuckles, inked creatures darting into his sleeves.

I'd known before I came here that he wouldn't be in the best place after what happened on Ceres, but we were both Company vets, and not wearing your full kit when going below was such a dumbass, rookie thing to do.

I touched my earlobe to turn down the music volume, interrupting the satisfying, jagged blast of "Sloppy Gods and Monsters" that was rattling through my skull, the latest release by Martian Rust out of Chryse Planitia.

"Get your gloves on, man. Last thing I need is you going geriatric on me and getting frostbite."

Jacob startled, and for a moment he seemed surprised to see me there, as if he'd forgotten where he was. But at least he dug his gloves out of his kit bag and pulled them on, sealing the click-seams against the cold.

"Sorry," he said, and looked it.

I shrugged it off, turned up the music again, and thought of Petra. I thought of her a lot lately. Thought of her grinning and cranking up her playlist at the start of a shift, the music ripping through us as we worked. She always had the best tunes, raw and gritty stuff that would make your heart pound and your head spin, the kind of old-school shit hardly anyone played anymore. I thought of her laugh, raspy and warm, big enough to hold the world and everything in it.

"You might have sold your bodies to the Company, and you might let them ship you from sea to sea, but they won't really take care of you. No one cares about us deepster punks, except other deepster punks. That's why we have to look out for each other. On every world. On every station. On every shift."

Petra told us that in training, twenty-five years ago, and it had been my mantra ever since. Any loser could become a diver if they went through training, but becoming a deepster punk meant something more. It meant living on the edge of the precipice where no one else would be stupid enough to go. It meant working the utmost depths for the

Company, surviving inside the system, finding fleeting moments of freedom and glory and togetherness in this goddamn profiteer's paradise of a solar system. It meant stripping your existence down to the bare necessities, traveling through life with nothing but your skin, your playlist, and your kit bag. Sometimes it was hard living like that, but no matter what bullshit missions the Company had thrown my way, no matter how long the hours or how dangerous the site, no matter who I'd been teamed up with for a job, Petra's words had been my guiding light.

I used to think those words were Jacob's guiding light, too, but lately, I wasn't so sure.

The pod surfaced in the grey water below us—a bright yellow, almost spherical sub-vessel, stamped with the Company's logo in black. We climbed down the ladder, and as the hatch sealed above us, we descended into the North Sea, trading the lashing wind and waves of the surface for the familiar murky stillness beneath.

"You okay?"

Jacob nodded, and beneath the ginger stubble, his face was still the same stiff mask of calm normalcy he'd worn since we met on the mainland.

I probably wore the same mask myself. As if everything was okay. As if Petra wasn't dead. As if she hadn't drowned, impossibly and inexplicably, inside that station on Ceres. As if Jacob hadn't been the only one there with her.

Petra.

The pain sliced through me, so sharp and jagged I had to close my eyes. She'd been the best of us. Our mother-goddess, our patron saint of safety first, and now she was gone.

I slid my hand over the front of my thermal suit, feeling the reassuring presence of the stun-baton hidden in the pocket on my thigh. It was small enough to fit in my hand, yet the charge could knock out a grown man, according to the trader I'd bought it from at the bar in Narvik.

"Knock out as in kill, or as in stun?" I'd asked while she pocketed her credits.

"Does it matter?"

No. What mattered was that it wouldn't be detected by the Company's security scanners.

Jacob was peering through the pod's single porthole. Layers of ocean drifted by, lit by occasional sparks of bioluminescence, gleams of life.

"Did you get to go home at all before you came here?" I asked. "Or did they send you straight from the debrief on Mars?"

He shrugged, as if it didn't matter. I guess it didn't, really. "Home" didn't mean a heck of a lot when you spent your life traveling from sea to sea, working your ass off in the deeps on Earth and elsewhere in the solar system. I'd bought an apartment in the Scandinavian sector a few years ago but it was agony to stay there for more than a couple of days, pretending I was enjoying my shore leave. Pretending I was home.

"Everything down there looks all right so far." Jacob projected his retina-readout between us—all the stats reaped from the station below us in Devil's Hole—water pressure, surface conditions, water temperature, ocean currents, station integrity and status.

"Looks that way," I said, even though nothing felt right. Jacob leaned back in the seat beside me and removed his gloves, working those fingers again like he had up on the platform. "What's wrong with your hands?"

He looked up.

"Nothing." He put the gloves on again. "Just a cramp or something. It comes and goes. Been bugging me since Ceres."

Ceres.

I thought of Jacob and Petra, working together on Ceres.

Goddamn Ceres.

Every deep-station was much the same once you were there, and none of them were exactly plush, but Ceres was one of the oldest builds in the Company's network of science outposts and resource extraction hubs. It was cramped, dark, cold, and working there was hard on your body and your psyche. Usually, the Company sent newbies there for short stints to make sure they knew what real deepster punk life was like. The idea was that after Ceres, every other Company facility would look pretty good. Why they'd sent two veterans like Petra and Jacob there together was beyond me.

I studied Jacob in the bleak light of the submersible. His face looked the same as it always had, just a few more wrinkles added to the dimples and cheekbones I'd fallen hard for when we were rookies together. And he still had that mess of short-cropped, reddish curls I'd pulled my fingers through a thousand times in bed and elsewhere. He *seemed* okay, but you never really knew what moved beneath the surface.

Deepsters snapped, everybody knew that. It wasn't unusual, really. Only, we were supposed to snap on our own time, with a bottle of home-brewed booze, the psychoactive substance of our choice, or occasionally, with a bullet or a noose. Not on the job.

I thought of Jacob's hands, opening and closing. Strong. Empty.

How much force would you have to use to kill someone like Petra?

How empty would you have to be to let them drown?

***

"Do you think it's sabotage, Becca?" Jacob asked when we stepped through the entry chamber from the shuttle, closing the pod's hatch behind us before the station-hatch opened and we could enter.

That got my attention. Nothing else he'd said today had really sounded like him at all, but now he gave me a shrewd gaze, looking almost like the Jacob I'd known for so long.

I kept my voice deadpan.

"Sabotage? I thought this was a routine maintenance job?"

Jacob scoffed. "Right. Ten major incidents all over the solar system in two years. Fatal outcomes on Enceladus and Ceres." He paused, as if he expected me to say something, but I didn't. "And now it's suddenly all hands on deck for routine maintenance from the North Sea to Ganymede. Something's up."

"You think all those incidents were sabotage?"

"I think the Company *hopes* it's sabotage, because if it's something *they* did, some design flaw, they're in the crapper with governments *and* shareholders. Sabotage? They'll just nuke a few of us and be done with it." The look he gave me sharpened. "Or, they'll set us on each other and try to clean house that way. Right, Becca?"

I flushed, not so much from anger as from annoyance at my own lack of a convincing poker face.

He nodded as if I'd confirmed his suspicions. "They asked you to watch me, right? Told you I needed babysitting after Ceres. That's why you've been staring at me like I might go off the rails at any moment."

I looked away. "You know it's not like that," I mumbled, but of course it was. *Ride with him for one job, and report back*, that's what the suits had said. *You're his friend. We just want to make sure he's in a good place. Guilt and grief can make people do stupid things.*

I'd said yes, because in the end, the Company would always get its way.

"Don't worry, I won't hold it against you," Jacob said, and kept walking, his voice so flat I couldn't tell if he meant it.

***

Usually, a two-person team would be taking turns on shift, but for this job, the Company had specifically requested we work together at all times. It was obviously another way to make sure we snitched on each other.

I stowed my gear in a locker, and when I got into the control room, Jacob was already there, standing by the view-window. It was dark outside of course, down there at the bottom of the Devil's Hole trench, except for a faint shimmer in the glass in front of him. A reflection, I thought, or something sliding across the surface outside.

"Jacob?"

Something about him, his stance, the outline of his body, felt wrong. Like maybe it wasn't Jacob at all, but someone else, someone I didn't know. Someone that should not be here. I shuddered. What the hell was going on with me? It was like I was a rookie again, seeing monsters at every turn.

Every deepster saw monsters. They were the imaginary creatures your brain stitched together from stray shadows, random movements, moments of oxygen deprivation, and bits of structural noise. It happened more frequently when you first started out, but no one was immune. And if you weren't careful, if your brain convinced you to believe in the monsters, you could end up doing harm to yourself and others.

I'd seen my share of monsters beneath the seas on Earth and elsewhere, but this felt different. This felt *real*. I slipped my fingers into the pocket, felt the smooth, hard surface of the zapper, the small indentation at one end that would activate the current.

"Becca?"

Jacob turned, and I saw his face in profile. The way the dim lights hit the angles of his nose and cheeks made me realize how hollow and spent he looked. Not a monster. Just Jacob, my friend, my on-and-off lover, my co-worker, and whatever else he'd been to me through the years. Good old Jacob, Mr. Easy-going, the guy everyone wanted to work with, and not just because he was good in the sack. The guy who brought the beer, no matter what planetary body you were working on, and made sure you drank it cold.

"You all right?" I asked, and switched on the exterior lights.

There was nothing unusual outside, only a section of the Devil's Hole extraction area, much the same as the Company's setup no matter where you went in the solar system: delivery tubes snaking through the sediment; the bots crawling everywhere, flat and multi-limbed like metallic crabs, helping the larger bots further out extract and transport the ore and minerals that would eventually be ferried to the mainland by the Company's delivery vessels.

"Yeah. I'm just tired. The debrief after Ceres was...rough."

I wanted to ask about that, should have asked, but we were on the clock. Instead of talking, I hooked my playlist up to the station's sound system and cranked up the music while we busied ourselves with the inspection, checking hardware, software, wiring, safety systems. Nothing we found was out of the ordinary, and just working together set my mind at ease. I fell into the routine of it, the easy muscle-memory of companionship, that comfortable ability to work together without talking.

While I worked, I thought about what Jacob had said, about ten incidents in two years. I knew there had been an increase in accident stats, but had it really been that many? I set the intra-net to do a rundown for me on my retina-screen, and he was right. It was all there, incidents strung out all over the system. Always water breaching the station. Usually moderate to severe injuries, but fatalities on Enceladus and Ceres.

A sliver of unease slipped in beneath my skin.

Petra had been the team lead on Enceladus. Petra had died on Ceres.

No. I shook off the chill. Jacob was right. The Company was probably trying to pin this on sabotage because if it was material fatigue or construction error, their bottom line would be in trouble.

***

After a few hours, we took a break for a classic deepster punk dinner, also known as hot tea and cold calorie bars. Jacob still brewed the best tea in the fleet, brought his own stash to make it, so at least that hadn't changed. And at the end of the meal, we ended up comparing new tats, because it's not a real deepster punk get-together unless there's an ink show'n'shine.

I showed him the school of dolphins I got on my back, tails flipping as they jumped over my shoulder into my bra, slipping down between my breasts. Jacob didn't say anything, but I knew that look, and when I zipped up, it lingered.

He hummed and hawed before stripping, as if he wasn't dying to show off, and sparring with him almost felt like old times. Finally, he acquiesced and unzipped the top of his suit, pale skin prickling in the chill station air.

Even at 40 plus, Jacob was still cut enough to make me ache, and animated tats writhed on every inch of his exposed skin—jellies, squids, sharks, narwhals, other real and imaginary sea creatures I hardly even recognized undulating across his arms and torso. Every image was aglow with bioluminescent ink—blue, green, red, shimmering black. A large Pacific octopus, rendered in hyper-realistic detail, swam around his midriff, and when I touched it, the creature twitched away, tentacles sliding around his waist.

My hand lingered in its wake, the music throbbing through me like a second pulse and I knew he felt it too. After all, how many times had we listened to this track together, "Blood Feud" by The Rowdies pumping through us, whether we were clothed or naked, fucking or not. In this life, there were some days, some nights, when the music and another body were the only things that kept you alive, that reminded you of why you kept going at all.

"What did that octopus cost you? It's gorgeous."

"Three months wages and a bit. All hand-worked by a lady on Mars, no ink-bots." He waved away my frown at his extravagance. "What else do we spend our money on? We've got no homes, no kids, no pets. The Company owns everything we are and everything we think is ours. All we have are these damn bodies. Might as well blow our credits on that."

"Bitter?"

"Hell no. Wouldn't choose any other life even if I could. You know that."

"Not even now?"

My hand still lingered on his hip and he didn't move away.
"Not a chance."

***

Every station had at least two bunk-rooms, always a relief on longer missions with people you didn't know or didn't like, but Jacob and I had shared rooms and beds since we were in training. I'd thought about using the second room this time, but I didn't.

At shift's end, in our shared bunk-room with the music playing between us, all rib-rattling guitars and drums, I watched Jacob undress. Then, he watched me.

The mutual titillation of that game between us was different now when we were getting close to 50 than it had been when we were in our twenties, but I still liked the way he looked at me, the way his gaze moved slowly over that aging body of mine. It was still a good body, strong and tall and pain-resistant, though whatever firm curves it had once held had been blunted by the years.

"Looking good, Becca."

"Not half bad yourself."

"I missed you," he said, tattoos slipping ever faster across his skin.

I knew he wanted to pull me down on the floor or on that narrow bunk with him. Part of me wanted it too. Badly. But instead, I sat down on my bunk, turned off the music, wrapped the sleeping bag around me and made sure the thermal suit was folded up nearby, the zapper within easy reach if I needed it.

"Jacob. Tell me what really happened on Ceres."

He winced. I watched his face, but most of all I watched his hands. He had moved them to his sides, fingers clenching, unclenching.

"I talked about it enough with the shrinks."

"I don't care what you told them. You're my friend. Petra was my friend."

Friend. How small and incomplete that word felt to describe Petra or Jacob.

"What do you want to know?"

The tattoos swirled over his skin, not as fast as before, but still animated, even though his face looked calm.

"Did you kill her?"

I almost thought he'd hit me for that.

"Is that what you think?"

"Or did you just let her die? Because there is no way Petra would have just drowned inside a station like that."

"It's more likely I killed her? Is that it? Is that why you brought that zapper?" He leaned over, grabbed my suit and threw it on the floor. "You think I didn't notice? Why don't you just take it out and fry me right now."

All the grief and anger I'd tucked away inside reared up at him.

"I brought it because I have no idea what the hell is going on. You didn't contact me after Petra died. I had to get it all from the Company. And now, you're talking about sabotage. Maybe there are people in this Company that want to sink it and don't give a shit how they do it. Maybe you're one of them. I don't know. That's why I'm here, that's why I brought the zapper. That's why I agreed to babysit you."

Jacob closed his eyes. His hands had stopped moving, and all the tattoos had gone still, glowing but slowly fading. In the low light of the bunk-room, I imagined I saw movement on his skin anyway, as if a shadow passed beneath the ink as it faded.

When he started talking, his voice had a hollow ring to it.

"They did it to me, too, Becca. That's why I was on Ceres with Petra. They told me to watch her. Told me to report back, let them know how she was doing. Told me they were worried about her after that installation on Enceladus went to shit. Babysit her on this one job, they said. We don't know if she's in a good place or not. You're her friend. Look out for her." He opened his eyes. Blue. Clear. Full of tears. "The joke is, I was going to tell them she was fine."

The fire inside me guttered out.

"Why would they think Petra was a problem?"

"Because she was the one running the show on Enceladus. They handpicked her for that brand new installation, a new world, all that glory, and in the end, her whole team almost died." He was quiet for a bit. "After Ceres, I looked at the accident statistics, like I told you. Managed to wrangle some docs from the Company data-pit. In every incident the last two years, at least one of the people present had been at the accident on Enceladus."

My limbs felt numb.

"What does that mean? What happened there?"

"Petra doesn't...didn't know. She couldn't tell me everything because a lot is covered by the Company's non-disclosure, but the last thing she remembered clearly was drilling down into the sediments. Next thing she knew, she woke up in the medivac drone. But something was off on that mission. There was a new guy on it, fresh out of training. He was the one who died. Petra said he freaked out when they did a dive near the initial drill site. He said he saw a monster, thought his suit had ripped, and he almost took down two others before they could sedate him. They checked him over, suit and all, and of course everything was fine, but after that, things got hairy. You know how Petra was. She made you think she was invincible, but Enceladus...that place got under her skin. Talking about it with me, she seemed rattled. Told me she saw monsters *everywhere*. That everyone did. Even on Ceres she..."

His voice faded.

"She saw them on Ceres, too?"

"Once. I think she was spooked and shattered by that rookie dying on her watch. You know how she was. Take care of each other, you know, her gospel. She felt she failed."

A thought skittered by in my head, out of sight. Something I couldn't grab hold of.

"Okay. Enceladus went to hell. Next, they send her to Ceres with you. What happened there?"

"Like I said, I thought she was pretty much fine." His voice changed, became clipped and serious, the way he'd probably laid it out for the Company psychs, over and over and over again in the debrief. "She was on shift. I was on sleep cycle. Logs show she went into the shuttle-pod chamber without her suit and somehow managed to cripple or disengage the pod, causing a leak. She was in the transit chamber between the station and the pod when the water rushed in. The station hatch was sealed, and I couldn't open it until I had sealed the exterior hatch and pumped out the water. It took too long. By the time I got to her, she told me to take her home, and then she died."

That unsettled skittering of something I ought to understand got worse.

"She *talked* to you? How long had she been in the water?"

He laughed, a sharp sound.

"You sound like the psychs, Becca. They told me she couldn't have said anything. That I imagined it. It's true I blacked out at some point. I can't even remember most of what happened before the evac-bots extracted us. The debrief team told me she must have been dead when I got to her, that she couldn't have said anything. But she did. 'Take me home.' That's what she said. And then she was gone."

***

Surface

The sea heaves around us, too cold, too deep, too vast. My suit is keeping us afloat, but Jacob is fading. Maybe he's already dead. The abyss is pressed up against me, heavy and cold.

We have nothing but our bodies, Jacob told me, but here, at the end, he doesn't even have that. Even that has been taken away from him.

Teeth chattering, I call his name, and then I sing him snippets of every song from my playlist I can think of, hoping the sound of my voice will keep him here, that it will remind him of who he is, who we are, and why he has to stay with me.

I think of Petra, our glorious deepster punk mama, telling us to take care of each other.

I tried, Petra, just like you tried. But it wasn't enough.

That's when I see the light. The platform. And taking flight from it, three rescue bots, roaming across the waves toward us.

***

Ascent

When I woke up in my bunk, Jacob was gone, his sleeping bag tangled as if he'd fought his way out of it. His thermal suit still on the hanger. I knocked on the door of the hygiene stall, hoping.

"Jacob?"

No.

I knew it, then. Knew what it was, the feeling that had skittered around my mind since we got here. I knew with absolute certainty, that something or someone was on the station with us. But was it just a monster, stitched together from my grief and anger, or was it real?

Heart pounding against my ribs, I put on my suit and followed the narrow hallway toward the shuttle-pod hatch, checking the small rooms as I went past. Part of me already knew where he was, but I kept hoping I'd find him on the way.

Again and again I called his name, but all I could hear was the hum of the station, and eventually, a muted alarm.

Jacob was in the transit chamber, between the station and the shuttle pod. Lights were flashing everywhere, wiring hung loose from a panel on the wall, as if he'd tried to disengage the shuttle-pod to let the water in. He hadn't succeeded, yet, but I wasn't sure we'd be able to get back to the surface in the pod anymore.

He stood there, naked, just like Petra had been, just like the guy they'd found dead on Enceladus, and none of his tattoos moved or even glowed. All his ink was dull and dead.

I pulled the inner hatch open and the sound from the alarm went from mute to an ear-shattering mayhem.

"Jacob. Don't."

His hand trembled on the panel beside the shuttle-pod. If he dislodged the seal now, with the inner hatch open, the station would flood, the pod would flood, and we'd be dead.

I stepped inside and sealed the hatch behind me.

He turned slowly, like he was surfacing from some place deep and mute, and in my head all the pieces were fitting together into a new kind of monster. The string of accidents after Enceladus. Always someone from Enceladus present. Except here. Here, it was just me and Jacob. Jacob, who had been on Ceres with Petra. Jacob, who was the only one with her when she died.

The accidents had been moving through the system. *Something* had been moving through the system, from one deepster station to another. Enceladus to Europa, Europa to Ganymede, and so on. Eventually to Ceres. Eventually here. Moving through us. Inside us. Inside other crew members. Inside Petra. Inside Jacob.

Jacob looked at me, but something else was staring out through his eyes.

"Take me home."

The voice was Jacob's, but I knew it wasn't him speaking. Just like it hadn't been Petra speaking to him on Ceres, because she'd already been dead.

Home. There was a yawning pit of despair and loneliness lurking beneath that word. The deep, dark waters of the North Sea were so very far from the depths of Enceladus—the abyss of outer space separating them. Separating whatever creature had entered a human body there, stowing away through us, through space, trying to find its way back to the ocean where it belonged.

"We'll find another way." I reached out for Jacob, hoping he was still there. "Whatever you want. Whatever you need."

In an instant, Jacob's tattoos flared to life, all of them glowing brighter than I'd ever seen before. At the same time, Jacob rushed me and knocked me down on the hard metal floor of the chamber. I scrambled to get up, but he was already at the broken panel, trying to activate the switch to blow the shuttle-pod, to let the darkness in. Or maybe, to let it out.

There was no time for finesse or subterfuge. I got to my feet, grabbed the stun-zapper in my pocket, trying to find the button, trying to turn it the right way around so I wouldn't knock myself out.

I yanked on Jacob's shoulder with one hand to pull him away from the panel, and with the other, I jammed the stun-zapper into the small of his back. He fell. Spasms. Screaming. The tattoos on fire, blazing, burning, until he passed out on the floor beside me. Looking down at him I saw a shadow moving underneath his skin, rippling past, diving deeper into muscle and bone to hide itself again.

Shaking, I opened the hatch to the shuttle-pod and dragged Jacob's heavy, limp body inside. After I'd made sure that the pod was sealed, I hit the emergency evac button.

***

Surface

I can still see the busted shuttle-pod drifting in the swell, rolling over heavily, half-full of sea water. At least it got us to the surface safely. At least we won't get the bends. At least the hatch didn't fail until we were up here. At least I got Jacob out before it started filling with water.

I keep my eyes fixed on the lights on the platform, on the rescue bots closing in, hoping they will get to us in time, but Jacob is so heavy. Even with the built-in floatation in my suit, I have a hard time keeping him above the waves, and I don't know how much water he swallowed since we left the pod. I keep singing, wishing I could blast the music into the night: staccato drums to make his heart beat, ragged guitars and vocals to make him breathe.

His body spasms again, just like it did below, and the tattoos come alive—writhing, luminescent. There it is again. Beneath the ink, the shadow moves as if it's trying to break out of his skin from the inside. I see it move over his chest and throat and then—a shadow, a mist, a ghost of a shape twitches loose from his flesh and bursts out of his wide-open mouth. For a moment, I almost see it clearly—undulating, shifting—then Jacob shudders and the shadow dives below us and is gone.

The whirring rescue bots are right above us, and I hold on to Jacob, shouting out his name above the noise, shouting that I love him, that he can't die on me.

Jacob said we don't have a home. But we do. Petra knew it. That's what she tried to tell us. She understood it long before I did. Space is cold as hell, and the oceans are deep and dark and full of monsters, real and imaginary. But we have a home. Home is right here. Home is you and me, together. Home is us, two old deepster punks, clinging to each other in the darkness and the cold, keeping each other alive. That's all the home I've ever had. That's all the home I'll ever want. All the home I'll ever need.

When the bots lift us out of the water with their retractable limbs, Jacob's tattoos shimmer to life, bioluminescent ink lighting up his body and his face. I curl up beside him in the rescue cradle, listening to the simple rhythm of his life-signs pinging through the CPR-bot, his chest shuddering with breath again. Looking down into the water, I see something in the waves, below the surface, or maybe skimming the waves—a gleaming shape of light, wrapped in darkness. For a moment it's there, then it's gone, and I can't tell whether it dives into the darkness below, or whether it takes flight into the darkness above us, headed for home.

THE ROOT CELLAR

GRANDMA'S ROOT CELLAR LOOKS LIKE a barrow in the gloaming: door facing north, yawning wide beneath the hill. Lintel so low it makes me crouch, threshold so high it makes me stumble. You might have laughed at that if you could see me, brother. I wish you would. I wish I could hear you laugh again. I wish I could hear you scold me for everything I've done wrong since we ran away from Father.

I think of Father every day, Jeremy, tracing the scars and memories in my skin.

You were too young to remember how he brought us to that barrow by the lightning-blighted oak. I was already six and worldly wise, I thought. Mother was long since gone, I don't know to where, though I often think of Father weeping near the frozen mere that winter when he said she left.

Our tallow candles burning low, he led us beneath the barrow's rock-hewn arch, beneath the hunched shoulders of stone and dirt.

"Hold still," he said when he laid us down on that flat stone table, and we did, though we'd seen the knife, flint and quartz.

He cut us, Jeremy, he carved his runes into our skin and fed our blood to the bones and shadows beneath the ground. I remember how you cried, how you did not stop wailing until you'd been given a cloth to suck, rough-spun linen dipped in sugared brandy. Afterwards, when we walked home beneath the cloud-wrapped moon, Father told me we'd be strong as rocks and roots now that the earth had tasted us, that nought below the sky could hurt us, not even the craft Grandma wove into the darkness below the spruce and pine.

I thought he lied, Jeremy, as he sometimes did when he'd been drinking. I thought all he wanted for us was the pain, but I was wrong. I understand it now. Even then, he was looking out for us.

***

The door to Grandma's root cellar creaks open, complaining to itself on rusted hinges, warped wood murmuring the secret sigils bound to it long ago. There's a space inside, between the outer door and inner, lined with wooden shelves on either side where Grandma stores her empty buckets and rinsed-out pickle jars. Almost I can see her there, peering through the darkness, round glasses slipping down her nose.

I close the outer door behind me, bracing the heavy axe I brought against the wood, long handle planted firmly in the ground. That handle fits so well into my hand, like it was made to measure: easy to grip and swing, even with just one hand. Slice and cut, chop chop chop.

I stop and listen for the scratch and skitter of eager bones outside; I listen for the pitter patter of rat claws, too.

No. Nothing. Not yet.

I've come for you, Jeremy; you, and my arm. The rats brought back to me everything I lost, except that. I've already searched Grandma's house: the cellar and the attic, the dank room beneath the stairs, the cupboards and the chests, the hidden spaces between the walls and floors—finding nothing there but rat droppings and silenced sparrow bones. But I'll find you, brother; you, and that wayward limb of mine. Then we'll go, the two of us, and make our way out of here, together. Could be, we might find Father, too, if he can still be found.

The inner door swings open as I step inside, beneath and under, into the chill breath of earth and damp. Jeremy, where are you? Beneath the ground? Will I have to dig? Might be I should have brought a shovel rather than an axe.

The lantern-flame flickers over the barrels and the baskets, the wooden crates filled with winter-stored potatoes, apples, carrots—last year's harvest brought beneath the ground to keep. Braided onions and garlic dangling low from the root-twined ceiling; rows of jars with jellies and preserves, pickled beets and beans, each labeled in Grandma's strong, sure hand. I grope and rustle among the tubers: searching, seeking, never finding.

Brother, are you here? Can you hear me whispering?

Such a sap I was, Jeremy. Thinking I was saving us that night we ran away, slipping through the pathless wood like the shadows of two birds while the house burned down behind us.

I didn't mean to do it, I swear it. I didn't mean to drop the kindling from the hearth, didn't mean for the flames to catch. And Father on his way home already, striding between the boles, carrying his saw and hatchet, having spent the day splitting logs and hauling timber, expecting his dinner set out upon the table.

It was best for us to flee, I thought, before he returned to see what I had done.

I remember the bitter taste of tears and smoke, how you tugged at my singed skirt as we ran, how you cried for us to turn back 'round. And me, prideful and foolish as I've always been, not listening. By the time I saw the truth of it, we were already lost, caught in Grandma's cunning weft. Father always said her power reached from tree to tree, far as anyone could walk: a weave too fine for eyes to see or hands to feel yet impossible even for breath or dreams to slip through.

But I've torn her weave, Jeremy. I've slashed it.

I chopped her head off. Knocked her over in the privy, pinned her down beneath my knee. Axe and block, chop chop chop. Last thing she told me was that I'd never find you. She laughed, and then I swung. I told the rats to help me hide her, and they did.

It was the rats that saved me in the end, Jeremy, the ones we fed the scraps and leavings from Grandma's larder. They followed me everywhere after you disappeared, snickering behind me as I searched, tangling in my hair when I fell asleep. But in the end, they pitied me, dragging my limbs and guts through Grandma's house, gathering me up bit by bit underneath the eaves. Last of all they got my head back: hair shorn off, mouth and nose askew from when it fell and rolled across the floor. You might've laughed at that, too, if you'd seen it.

I should have done better than to lead you here, Jeremy, but I will make it up to you, I swear it by my bones and marrow.

If only I could find my arm! This one's already dangling loose, I was in such a hurry when I stitched it on. But I've searched all the crates and barrels, and there is not a whiff or whimper of it, nor your skin and bones.

Grandma came for me two nights after you'd gone missing, brother, her voice all soft and cooing as she woke me in that narrow bed you and I had shared. The rats squeaked my name, their shrill voices muffled by the mattress-straw, but I did not listen. Grandma said she'd found you, said she'd show me where. And I went, even though the faces in the mirrors shook their heads. They knew. But they're the kind that cannot speak unless spoken to.

"Look behind the woodpile, Amadine." And I bent down. Stupid girl.

I fought her, Jeremy, tearing at her hair and apron. That's when she took my arm, hand still clenched into a fist. Right before her blade sliced off my head.

"Every life has power, girl, and children most of all," she told me as she took me apart like a clock upon her table, laying aside my teeth for necklaces and charms, hanging my skull from the rafters to dangle with the hams and herbs.

Father always said there's worse things than being eaten, but I'd not believed it until then.

Oh, Jeremy, there's nothing here, nothing but the smell of dirt and roots, the chill of winter and trampled earth. No arm, no you. Just me, unraveling.

I know she's coming, Jeremy. The iron bands weighing her down at the bottom of the well won't hold her long. Neither will the spells I wove. I listened to her, brother, while I dangled from the wooden beams; learning the craft that binds and loosens, the runes she speaks and carves.

Can you hear that? That's her hands crawling up the well. She'll be here soon, trying to rend my flesh asunder one more time. Oh, Jeremy, I don't know if I can do it, not again, knitting flesh to bone, nerves to veins. I'm no great seamstress and I made such a mess of it the first time: legs all crooked, spine askew, neck and nose turned and twisted. Wouldn't that have made Father smile? Like he smiled at me right before he cut us in that barrow long ago.

"One day you'll thank me, Amadine," he murmured as I whimpered beneath the knife, "though I might not be there to hear it."

My knees snap and sway as I sit down on the floor, the seams I stitched through joints and gristle showing flaxen-pale on dirty skin, all that thread unraveled from Grandma's linen curtains. I've brought enough thread for you, Jeremy. A needle, too: sharp and good and strong. I'll put you back together, if only I can find my arm.

That's her again, that creaking. She's hauling up her limbs from the well, rope and crank and bucket. But I'm sitting quiet, like you would do if you were me, humming words of finding sweet and low as I shut my eyes, pawing through the spilled parsnips and rutabagas on the floor.

There. Down in the dirt, I feel it: elbow, wrist, and fingers. I still can't see it when my eyes are open—then it just looks to be an errant root half-buried in the floor, but my fingers cannot be fooled. It's my arm, twitching there to greet me, fist unclenching in the dust, letting go what's been held inside all this time, bent and twisted: golden wire, glass.

Little brother, you should have seen how Grandma searched for those spectacles of hers, even thinking that the magpie might have carried them aloft. She never noticed, never felt my hand grabbing in her apron pocket, right before she twisted my arm out of its socket.

I slip them on, feeling the pinch around my nose, looking through the lenses streaked and cracked. The lantern-glow shifts and trembles, crates and barrels wobble and reshape, the glitter of the pickle jars twisting inside out.

Oh, Jeremy. I see you now, you, and all the others: your hair and fingers turned to braided garlic strings; your eyes peering at me between the pickled beets; your heart beating slow in the jar of jellied apples; your bones and sinews in the barrels, packed down nice and neat in salt and brine.

This place was never built for potatoes and preserves. It is just another barrow, made to keep those things that should be underground: grave and cellar, both, dug beneath the hill.

Don't worry, Jeremy, I have my needle and my thread, I have Grandma's spectacles to see with, and as soon as my arm is back on I'll make you whole. My needlecraft might leave something to be desired, but I'm quick, and the thread is strong.

Never mind Grandma's knuckles rapping on the door, brother. I won't let her in, not until we're both good and ready. Not until the hungry rats have gathered kith and kin, come to take another meal from the scraps we might leave behind once we've said our last farewell to Grandma.

A STRANGE HEART, SET IN FELDSPAR

Beneath

ALICE IS KNEELING IN THE darkness, breathing hard, heart thumping behind her ribs.

The kids are gone. She feels it in her cold flesh and aching bones, as surely as she felt them being pulled out of her body at the hospital when she gave birth to each of them all those years ago.

She calls their names anyway: "Anne! Lisa! Eric!" But they don't answer.

The guide is nowhere to be found either, but she doesn't really want to think of him anyway, that smile turned to lips and teeth, the way he shook his head when she asked for help before he sunk into the darkness without a trace.

The tunnels of the old mine seem to throb and twist and shift around her, like the intestine of some strange, gigantic animal; she has to reach out and touch the rough walls on either side to steady herself and stop the world from lurching.

What now?

She can keep going deeper into the mine, without the guide, without the light. Or, she can turn around. She knows the way out, just follow this tunnel back about forty steps, then turn left and right, and she'll be standing at the ladder, below the open sky. Climb up and out, call the police, wait for rescue. Wait for someone else to tell her the kids are gone.

In the silence, in the darkness, she turns the choice over, the rough and the smooth of it.

They don't want me to find them. That thought is barely a whisper, small and cold and slippery, like a worm wriggling in a festering wound. *I told them to stay with me but they never ever listen.*

A breath shudders through her lungs.

They would have listened to Bill. They always listened to him.

But Bill's dead. He's been dead for two years. He should have seen that truck coming at the intersection, but he didn't. Instead, he left her alone with the mortgage and the bills and the kids and this goddamn life to live. Two teens and an eleven-year-old. How the hell is she supposed to deal with that? She never signed up for this single-parent bullshit, and now she's failed the kids again. Maybe for the last time.

She gets up, knees still shaking but getting steadier.

I'll bring back help, she thinks, and begins to retrace her steps, knowing full well there is no help to give or receive anymore.

She's almost at the second turn when she hears the first scream.

Above

"Mom, this can't be the place."

It was Anne who said it out loud—what they'd all been thinking for the last half hour while she drove deeper into the woods along the winding gravel road. The kids had already hopped out of the van and were staring at her through the window, shivering in jeans and fleece sweaters in the early Swedish sunlight, pale faces miserable and accusing. They reminded her of birds, crows or some other kind of scavengers—watching, waiting for her to fail them again.

For a moment she just sat there, staring back at them, hands on the wheel, engine running. She was so tired. Of being here in Sweden. Of this so-called holiday. Of herself. Of them. Of the fractious, needy, collapsing *us* that was her family.

Looking at the kids, she considered locking the doors, turning the van around, stepping on the gas, and leaving them standing there. Only for an hour or so, of course. They weren't babies anymore, they could handle it. To teach them a lesson. To get a moment's peace from the whining and the arguing. It would be so easy. Just drive fast and don't look back.

As soon as the thought took shape, guilt flooded her. Of course she couldn't do that. She was their mom. The mom who had gotten them out of bed early, harassing and cajoling. She had even skipped her own morning coffee for this.

Zipping up her jacket, she stepped out of the rental van and looked around at the tall, skinny northern pines, the dense underbrush between them—plush moss and glossy lingonberry leaves studded with pale-pink flowers. The June morning was sunny, but the air was cold enough to make her shiver.

"Come on!" she said, trying to sound bright and chipper. "It's got to be around here somewhere, right?"

Eric ambled off, his voice a hushed grumble, but the girls barely moved.

"Let's go back to Skellefteå," Anne said, swatting at the mosquitoes.

"Yeah," Lisa joined in. "Seriously. Let's get back to town. There's no adventure park or whatever that guy promised here."

"There's not even a pit toilet," Eric whined.

"You're a guy," Lisa scoffed. "How hard is it to pee in the woods?"

"That's barbaric!"

"Not as barbaric as a pit toilet," Anne mumbled, making a retching noise to underscore her point.

"I didn't even want to come," Lisa fumed. "I knew it was going to be like this."

"You never want to go anywhere," Alice heard herself say, regretting her tone and the words as soon as they were spoken.

"Not with *you*. Or with these two losers."

"Grow up, baby-face!" Anne growled, and then the girls were fighting again. Third blow-up this morning, or maybe it had just been one continuous, never-ending argument since they woke up.

Alice didn't even try to stop them, knowing they'd only turn on her instead. She looked at the GPS coordinates. They matched the numbers on the flyer she got from the man who had approached her at the gas station yesterday. "Want to do something fun with your kids?" he'd asked while the children were yapping at each other by the ice cream counter. Something about his voice, the way he spoke English with that pleasant, soft lilt, had caught and held her attention. "Come hang out at the old mine. Caves and tunnels underground, that kind of stuff. Really old. All sorts of stuff to learn. I'm a guide there."

"What is it?" she'd asked. "Like, an adventure park?"

He'd smiled and handed her a colourful, tri-fold flyer.

"Yeah, like an adventure park. Great for kids and adults." At the top of the flyer it said, "Explore the Abandoned Mine!" in letters dripping with gold and scarlet. "Be there at eight o'clock. I promise it'll be worth it."

It was eight o'clock, but there was nothing here. No guide, no buildings, no parking lot, not even a sign. What had she been thinking? Dragging the kids into the woods like this. Dragging them from Canada to Sweden at all. A holiday to connect with their family's roots had sounded nice in theory, but the kids had moaned for most of it as she hauled them through the houses of distant relatives, and through old buildings and museums where nothing, ever, seemed to interest them. Today was just another disappointment. Another shitty day that was all her fault.

"Mom, is this it?"

Lisa held up a hand-painted, arrow-shaped wooden sign that had fallen over in the tall grass and daisies by the roadside. "Abandoned Mine," the sign spelled out in gold and scarlet, and walking over, Alice saw that it marked the start of a narrow, almost invisible trail.

They headed into the woods, and when Alice turned around after a few minutes, she couldn't see the van or the road anymore. There were only the trees, only the trail, only their own voices mingling with the breathing wind.

Beneath

It has to be Anne. The pitch and volume and sheer endurance of the scream tells her as much. Even as a newborn, Anne could scream loud enough to wake the neighbours.

For a moment, that scream burns away all fear and indecision, and she runs back into the belly of the mine, towards the sound, away from the coveted safety of the entrance and the glimpse of daylight beckoning ahead. She stumbles, falls, scrapes her hands and knees, but keeps running, one hand trailing along the wall so she won't lose her way in the dark, keeping track of steps and turns as carefully as she can with the panic cutting through her. Anne sounds so close but the scream is always out of reach, and eventually it fades and disappears.

"Anne!"

Nothing. Barely even an echo of her own voice in spite of all the stone.

Alice stops. She knows she's deeper into the mine than before, knows she cannot run heedless into the dark. Desperate, she grabs her phone, but like before, the screen is dead. "Something to do with the properties of the rock," the guide told them when they entered the mine, and for some reason she didn't question him further, even though it's clearly a bullshit explanation.

Tucking the phone back into her pocket, she bangs the fickle flashlight against her palm, and to her surprise, it glimmers to life, faintly illuminating the rock around her. The pale glow wavers over the rough, damp surfaces, making amorphous shapes and shadows scurry away into the dark.

The flashlight flickers, and she tries to absorb all there is to see before it goes out.

A few steps ahead, something glistens on the ground. It is a vast, black puddle, a pool that fills the curved tunnel in front of her. The surface ripples slightly, shivering with light. Alice crouches down to touch it. It's so cold it feels like ice, and when she withdraws her hand, there's a tingling numbness spreading beneath her skin, as if the cold is seeping into her.

Standing up, she points her flashlight down the tunnel. Thirty metres away, maybe more, she glimpses another crouched form, almost a mirror image of herself, though this one seems to be holding a reddish, sputtering flame aloft, rather than a failing flashlight.

"Anne?"

The ruddy glow slips over the features of the shape beyond the pool, but before Alice is sure of what she's seen, both lights go out.

Above

The kids were already whining about the long walk when the forest suddenly opened up into a wide clearing where the ground was littered with rocks of various sizes, from pebbles to boulders, rough and smooth, all in different hues of grey. Beyond the rocks was a small rise, and the narrow trail wound up the slope and disappeared over the top of it. All around, the forest loomed, the sky cupped like a dome of brilliant blue glass above the treetops.

"This place is cool," Lisa said, and stepped into the clearing, Eric and Anne following close behind.

Alice hung back, breathing in the scent of pine and sunlight, revelling in the stillness. Even though she knew they were only fifteen minutes walk from the road, this place felt impossibly far away from everything she'd ever known, and at the same time it was as familiar as a recurring dream.

Maybe Grandma had mentioned it in one of her many stories about the Swedish woods, about lingonberries and midwinter snow, and faded folklore creatures snaring the unwary.

She was about to check their location on her phone when the smell of coffee wafted through the air.

"Hello?" Her voice sounded small and uncertain in the silence.

"Hej! Hello! Over here!"

The voice came from the trees near the ridge, and as they walked closer, the smell of coffee got stronger. On a log beside a small campfire sat the man from the gas station, tending to a blackened coffee pot hanging over the flames.

"Welcome! Coffee?"

"Yes, please."

He poured her coffee into a hand-carved wooden cup with a curved handle of polished reindeer antler. Small symbols were scratched into the handle, similar to ones she'd seen in photos of stone carvings at the local museum—sun, boat, fish, moose. The coffee was strong, made the way her grandparents used to make it: the coffee grounds scooped into boiling water, left to steep and settle.

"Good?" he asked.

"Good."

While she drank her coffee, the kids scrambled over the rocks, their mood shifted same as her own. They were no longer fighting or whining, but laughing and playing. Alice couldn't even remember the last time she'd seen them like this.

"They're having fun already," the man remarked. "How about you?"

"So far, so good," she said guardedly, but she felt it too. Something good. Something that was almost contentment.

"That's what we do here. Take people back to a simpler time." He gestured vaguely at the sky and trees and rocks. "Help you find your way back to what really matters."

She nodded but wasn't really listening. He'd told her something similar when he gave her the flyer, some new-age bullshit about "finding your way" and "reconnecting." She'd heard too many of those kinds of platitudes since Bill passed, but the coffee was good, and hearing the kids laugh was better. And there was something about the place that appealed to her, a peacefulness, maybe even that elusive sense of home and belonging she'd been searching for this whole trip.

"Where are all these rocks from?" Anne asked, climbing up a nearby boulder.

"Some were brought here by the ancient ice and seas, but a lot are from the mine. Gunnar, the guy who started mining here in the 1930s, carried many of them out, hoping they'd be worth something. This was a few years after they found gold in Fågelmyran not too far from here, so he was hoping to get rich."

"Did he find gold?" Lisa asked, ambling over with a rock in her hands.

"Not here. He kept looking, though, digging and drilling deeper and deeper. People said he was a little odd, and no one thought it very strange when he eventually disappeared in the mine."

"Disappeared?" Eric stopped mid-stride with a lichen-covered rock in either hand. "You mean there's a dead guy in the mine? It's haunted?"

"That's not what he said!" Alice protested, but the man's smile only widened.

"Maybe. Some people say they still see Gunnar here, sometimes, carrying rocks out of the mine."

"Anne loves creepy shit like that," Lisa said, watching her older sister flush.

"Does she now? Well, there are more dead people around here. Just a bit further into the woods are some old gravesites."

They all turned as one, looking in the direction he pointed.

"Like, with real bones and stuff?" Anne asked.

"Yeah. It's just a few simple cairns, and the archeologists took most of it away, but there were human bones, stone tools, some fish hooks made of bone. Nothing fancy, but proof that people have lived around here for thousands of years. From back when this was the coastline."

"There's no sea here," Lisa protested.

"Used to be. All of Sweden is rising slowly, has been, ever since the Ice Age when the land was pushed down by the weight of the ice. Even now, the land rises a little bit every year, and thousands of years ago you could push your boat out and go fishing right here."

Alice looked at the glade. She could almost see it—water lapping the rocks; a simple wooden boat, cleaving the waves.

"Dad would have loved this place," Lisa breathed, then yelped when Anne smacked her arm. They both glanced at Alice. She felt the burn of their gaze, the worry, the fear. They still thought she might break. As if she wasn't already broken beyond repair.

The guide glanced over, then stood up, poured out the dregs of his coffee, and clapped his hands together.

"Let's head into the mine!"

Beneath

The flashlight won't come on again, so she stumbles back through the darkness, but even though she's carefully counted her turns and steps, she cannot find her way back to the entrance. Every tunnel seems to have twisted out of place, and in the dark, her senses are playing tricks on her. She hears the children's voices, her own voice, too; echoes of conversations and arguments and fights through the years. She hears her own thoughts whispering between the rock walls, hears the children scream again and again, always out of reach.

At first, she screams, too—screams for help, screams the children's names, but it only makes the silence worse afterward. It's better to stay quiet, better to try to find her way.

Twice she comes back to the immense black pool, twice she turns around and tries to find another way.

An unexpected breeze tickles her face as she staggers into a wider space, and for a moment she thinks it's the cave where they entered the mine, but there is no ladder, no hole showing the sky above. Instead, there's a dim light, the smell of smoke, and a group of huddled shapes by the opposite wall, gathered around an object in their midst—a large rock with a dark and distant crystal heart glowing like embers beneath ash, set in pale feldspar. One of the shapes turns toward her and his face is the guide's face, his smile a glint of wolfish teeth. Then the vision falters, and she's alone again.

Between

The entrance to the mine was a manhole-sized fissure in the ground just beyond the crest of the rise, with a rope ladder attached to a log dangling into the dark. Handing them each a flashlight, the guide shone his own light into the hole, illuminating the floor six metres below.

"It'll be a bit dark going down. Who's going first?"

Anne grabbed the ladder, didn't even hesitate. Then Eric, then Lisa.

"Mom! Mom! Come on!"

They called out to her from below, their upturned faces lit from above.

"Maybe I'll just stay up here and drink some more coffee," she called down, only half in jest. Part of her wanted to stay in the glade, in the sunshine beneath the translucent blue sky; wanted to just sit and dream of the ancient sea, and of Grandma and Grandpa, who had left this place so long ago. Instead, she took a deep breath, tucked the flashlight into her jacket, and climbed down the swaying ladder.

Once she stood on the floor of the mine, she lit her flashlight and swept it over a large, round cavern with several rough openings radiating out from the central chamber. Some tunnels looked big enough to walk through, others had collapsed or seemed too narrow or low to enter. A strange assortment of tools was on display around the walls, and the kids were already hefting various sledgehammers and pickaxes.

"Is that safe?" she asked when the guide came down the ladder behind her, recalling the mayhem that usually ensued if the kids armed themselves even with something as simple as cardboard tubes.

Standing there, underground, it occurred to her that while she had mentioned to one of her many Swedish second cousins that they were going on an excursion, she hadn't given anyone an exact location, or a time when to expect them back. She grabbed her phone to text the details to a couple of those second cousins, just to ease her mind, but the phone didn't turn on.

"Electronic devices don't work down here," the guide informed her, still smiling. "Something to do with the properties of the rock."

His reassuring voice smoothed her worries, and she put away her phone, even though a sense of unease still prickled down her spine.

"Alright. Let me give you the educational tour before I let you roam. This mine started out as just a cave back in the Stone Age. It might even have been used by those Neolithic inhabitants I told you about, the ones buried beneath the cairns. There are a lot of old tales around here, you might have heard some of them from your Swedish family, about trolls and vittra and other strange creatures living in this part of the woods, but for all intents and purposes, this cave was overlooked until the 1930s when local villager Gunnar Marklund started mining here, looking for gold, like I told you. Mostly, he found pegmatite, quartz, and feldspar instead."

"So there really is no gold here?" Lisa said, sounding disappointed.

"No. But he still made a living from the mine. The quartz was sold to the local copper smelter, and the feldspar, which is a very common mineral, was sold and used to make china plates and porcelain. He also found a kind of rock that was previously unknown to geologists."

Bending down, the guide picked up a large rock from the ground and held it out so it caught the sunlight from above. It looked heavy and jagged, about the size of a man's head, and while the outer part of it was pale and matte, its dark, glassy center sparkled in the sunlight, reflecting and refracting it. Leaning closer, Alice could have sworn she saw something move inside the crystal—shadows flickering below the surface.

"Feel it," the guide said, and held it out to her.

As soon as Alice touched the glossy crystal surface, a shiver ran up her arm and down her spine, as if the rock had given her an electric shock.

"The light-coloured part is ordinary feldspar," the guide continued, and passed the stone around, giving each of the children a turn. "But the dark part, the heart of it, that's something else. It's a mineral that has not been found anywhere but here."

Eric was the last to touch the rock, and when he was done, Alice reached for it one more time. It made her skin tingle again, and now there also seemed to be a buzz, a whisper, at the edge of her hearing, as if the rock was making either the air around her, or the bones inside her, vibrate.

"It's beautiful," Lisa whispered. "Can we keep it?"

The guide grinned, his smile all teeth.

"Sorry, but no. It's one of a kind." For a moment, his face turned utterly serious, almost menacing. "It can't ever leave this mine." Gingerly, he put the rock back on the ground, and when he looked up, he was smiling again. "Take a look around. Everything you see here, all the tools and the tunnels, is pretty much the way it was when Gunnar disappeared in the 1940s."

"Where did he really go?" Eric asked. "He can't just have disappeared."

The guide shrugged.

"Who knows? While this mine has only one entrance, there are many different ways out of it, but every person has to find their own exit."

"What the heck does that mean?" Alice asked, but he was already heading down one of the tunnels, the children ambling in his wake. "Stay close kids," she called out, but of course they didn't listen, too enthralled by seeing what lay ahead.

She followed them, only half listening as the guide spoke of old mining procedures. How one man held a hand-drill while another hit it with a sledgehammer, how the drill had to be repositioned and turned after each stroke. She even thought she could hear it, *thump thump thump*, and wondered if they'd installed a sound system to make the tour more realistic.

While the children investigated an old wheelbarrow and its load of rocks, the guide turned to Alice.

"Didn't you say your Swedish family came from around here?"

"Yeah. My grandparents moved to Canada in the 1950s, but *mormor*, Grandma, grew up in the village we passed on the way here."

"What was her name?"

"Elsa. Elsa Viklund, before she married."

The guide nodded.

"Elsa. Yes. I remember her. Such a good girl. Used to pick lingonberries around here every fall."

Alice turned her flashlight on the guide's youthful face. He could be no older than thirty, forty at the most.

"Excuse me? You remember her? How old are you?"

The guide's grin bent and twisted into something sharper, and then all the flashlights went dark at the same time.

Beneath

After roaming through endless tunnels, the pool bars her way again.

This time, there's a faint, silvery light coming from somewhere further down the tunnel, beyond the pool. In the eerie glow she sees footsteps in front of her, disappearing into the pool; sees three piles of clothes left discarded on the ground.

A sobbing, cold breath fills her lungs, but she's still drowning.

She'd call their names if she thought it would help, but she understands now that words and names have no power here. The only thing that matters is what she wants to find: a way out, or the kids.

When she first realized they were gone, something stirred beneath her fear and panic, something small and cold, hidden in the deepest folds of her mind. She didn't want to feel it, but it wriggled free anyway, a maggot gnawing its way out of rotting flesh.

Relief.

Relief that she could give up, that she could finally run away, and ask someone else for help.

Life's been so hard for so long. Trying to be a good mother, trying to keep it together, trying to be everything the children need, trying to do the right thing, trying not to break and shatter, every second and minute of every day. Always failing. Always falling short. Always thinking they'd be better off without her, if only Bill had lived instead of her.

But it's too late to run away and ask for help now. It is the fourth time she's come back to this spot, and she understands now that no matter which way she chooses, no matter how she counts her steps, there's only this place, in the end.

She found her way back to the entrance once, but she chose not to leave, chose to run back when she heard Anne scream.

"While this mine has only one entrance, there are many different ways out of it, but each person has to find their own exit."

When the guide said it, she thought it was yet another empty, new-age metaphor, but she has come to the belated realization that nothing he said was metaphor. This is real, all of it: the fear and the pain, the voices and the screams, the darkness behind her and the light ahead.

I told them to stay with me, but they never ever listen.

But it's too late for I told you so's. Too late for everything. Too late to find another way.

Between

When the light went out, the children screamed. She reached for them and found Lisa and Eric right away, but not Anne.

"Anne!" Her voice splintered into echoes.

"Mom?" Anne. Right beside her.

"Just stay where you are, kids."

She let go of them and tried to get her flashlight working, but it would not come on, and when she reached for the kids again, they weren't there.

"They're gone," the guide said, appearing in front of her, his face dimly lit. She wondered where the light came from, until she saw that he was holding that rock again, that strange heart of crystal, set in feldspar. The shadows inside it moved faster now, a churning vortex, and its whispers were more insistent and urgent.

"Where are my kids?"

"I don't know."

"Please. Just tell me where they are."

"I can't. You're their mom. You have to find them. If you want to find them."

She trembled.

"What do you mean?"

"You know what I mean, Alice. Don't you? Sometimes it's so easy to guide people. As soon as I see them, I know they're unhappy, and I understand right away where they need to go, what they want to find. Like Gunnar. He wanted to find gold. Others wanted to find other things, other places. Your kids, they were easy to guide because they knew where they wanted to go. But you... I'm still not sure. Do you want to find the kids or a way out?"

She stared at him, her heart beating so hard she heard it echo through the tunnel.

"I don't understand. Just help me find them."

"No. You have to find your own way out. Everybody does."

And then he disappeared, too.

Beneath

Alice kneels in the darkness, by the cold water's edge. She shivers in the pathetic human husk that is her body, the broken remnants of her soul rattling around inside it. Then, she sheds her fear and doubt and garments, leaving them on the floor next to the children's clothes.

Eyes closed, head lowered, she inhales the darkness and feels it settle and harden inside her, sharp and heavy. There is a new heart beating behind her ribs now, slow and purposeful, dark and opaque, set in her otherwise unremarkable flesh.

Do you want to find your kids or a way out?

She didn't know the answer then, but she knows it now.

Alice walks into the water. The pool is deep and cold. She wades until she has to swim. The liquid feels heavy, as if it resists the movement of her limbs.

When she reaches the other side, the tunnel narrows until she can barely fit through it. She has to lie down and wriggle and push and drag herself through it while the rock rakes her flesh and skin. But the light ahead is getting brighter, and she moves towards it, no longer sure if this is a dream or nightmare, a heaven or a hell, but it really doesn't matter. She smells fire, earth and rot, damp and blood. Then, the tunnel widens slightly. The light turns into the moon, and the air on her face is cold and smells of pine and smoke as she crawls out of a crack in the ground into the forest by the shore.

She stands there in the moonlight on top of the ridge, her skin streaked and slick from the pool, bloodied and raw from her passage through the rock. Below, there's a small fire near the water's edge, a boat pulled up in the shallows, and three familiar shapes clad in skins and fur are huddled around the flames.

She looks down at the ground beneath her feet, searching for the crack she came through, but it isn't there anymore.

One way in, many ways out.

The three below look up and call out to her, joyfully and loud. "Ma! Ma!" they shriek, shaking bows and spears. She raises her arms in greeting, and walks down the slope until she's home.

THE BRIGHTEST LIGHTS OF HEAVEN

I HAVEN'T SEEN MOIRA FOR fourteen years, but I dream about her all the time. The dream is always the same. We're six years old and we're dragons again—jumping off the roof together—but this time we don't hit the ground and we don't end up in the hospital and we don't need any stitches. Instead we just spread our wings and fly.

Last time I saw Moira in the flesh, she was eleven—gap-toothed and nearsighted. I was eleven, too—all gangly energy, frizzy hair, and braces. It was the same night our last game began, and it was also Moira's last night in Canada. Her parents had divorced the year before; now her dad was gone and her mom had decided to move back to Australia, taking Moira with her. I didn't want her to go, didn't even want to think about what my life would be like without her, but Moira said we had time for one last game, and I wouldn't have missed that for the world.

She always made up the best games: zombie tag, cops and aliens, wolves and hunters, vampires and slayers. Ever since preschool, she'd been turning yards and playgrounds into battlefields of fear and glory; turning us into something other than what we seemed to be: generic girls—awkward, studious, shy.

We already knew we were different than people thought we were, knew enough to hide it, too. We knew that beneath the surface we were something else entirely—something hungry, something jagged, something crooked and impatient.

That night we met in an empty storage locker in the basement of the rickety old apartment building she lived in with her mom in Burnaby. We'd sneak down there as often as we could, a fickle flashlight our only protection from pervs and ghosts. That night I brought my incense sticks and a box of matches. Moira brought a book on witchcraft and her penknife.

The book was from the library, dog-eared, severely overdue, its plastic slipcover torn. We took turns reading spells and stories from it, looking at the pictures while the incense made the small space smell like Friday nights at my Aunt Jackie's house.

"Mom says I'll forget you," Moira said, holding on to a lit match so long the flame singed her fingertips. "She says you'll forget me too. Everyone forgets, she says. When they get older. It's better that way. Easier."

I watched the match burn between us, my eyes stinging.

"That's stupid." The words hitched in my throat. "You won't, will you?"

She shook her head. Another match—lit, burning, singeing, extinguished.

"One last game, right?" she said, and I nodded. "But you have to promise you won't chicken out on me. It won't work if you chicken out."

"I won't. I promise." And I meant it.

When we were six, we played knights and dragons for a whole day in the backyard, taking turns wielding swords and claws, shields and fangs. Right before Moira had to go home for dinner, she changed the game. She told me we were both dragons and made me jump off the roof with her, saying we could fly. I knew we'd probably die, but I jumped anyway. Ten stitches and a fractured ankle was a small price to pay for that one dizzying moment when we were airborne, when we were dragons—scaled and fanged, hands entwined—together.

Our parents must have figured we'd grow out of playing those kinds of games, but we just got better at hiding what we did. At age eleven, sitting in that patchouli-scented basement, all I knew about myself for sure was that I never wanted to stop playing with Moira, and that I would never be what my parents expected me to be. Moira knew it too, of course. She knew me better than anyone ever has, before or since.

"Hold out your hand," Moira said, after sitting quietly with her eyes closed and the book open on her lap for a long time. She brought out the penknife, wiping the blade on her shirt, and I felt the darkness quicken around us, tickling my face and limbs with ghost breaths and spirit sighs.

She grabbed my wrist, harder than I thought necessary, and cut my palm with the knife. It took her a while to work up enough determination to penetrate the skin with that small, dull blade, but I kept still the whole time. Next, she cut her own palm—quicker then—and we clasped hands in the coiling tendrils of scented smoke, blood dripping on the floor between us.

Moira leaned in close—face lit by the flashlight, thick glasses framed by yellow plastic distorting her blue eyes.

"I had a vision, Rae." Her voice was an unfamiliar, hoarse whisper, skittering up my spine. As if she'd found another voice in the dark. As if another voice had found her. "You are a daemon escaped from the deepest depths of the void. And I am a daemon hunter blessed by the brightest lights of heaven. We are enemies henceforth. Before we both turn twenty-five, one of us must kill the other."

My palm stung and I felt dizzy. I already knew it was more than pretend, more than imagination. Moira had always made our games seem real, but that night was different. I felt the blood and smoke twitch together between our palms, as if we had stirred up something sleeping, something dormant—whether within or without, I couldn't tell. I felt it shudder and twine, snaking around my flesh and bones. Words and smoke and blood binding me, changing me. Changing Moira, too.

"We did it," she said, and laughed out loud, her voice her own again, though it scared me still.

***

The next day, Moira was gone.

"She'll probably write, once they've settled in," Mom said, but I knew better. I knew the game was on. I knew something had wriggled its way into this world, that Moira and I had made it real, and that she would stick to the game no matter what I did or didn't do.

Don't chicken out, Moira had said, and I knew she never would.

***

After Moira left, nothing much happened for a few years, though there were flickers and murmurs of something stirring. An open window Mom said she'd closed before she went to bed. A dead crow in the yard with its eyes gouged out. Our cat, gutted in the street. Run over by a car, people said. They didn't see the runes drawn in blood on a wall nearby. I'd seen those runes in the book—the book that was still in Moira's possession, as far as I knew.

***

The first murder didn't happen until I was twenty. I was at university, and one Friday my roommate asked if she could have our apartment to herself over the weekend. On the Monday, police tape was strung across the door, blood was soaked into the mattress, and her mutilated body was removed from my bed. Everyone always said the two of us looked alike, even though I could never see it. The room smelled of cheap incense and there was a pile of fragrant ash on the floor but, in the end, the police pinned it on her boyfriend, who was nowhere to be found.

I tried harder to find Moira after that, searched for her online and elsewhere, but turned up nothing. It was as if she'd been extinguished and erased, or maybe her mom had just changed their last name. Either way, I couldn't find her. All I had left to prove that she had ever existed were my old class photos where she stared at me through those thick glasses: awkward and forgettable, just like me.

Then Aunt Jackie died: diabetic coma. That familiar smell of incense wafted off her corpse when she lay in the coffin, but it didn't mean anything to anyone but me. Jackie's place always smelled of smudge sticks and incense and vegetarian chili—all the better to cover up the pot she smoked.

Mom cried and so did I, my hands clutched in prayer as I sat in church between her and Dad.

I prayed to find Moira, but I didn't.

***

A year after we buried Aunt Jackie, one of our old teachers was killed in a hiking accident. I'd called her to see if she might know where Moira had ended up. She didn't, but said she'd ask around. A week later that same teacher made the evening news: she'd fallen into a ravine on a North Shore hiking trail. Fractures, broken neck, contusions. Convenient.

"For fucks sake, stop it with this black magic shit," my boyfriend at the time told me after we got drunk one night and I spilled my guts about Moira. "You were kids and played a stupid game. You're so fucked up sometimes."

But he was not a daemon, nor a daemon hunter, so what did he know? He certainly didn't know what it was like that first time you wake up in the middle of the night and feel your teeth suddenly too sharp beneath your tongue, your vision too clear in the dark, your skin scaly and feverish, your flesh crawling like maggots and beetles, and you run into the bathroom to see, to see what a daemon really looks like, finding only your own face in the mirror.

That boyfriend is dead too. Pickup truck. Highway. Ice. Pole. Goodbye.

I never did manage to track Moira down.

Maybe my parents could have helped me find her, but Mom died in hospital two years ago, that year the flu was so bad. They thought she'd be okay but overnight, she slipped away. Her hospital room might have smelled like incense, but what difference did it make? No one cared. She was dead. Dad died shortly after. A ferry sank when he was on holiday in Thailand. Lots of people died. He was a lousy swimmer.

That was a long summer.

***

I'm turning twenty-five tomorrow. It's Moira's birthday in a week. Suck on that: all the birthdays we've almost shared. And here I am, outside a club in downtown Vancouver saying goodbye to all my almost-friends from work, turning down the offer of a ride home. An icy tendril slithers up my spine and I know Moira is close. I feel her presence as I walk up Granville Street, as I ride the SkyTrain home. The words she said so long ago twitch and squirm beneath my skin, through my veins: worms and leeches bred in darkness.

Last year someone plowed into the car I was sitting in on a side street in New Westminster. A hit and run. The doctors couldn't believe I got away with only scrapes and bruises. I was in hospital for a few days afterward, for observation, waiting every minute for Moira to come and finish what she started. She didn't. There were flowers though. No note. I felt Moira's presence real close that time.

"You don't know what it's like," I told Mom once, "to have to wait for Moira to hunt me down, for the game to play out to the end."

"Who is Moira?" She didn't even remember.

"My best friend, the one with the glasses."

But Mom didn't remember until I showed her the class photo.

"Oh, that girl. I thought they moved to Australia."

Right.

"Moira said I was a daemon," I told Dad just before he died. "I'd never felt like one until she said the words. But for a moment in that storage locker, it was like I forgot who I was. Or maybe I remembered. I mean, everybody has a wriggling bit of darkness inside them, right? A worm in the flesh, hatched in the warmth of your pulse. Fed by hate and anger and depravity, growing fat and lush through the years, like a leech. But I know I never even dreamed of being a daemon until Moira told me I was one."

That was the same day Dad told me I wasn't his. That Mom had already been pregnant when he met her. She was dead now, so he could tell me, he figured. He cried about how hard that had been for him, and how sad he was that they never had any kids together.

Thanks, Dad.

I'm walking down the street from the station. We're really playing the game out to the very end. No surprise, really. I knew she wouldn't chicken out, and neither will I.

"You're a daemon," she'd said as the incense burned.

Why did I have to be the daemon this whole time? Being a daemon is hard work, and I should at least have had a say. But she just stuck me there, in the deepest depths of the void, and for almost fifteen years I've had to make the best of it.

I open the door to my apartment.

Even though I know Moira is there, I close the door, locking it behind me, securing the chain and deadbolt. I can feel the shift in the air, the smell. It's not incense, just her skin, just her breath. She's been here for a while, waiting for me to come home. Rifling through my belongings, no doubt. Looking for daemon spawn and daemon spells and daemon food: Tupperware containers filled with blood in the fridge; Ziploc bags of human flesh in the freezer. I don't know what she might have found.

Most nights, this daemon prefers sushi or Mexican.

"Hi, Rae."

She's sitting on my couch. No lights. Just us.

"Hi, Moira."

I feel my palm pulsing where she cut me all those years ago. I feel the words and blood twitching in me, livelier than they've been for a long time—since Dad died, really—twirling tighter around veins and marrow.

"Where've you been, Rae?"

"Oh, you know. Around."

"Yeah, I know. So busy playing."

"You've been busy, too."

"Not as busy as I should have been. Took me too long to get back here from Australia, but airfare is so goddamn expensive. You had time to kill a lot of people. Just like a good little daemon should."

"Me? Kill people?" I give her the wide eyes, the meek smile: the mask of skin and pretense I've used to hide my true features all these years.

Moira laughs, ever so softly.

"Oh, Rae." Her tone is one of admiration. "You've got guts and flair. Always did. That's why I love playing with you."

It feels good, even now, even here, to finally get the credit I deserve.

I lick my lips and feel the sharpness of my suddenly razor-edged teeth. My tongue feels rough and long as it flicks in and out, tasting her on the air. My nails are claws now, scratching my skirt, my thighs beneath, my scarred palm so hot that I can feel the flesh burning, sizzling, steaming.

"Well, what could I do? You turned me into this."

"We turned us into this." Her eyes shine a luminescent blue, reflecting the light from the street outside. "All I wanted was a good game, something so good we couldn't forget each other. And what a game it's been. The best, right?"

"The best," I whisper, and then I run at her, trying to slash her throat with my claws, but she evades, a silver blade etched with runes cutting into my arm. That hurts. Silver is bad for daemons. Just like it said in that library book.

And Moira has more. She's remembered it all: spell-wound spikes of ivory, holy water, an amulet of malachite and black onyx around her neck to sap my strength.

We fight: parry-strike-parry-slash. Things around us crash and break: TV, vase, glass-topped table. My arm breaks too, and I heal it up as best I can. Good stuff, these daemon powers. They're the bee's knees after single-car accidents on icy roads. (Come on. I just tugged the wheel a tiny bit.) They can even help you crawl out of the wreckage and get away scot-free while your fucked-up boyfriend's innards spill over the seat.

Moira's got some moves too and, in the end, I'm bleeding everywhere and so is she. She ties me to the bed, my scaly arms twitching helplessly as she binds me with a rope soaked in holy water. It sears and burns my wrists, but I don't hold that against her. It's all part of the game, after all.

"You should have made me the hunter, you the daemon," I tell Moira. "You'd be good at it. Even better than I was."

In the red and blue light from the neon sign across the street I finally see her face clearly, and she's smiling. Such a wicked good girl.

"What are you waiting for?" I growl. "Game's over. You made me. Now unmake me."

My life flashes before my eyes while I wait for Moira to get on with it. That roommate at uni, she might have looked like me, but her blood tasted ever so much sweeter. Mom's machine unplugged in that hospital room, just for a little while. Her soul slipping out at last, tender and quavering. Bye bye. Dad on that ferry as it went down, and me, beside him in the water, watching him sink. His soul took its time to leave: a cold sliver of life, bitter and stale when I devoured it. An acquired taste, I guess. That father-daughter trip to Thailand was so expensive, and I didn't much like swimming with all those corpses until the rescue boats came, but whatever.

There are others too—the cat, the crow, Aunt Jackie, that nosy teacher (I barely touched her, just gave her a little nudge)—but you can't expect a daemon to keep an accurate body count.

Moira's silvery blade shivers at my neck.

"I missed you," she whispers, leaning close, words and breath tickling my skin.

"I missed you too," I whisper back, and I mean it.

"At least you didn't forget about me."

I watch the light change colour between us—red, blue, red—my eyes stinging.

"You didn't forget either," I mutter, words hitching in my throat.

Next, I smell incense. The same kind I use before a kill—patchouli, the cheapest stuff—and for a moment I think the game is over. For a moment I wonder what will be left of me once it's done, and who I would have been without this game, without Moira.

Awkward, studious, shy.

Bored. Generic. Alone.

"Moira..." I whisper, doubting everything, past and present, future imperfect.

Moira rips my skin with the knife, but the cut is shallow and reluctant. She cuts me again, but not my belly, or my chest, or my throat. Just my palm—the other one—slicing deep and true.

"I had a vision, Rae." The voice is a familiar hoarse whisper in the dark, the face a mask of shadows slipped over Moira's features. "I am a daemon escaped from the deepest depths of the void. And you are a daemon hunter blessed by the brightest lights of heaven. We are enemies, henceforth. Before we both turn forty, one of us must kill the other."

Our bleeding hands clasp and hold fast, the darkness around us quickening with ghost breaths and spirit sighs and oh, oh, there it is again: that jagged and impatient hunger, words and blood and smoke twitching together between our palms, shuddering and twining around my flesh and bones. Unmaking. Remaking.

"Don't chicken out on me," I whisper, relishing the pain, relishing the feeling of her hand in mine.

"I won't."

I see the glint of fangs where none were before when she smiles, the flick of that cloven tongue between her lips. She likes the feeling of it, the strength and daring, I can tell. I liked it too. Now I'm kind of relieved to be rid of it. Being the daemon can be a hard slog, as she'll find out soon enough.

Then Moira laughs and so do I because, for one dizzying moment before the new game begins, before the words and blood take hold, we are the same. We are twins, airborne, suspended between the void and heaven—cursed and fanged, blessed and brightest—hands entwined. Together.

METAL, SEX, MONSTERS

YES, OFFICER: I DO REMEMBER my first time. I was thirteen, and the room smelled of drugstore perfume, apple-scented shampoo, and sticky lip gloss. I remember what the boy tasted like, too: potato chips and popcorn, teenage sweat, and bated breath. It was in the basement of a friend's house, a party, out of sight of the parents, and Judas Priest was playing on the stereo when someone turned off the lights and said we were playing a kissing game: everyone had to walk around in the dark and kiss whoever they could get a hold of. It sounds kind of louche now, I guess, but it was 1981, and it's not like we were drinking anything but soft drinks mixed with lemonade.

The boy's hair and eyes were brown and I'd had a crush on him since grade two, though I'd never considered doing anything about it. I'd never kissed anyone before, either. But in the dark, with Rob Halford screaming about working class frustration in Margaret Thatcher's Britain, he grabbed hold of me, probably out of pity, and kissed me.

I liked kissing him: liked the rush of blood to my head and groin, liked the way he held me. He might have tried to pull away soon after, or maybe he was just trying to breathe, but I persisted and he acquiesced, and when his lips parted just a little, I kissed harder, penetrating his wet, warm mouth with my tongue, nipping at the flesh. There was a taste then, familiar and new at the same time, slipping through me, of salt like tears, of rusted iron and oxidized copper.

I probed and bit and licked as something shuddered awake deep beneath my skin, rippling like the surface of a submerged dream, its sudden heat radiating through my capillaries, burning through my eyes and fingers, blistering my lips and cheeks.

Will you look at that? Look at my hands. Even now, thirty-five years later, the memory of it makes me tremble.

No, officer. I pulled away. He caught his breath and I thought he'd scream, thought he'd tell everyone that I had bit him. The blood was there to prove it, on his lips and chin, on my tongue as I swallowed. But he just put his hand to his mouth and looked at me, as if he'd caught a sideways glimpse of the hunger lurking inside me.

His family moved away later that summer. Probably just as well, even though I missed him.

But that's not what you want me to talk about. You brought police photographs.

Let me see. Yes, they were all mine. Such gorgeous boys. Hell bent for leather, wouldn't you say, each and every one. But then, rock and heavy metal gigs have been my venues of choice from the start. I love the music, of course, always have, and I figured those places were good for hiding in plain sight. There, I was just another hungry groupie, just another starving fangirl jonesing for a fix: unremarkable, disposable, forgettable. Considering how long it's taken you to find me, I guess I was right about that. But it's the bodies I love most of all. That's what kept me coming back. All that lovely flesh wrapped in sweat and studs and tight denim, bones reverberating with the amplified sound of guitars and drums and bass, shouted vocals clawing at their throats, the air thrumming with scent, everyone resplendent in eyeliner and hairspray, lace and spandex. All those beautiful people: souls loosening their grip on mortal coils, words and breaths and hands rising, each one wanting to taste blood and skin, wanting to disappear into another, to be devoured by the music and the crowd...

No, officer. I don't need anything to drink. I just need a moment.

The second boy I kissed was the first one who went all the way. I waited for him in the shadows on a street corner, after the club had closed: I was eighteen and starving. I wonder if you've ever been as hungry. Maybe you have. I'd been good for so many years after that night in the basement. It was hard, but school's important, and besides, it takes more than hunger. At least for me. Something has to turn me on, there has to be a spark—heat, lust, love—call it what you want, but if I don't want them, if they don't want me, it's no good at all.

Sorry. You look uncomfortable. Is that too much information? But then that's what you want, isn't it? Information. That's what you said when you brought me here.

But I was telling you about the second boy.

Inside the club he'd slipped his arm around my waist and I'd left it there. He was barely older than I was, all strut and swagger in his leather jacket when he followed me outside and offered me a ride on his motorcycle. I held on to him, speeding through that gossamer night, my body bursting, flaring at the seams and joints with heat and hunger, trying not to take him too soon, too quick, trying to make it last.

In the tall grass by the river he took off my bra and I took him into me, whole and screaming and unwilling. He was my first, and I wasn't as gentle as I should have been, as I've learned to be since. But that mingled taste of him—leather, beer, and cigarettes—it whets my appetite even now, just thinking about how he scraped and rubbed against my viscera as I brought him deep inside of me.

That was a long time ago. I've devoured so many boys and men since then.

How many? I couldn't tell you. I've not counted them. But, yes. More than in your photographs, certainly. If I wanted them, and they wanted me, then I took them. And when I reached out, when I opened up and they saw me in my glory, when they were blinded by my bliss and consumed, they were not afraid. Not in the end, at least.

Are you afraid, officer? Or is that too personal a question to ask?

What it's like? Why would you ask me that? You said you have video footage, so you must know. I don't know what it's like from outside. I only know what it feels like from within.

...heat and light, ignited and extinguished in the same moment

...reaching out through flesh and bones and web of veins and skeins of nerves

...unfurling myself

...unleashing myself

...unhinging myself

...unmaking them

...savouring the quavering tissue of life and memories, their first and last flashes of pain and ecstasy, the moment of their birth and the instant of their death.

Afterward, I can still feel them inside me for a while: plucking them like strings to hear the whispered echoes of who they were.

Yes, thank you, officer. I do need something to drink now.

What I am? Don't ask me that. Tell me what you see, instead, when you look at me.

I don't know what I am. I don't know what awoke in that basement when I was thirteen, with British Steel pounding beneath my flesh, blood riveted to my tongue; when I awoke and knew that I was no longer what I'd thought I was, that I wore the body I'd thought was mine like a second skin pulled tight over my true self.

I've thought about that kiss, that boy, every day since.

Something was different that time. I know that now. I sensed it, but didn't understand it until later, maybe not until tonight. That he was like me. That he hungered, too.

I wonder if he's looked for me like I've looked for him.

I'd know him anywhere. I'd know his dark brown eyes, would know his hair even if it's thinner and streaked with grey, would know the scent of him even thirty-five years on. I'd know him no matter where I saw him, or what uniform or badge he wore.

I'd know the heat, radiating from his skin before we even touched.

Yes, officer. I would know you, even if I'd waited decades, trapped and lonely inside an aging husk of skin and flesh, even if I'd lingered, sleepless for a million years in an empty space of stars and quantum rifts. I'd still know you.

Do you remember it? The dizzying taste of me in you? The fleeting promise of it on your tongue? Of course you do. That's why you brought me to this bar rather than the police station.

And if we kissed again, you and I, here and now, with this Judas Priest song cutting through us like a screaming metal blade, cutting all our memories open; with the noise and blood and hunger throbbing in us like when we were thirteen; if we kissed now, what would we become then, you and I, if we unfurled, unhinged, unleashed ourselves together, devouring each other, our light and heat bleeding into the other, pulsing, flowing, mingling, fusing into one?

What, I wonder, will we become now?

CLEAR AS QUARTZ, SHARP AS FLINT

IN EARLY SUMMER, BEFORE SOLSTICE-night, when the child is not yet so heavy inside her, Jenna climbs the hill to the ring of stones. She knows she shouldn't, but it's the kind of day when nothing seems perilous, not even those pale-grey sarsens looming on the tor. The breeze is soft, and the first bees, drunk on nectar, buzz through the pink sheen of heather spread across the moor. Father's sheep graze on the hillsides while the herding dogs lounge in the sun, their keen eyes on the lambs and ewes.

Jenna climbs the hill because she hears the stones sing.

Don't listen to that old stone-song, Grammy told her. That's what everyone says. Yet it is hard to ignore that call once you've heard it.

The first time Jenna heard the stone-song was in midwinter, that night when she let Keff into her bed while everyone was at the sun-feast. Only Grammy's wooden god watched them from the wall. When Keff moved inside her, the song thrummed so low and deep within she thought it was her own heart beating.

She heard that same song the day the baby quickened. Heard it again when Grammy laid her hands on her belly, shaking her head, muttering of ill-made children, saying that the stones would claim what the wooden god would not.

Lately, Jenna hears the song every time she walks past the smithy, every time Keff turns away rather than look at her.

***

Jenna climbs and the song quivers inside her, making the child stir—whether it is eager or uneasy she cannot tell. The song has words, but she cannot hear them yet. All she hears is the melody, like a cold trickle on hot skin. Like a drink of something cool when you're parched. Like sharp teeth sunk into warm flesh.

She climbs, feet slipping on rocks and tussocks, hands grabbing hold of dirt and roots, skin slick with sweat beneath the wool and rough-spun linen.

On the hilltop, the stones loom, worn smooth by age and craft, brought here so long ago only the sky remembers when, their grey bulk sunk deep into the hard ground. Jenna steps inside the ring, the song throbbing in her veins and marrow. She turns and turns again, eyes closed, the child gone still inside her.

If her eyes were open, she would see the whole world from this high perch—the village with its sod-roofed houses and sway-backed byres, the gleam of ocean just beyond, the undulating horizon. But she does not look. She just listens to the voices of the stones—whispering, rumbling, crooning.

Jenna sheds her tunic and her breeches, leaning naked on the tallest stone, arms outstretched, round belly pressed hard against the rock, every ounce of warmth leaching out of her. On the slope below, the sheep keep grazing undisturbed, while the dogs whimper, ill at ease.

She lets herself sink into the cold, until the chill breath of the rocks and the darkness writhing beneath the hill heave and twist inside her. Until she hears the words; until they cut her. Clear as quartz, sharp as flint.

The song remains inside her through the summer, voices shivering through her womb while the sarsens watch and wait on the tor.

She does not climb the hill again.

***

Now's the first day of autumn.

Late night. Early frost. Sickle moon slung low. Almost time for reaping.

In Grammy's house, Jenna shivers by the fire, swathed in bloody wool and soiled linen. The wooden god watches her, unmoved.

Even as Keff turns to leave, even as Grammy carries the little one away, all Jenna hears is the stone-song and the words the sarsens spoke when she stood inside the ring.

***

Within the ring of stones, the child is on the ground—crooked legs streaked with afterbirth, severed cord wet and supple, heavy head pillowed by the frost-nipped heather.

All around, the stones loom and whisper.

The child remembers a woman, face worn and sweaty in the firelight.

It remembers a man, turning away. It remembers one word spoken: "ill-made." No other name was given.

The stones remember the old woman who carried the child into the ring. They remember the sign of warding she made before entering.

They remember the warmth of Jenna's skin and womb. They remember the blood, thrumming inside her veins. They remember life. They remember hunger. They remember and they sing, leaning close while the baby cries.

Above, the sickle moon gleams between the clouds, its edge unsheathed. Clear as quartz, sharp as flint.

***

It's almost dawn. Frost bites deeper now.

On the tor, the wolves sniff the wind and heather, burrowing into the tiny carcass. Grey muzzles tear and eat.

When the wolves have fed, the child gets up. A shadow quivering above the hilltop, shrugging off its pain, shrugging off the last remnants of bones and flesh. For a moment, it flits inside a wolf and feels the lure of being wolf, of warmth and strength, of den and pack. Then, it slides through fur and marrow, back into the night.

All around, the stones hum and whisper, and the child listens, wavering. It longs for the safety of the ring; for the deep power of rock and roots. But it longs even more for a worn and sweaty face glimpsed briefly in the firelight.

The child turns. It runs toward the hearths and the smoke; its yearning like a cloak billowing in its wake. It runs, leaving its bones and doubts behind.

***

Beneath the covers, Jenna stirs. She still hears the stone-song, feels its chill below the fever burning through her. The cold, writhing darkness of those pale-grey voices fill the hollow space inside her. She hears the words—the only words ever spoken on that hill:

Feed us.

And when there's a scratching at the door, when a slip of shadow creeps across the threshold and darts across the floor, when the darkness scuttles beneath the covers, she clutches it to her breast and lets it suckle.

IT'S EASY TO SHOOT A DOG

IT'S EASY TO SHOOT A dog. Susanna watched Papa do it one bitter morning, winter before last, when old Karo couldn't get up off his blankets, so she knows how it's done.

You tie the dog to a fence post, put a soup-bone on the ground, load the musket with the right measure of powder and a lead bullet, aim it at the dog's head, and light the charge with the match-cord. Long as your hands don't shake, and the dog doesn't move, you'll blow its head clean off.

"It is an act of kindness and of mercy," Papa told her when he saw her watching from the porch, "to spare him the suffering otherwise to come."

Then he lit the powder, rough hands steady as the discharge scattered a flock of crows into the clouds.

Restless now on her cot beneath the rafters, listening to the quiet breaths of her own dog asleep beside her on the floor, Susanna hears that musket blast again, feels the shudder of the recoil through her bones, the sting of powder in her nostrils sharp enough to make her wince.

Judging by the moonlight, it's long past midnight and she knows it's time to go, yet she lingers beneath the covers.

She thinks of how she brought this dog home as a pup one October day ten years ago when she was seven, same year as Mama raised a stone with her brother's name in the boneyard; thinks of how old Karo took to that pup right away, watching it with kindly hang-dog eyes as it blundered wobbly legged through the yard and garden.

That pup grew up with her; became this rangy, flop-eared mutt that curls up beneath the table when she eats, sniffs out hares and grouse in the woods for her, twines its body 'round her knees to greet her when she comes in from the barn. For ten years, she's cared for it with gentle patience, the way no one's ever cared for her, and for ten years it's followed her wherever, sharing her bed, her paths, her warmth; its soul and shadow mingling with hers beneath this tarred roof, beneath this well-worn patch of sky and heaven.

It's easy to shoot a dog. Easier still if you don't think about it too long; if you can heft that musket clean of doubt or guilt.

Cold floorboards bend and creak beneath her stockinged feet as she gets up, reaching for her clothes in the darkness. There's the gleam of frost outside, even though it's only early fall, but then, it's been a hard year already. A year of bad omens; a harsh winter followed by a slow spring, wolves ravaging sheep, church-silver stolen off the altar. They even burned a witch in town, just after Easter. She went to look, but though the woman's hair was shorn and she was already burning, Susanna could tell it wasn't anyone she knew. After, when the bones still smouldered, the priest in his stiff black cassock puffed himself up before the crowd, assuring them the witch's spells and crafts would all unravel now that she was dead. Susanna stood there until dusk, waiting to see if anything would change, but the world remained the same as far as she could tell.

Beneath the shearling coat and felted woolen breeches on the chair beside the bed, Susanna's fingertips brush the embossed cover of Nana's ancient hymnal, but tonight she has no prayers to tuck between its yellowed pages. Instead, she reaches down, finding the warmth of fur and breath that has always been more dependable than faith and supplication.

The dog yawns as it stretches, gazing up at her with brown and faithful eyes, jaunty tail already wagging. It's eager to go with her, watching as she gathers up Papa's musket, tucks the tinderbox into her pocket, slings the supple leather pouch that holds the powder and the bullet across her chest.

"Come," she whispers so as not to wake Mama or Papa, and heads downstairs, slipping into the dark with the dog trotting keen on white-toed paws, following.

***

Far back as Susanna can remember, she always wanted a dog of her own, but Mama and Papa would not allow it. No matter how she begged or pleaded, they did not relent. Mama even struck her at the end of one long day when she got tired of her cheek. Old Karo was enough, they thought, keeping the yard and barn safe with his growl and bark; but much as she loved that jowly hound, she knew he was not wholly hers, knew he loved her Papa and her waddling, weak-chinned brother more than her. She craved a creature that would be bound to her, to love and roam with as she saw fit.

For months she prayed for a puppy, hands clasped around Nana's hymnal every Sunday as she sat in church beneath that soaring vault crowded with angels and apostles. Peering up at the Mother and the Son, at the vines and doves; staring at the polished silver cross studded with sardonyx and amber above the altar.

But God did not relent either, and one chill October morning she wandered off into the forest to find a pup herself. She was seven years old, hemmed in on all sides by chores and rules and commandments, her brother scampering in her wake. As always, she was supposed to watch him, the louse, same as every day since he'd been born.

"Stay here," she ordered, telling him of the ravenous wolves stalking the glades and paths, of their howls threading through mist and moonlight; of the witch weaving blood and bone into magic spells, changing children into pigs and sheep before she took their skins; of the trolls lurking 'neath the bridges and the rocks; of the vittra roaming the dells and hollows, snaring the unwary.

But he would not leave her alone no matter what she said or did, toddling along behind her undaunted.

At first she followed the trails she knew, to the places she'd gone to gather firewood and berries, to harvest birch bark for baskets, to forage for sticky-capped mushrooms in early fall and bright green spruce-shoots in spring. Then she wandered farther, across the bridge, across the river, to where she'd sometimes let the goats graze, meadows hazy with tall timothy grass and yarrow in summer, yet no dog could she find in that frosty wilted pasture, nor anywhere else her feet would take her.

"There *is* a pup," she told her brother, when he wept and said that he was hungry. There were countless places in the woods where a pup might hide, waiting to be found, waiting to be saved. "We just have to find him. Just a little farther."

She kept saying it, clinging to the words as if speaking them out loud would make it so.

Her brother cried most of the way. Because his ankle twisted. Because he was four years old. Because the wolves howled. Because he was cold and she'd forgotten to bring his mittens. Because he was too far away from Mama, no matter how hard and unforgiving her callused hands were most days.

When darkness fell, they trudged on, her brother sucking his fingers and holding on to her coat. He followed her wherever, because that was the way it had always been, since the first day Mama placed him in her care.

***

Ten years ago, when she walked home through the woods with that new pup whimpering in her arms, when she snuggled it close and felt the warmth of its soft, pink belly, she did not regret the choice she'd made. She did not regret it even when Mama and Papa shrieked and cried, asking where she'd been, asking about her brother. She told them he'd run off, that she'd followed but could not find him, no matter how she looked.

Even at the age of seven, the lies felt smooth and true upon her tongue.

And Mama wailing, like she'd ever cared for him, and Papa's face gone hard as rocks and iron, as if he'd even once held him close.

"You were supposed to watch him," Mama said, her voice so rough with anger it raked Susanna's skin.

"I did. I tried."

Papa saw the pup then, cowering between her legs.

"I found it in the woods when I was searching," she said, and picked it up, felt their two hearts pounding, close like breath and blood. "It's mine to keep."

Papa raised his hand. Mama raised her voice. But what could they do? They placed a stone with the boy's name in the boneyard once they'd combed the woods in vain. After that, Papa went back to the fields and forest and Mama went back to washing laundry for the burghers.

***

Susanna had spent three days and nights wandering the woods with her brother, scrounging for frost-bitten berries off the rowans, chewing bark and pine sap to fend off the hunger. In the dark, she whispered lullabies to hush her brother up, trying not to shout or strike him, even when he would not stop wailing.

By the time the old woman found them, they were chilled through bone and marrow; her brother sniveling snot and tears. Susanna was crying too, at least when no one saw. The old woman looked them over long and thoughtful, her gnarled hand resting on the curved blade tucked into her belt, though Susanna did not think she'd need that steel to end them. Once they'd been weighed and measured beneath that gaze, the woman took them to a sod-roofed cottage, evergreen ivy and withered bougainvillea snaking up the timbered logs and eaves, skulls and bones dangling in the trees outside, fresh hides stretched tight in wooden frames for tanning in the yard.

The woman fed them mutton soup and fresh-baked bread. She combed the pine needles and mud out of their hair. She put a fatwood pine-root on the fire to warm them. She wrapped the boy in a sheepskin and laid him down on a cot by the hearth.

Susanna sat at the table, sipping soup and watching. She saw the way the old woman used her mortar and her pestle, the way she hung the bunches of gathered herbs from the rafters, the way she mixed the potions and the salves on the counter below the deep-set window, the way she opened that heavy black book of hers, inked letters twined about with gold and scarlet. She listened to her sing, chanting words over her brother to mend his broken foot.

She knew what that woman was, and the woman knew she knew it, but neither of them spoke the word.

"All I wanted was a dog," Susanna said, though no one had asked for any explanation. "I'd give anything for a pup of my own."

The woman shook her head, her small bird-bone earrings clicking beneath her waist-long, grey-streaked hair. "Silly girl. Pups come along all the time. Wait till spring. They'll be rolling out of every barn and cottage."

"I've waited years already. I want a dog to care for now, before winter comes."

The woman laughed at that, at Susanna. Yet she looked at her with something akin to understanding.

"No patience in you, is there? Don't go looking for things to love, girl. Life's easier if you're not shackled to another." She nodded at the sleeping boy, gave a knife's edge of a grin. "One such chain of care has been slipped on you already, and as you grow there will be others, and they will be tighter still."

Susanna looked at her little brother. He was quiet then, but well did she remember his whining and his weeping, how he slowed her down and clung to her at every step.

"You're a clever girl, I can tell. Once I, too, was a clever girl who wanted things that would not be given to me. There are ways to get the things you want, but the getting's rarely free or easy." She gazed at Susanna, then turned away. "No. I do not think you want the dog that I could give you. Go home. Obey your parents. Become what they want you to be."

Susanna looked at her, thinking of the black book the woman had closed when she saw Susanna peeking, of the words she'd sung to change and heal the boy's bones and flesh; she thought of whispered winter-tales of children gone astray and of the raging hellfire awaiting those who used charms and curses to get what God and prayer would not supply.

"I'd give anything for a puppy."

The old woman turned from the cauldron, a gleam of embers in her sharp blue eyes as she peered through the murk of smoke and steam, seeing true and through. "Not many are willing to give **anything**. What would you give to get what you want?"

Susanna swallowed another mouthful of that soup, listening to her brother snuffling beneath the sheepskin; looking at that gnarled-root of a hand stirring the cauldron, and she thought she knew what the question and the answer meant.

"Anything."

***

Ten years on, Susanna is walking through the woods with the dog scampering in her wake. Might be his gait is stiffer now, might be his maw is grizzled, but he still follows her wherever; his soul and shadow still mingled with her own.

"There's a price for everything," the old woman told her that night beside the fire, "but you are only seven, and clever as you are, I'll still give you ten years until payment's due for what I'll give you. By then, the shackles of your life will be chafing both your skin and soul. Then you must bring yourself to me, to learn and listen, to stay beneath my roof as long as I see fit. And you must bring back what I gave you, for me to keep."

Ten years ago, as Susanna gazed at the fatwood smouldering low, as she listened to her own fiery heart burning hot and greedy beneath her ribs, the deal she struck seemed a well-considered bargain. She never thought ten years would pass by so quick—and if she thought of the deal at all those first few years after the old woman showed her the way home, she mostly thought of the snug bed in that small cottage, of the smell of herbs and mutton, of days without chores or errands, of the inked and illuminated pages of that heavy book, of the liberty to roam beneath the trees rather than feel the burn of lye as she helped Mama launder sheets by the creek.

But lately, as the years have run down through the glass, she's turned and twisted all the words the old woman spoke; she's run her fingers over them, the smooth and the rough, pondering their full meaning as she's laid awake at night with the dog warm and heavy by her side.

Bring back what I gave you, for me to keep.

She's thought of the scraped-clean skulls hanging from the branches, of bones boiled white, of hides stretched and drying beneath the trees. She's thought of the wicked knife in the old woman's belt, of the claws and teeth dangling from the charms. She's felt the dog's soft ears between her fingers, felt the curve and sleekness of his skull and jaw beneath the silken fur. And the fear that only tickled 'neath her skin ten years ago has turned into a constant itch and ache.

She's tried to find a way out. She prayed for salvation in church, with the wine and bread burning on her tongue, hands clasped around Nana's hymnal, even though she knows neither the Mother nor the Son nor the angels and apostles will help a girl like her.

It's easy to shoot a dog. As a kindness, as a mercy, to spare it the pains and suffering otherwise to come (beneath that wicked knife and chanted words). Susanna has held the musket more than once; felt the weight of it, heavy like her own heart in her hands.

Ten years. It is a decent length of life for any dog; yet even so, the old woman's words no longer seem like a fair trade or trusty promise. They seem a threat and portent, a shadow creeping ever closer through the pines and spruce. Susanna knows the payment's overdue. She knows the old woman will claim it, one way or another, whether Susanna goes to her or whether she waits for her to come knocking on the door.

She knows the price; knows what she would lose and gain if she were to pay it.

So she's learned the things that might confound an old woman such as that: sardonyx and amber, salt and silver, mistletoe and iron, scattered pebbles on the path, a hag stone on the fencepost by the road, hazel planted near the house.

Even so, her fear runs deep. How many times has she stayed awake listening for the old woman's steps coming up the pebble-strewn path, crossing the line of salt she laid at the threshold, climbing up the creaking stairs? How many nights has she waited for her barred door to shiver, for the latch and hook to bend and warp and snap, for the hinges to break, the wood to crack beneath the old woman's power?

It's easy to shoot a dog.

It's harder to shoot a witch.

***

The bright frost shatters beneath Susanna's boots as she heads deeper in between the boles, searching out the way she came and went ten years ago.

She's never cried, not in ten years; not once. Not so as anyone could see or hear it, anyway. And even if she tasted those tears, even then, she knows she'd make the same bargain again.

Anything, is what she said. But whatever promise she made when she was seven, she knows now that she cannot give up this dog, cannot let him suffer beneath the knife, cannot let his skin be taken, cannot aim the muzzle at his head even to spare him the pain otherwise to come.

Susanna walks with one hand on the musket, treading through dawn and day and dusk, into the shiver-dark of another night with the dog beside her. She walks until she finds the sod-roofed cottage, one candle lit in its northern window. In the rippled moonlight slipping through the chasing clouds, she sees the pale skulls hanging from the trees, hears their hollow song of wind and bone, and she sees an empty frame set up to tan a new hide behind the house, wooden pegs and sinew-thread ready for the stretching.

The old woman knows they're coming, her heavy feet already treading the warped wooden boards within the timbered walls. When the door glints open, there's a breath of utter silence when Susanna thinks she might turn back or falter. But no. There the old woman is, in the doorway, grey hair tangled 'round her brow, blue eyes peering through the shadows. Just a thin line of darkness between them now.

"Come inside," the old woman coos. "I thought you might not come. Thought you'd changed your mind. Thought they'd found a way to hinder you, perhaps. I should not have worried. At seventeen, you are still a clever girl."

The wood and metal of Papa's musket is smooth and heavy in Susanna's hands. She can smell the powder, smell the slow-burning match-cord—woven hemp cooked with saltpetre. In the darkness, she puts one hand on Brother's head—to calm him, to calm herself. And yet they both tremble.

"I told you I would teach you, and I will," the old woman whispers, soft words snaking 'round Susanna's pounding heart. "I'll teach you all the things you'll never learn at home, not from the preacher, not from that good book of yours, nor from any husband they might choose for you. I'll teach you all the craft a clever girl might want to know."

Susanna knows it is the truth. She knows she could reach for all that power, pay the price, watch Brother's hide scraped and stretched in that yard and be done with it. She knows the old woman could teach her how to grasp the forces of earth and sky and fire, of wind and water, and bend them to her will. She knows the old woman would open that heavy book and let her read its pages, learn the chants and verses written there; stranger songs than any printed in Nana's hymnal.

It would be easy to keep the bargain, to pay the debt she owes, leave everything behind. Easier than trying to take it all with naught but a loaded musket in her hand and Brother by her side.

Behind her, Brother stirs, his growl no more than ragged breath.

"You've brought him, as agreed. Good. A fair trade for both of us. Let me take him off your hands before you step inside, because I allow no shackles of love nor duty here. It's best to put away such childish things, and you'll soon learn that freedom's ever so much sweeter than the fetters you have known."

In the wan light, Brother's eyes are fixed on Susanna's, brown and faithful even now. Even now he hearkens to her. Even now he trusts her.

It is right that he should trust her. After all, what would he have been without the deal she made? Nothing but another useless crofter's runt, working his fingers to the bone, staggering beneath some richer man's yoke, bending his knees and back beneath the priest's commandments.

She does not want Papa's musket or the witch's knife to end Brother's life. She does not want her own life to come undone either, and to see her sin turn into human flesh again. She wants it all, just as she always did—the dog by her side, the magic between the illuminated pages hers to wield, this cottage their new home.

Standing on the threshold, Susanna knows there is a price for everything: for love, for knowledge, for life. For betrayal, too.

The musket's loaded, just like she's learned from watching Papa, even though he never would teach her. Here's the match-cord lit and smoldering, threaded through the prongs atop the lock. A bit of priming powder in the pan. The right measure of powder down the barrel, too, and a bullet, as smooth and warm and heavy as her guilty heart, as her tarnished soul.

She's already dropped that bullet down the muzzle, tamping down ball and powder with the scouring stick. And now she stands here, the lit end of the match-cord glowing hot and red like a demon's eye in the murk.

She thinks of all the things she'd give right now, rather than Brother's skull and hide. Even Mama's and Papa's lives she'd trade without regret. But not him. Not this dog. Not Brother.

The old woman sees the musket, sees Susanna raising it, aiming it at her head, but she's not worried. She thinks it's loaded with naught but a ball of lead, easily averted. She does not know how patiently Brother waited at the church door while Susanna snatched that hallowed cross off the altar—the Mother gazing down upon her sacrilege. She does not know about the silver Susanna snipped off that cross with Papa's tongs to melt and put into the bullet mould. She does not know about the sardonyx and amber Susanna pried off it and dropped into the ladle as the molten lead and silver swirled there, glossy-hot and grey. She does not know about the three long grey hairs Susanna plucked off the old woman's cloak ten years ago while she lay sleeping, while the fatwood burned low, while a seven-year-old girl pondered the deal she'd made. She does not know how safe Susanna has kept those grey strands, tucked between the pages of Nana's hymnal.

There is no going back. Not to who she was ten years ago, before her hot and greedy heart burned away all chances of salvation. Not to Mama and Papa, telling her each day to marry and be gone. Not to church, with the priest leaning close in the confessional, asking about those dog-tracks in the snow beside the church gate, about the errant boot-prints by the altar.

But if the bullet finds its mark, if the witch's craft should come undone, if her skein unravels here, what then for her, what then for Brother, what then for both of them? For him, the slow death of a stunted life. For herself, the stocks, the pyre, a shallow grave in unhallowed ground.

Susanna grips the musket firmly, Brother quivering at her side. He won't leave her, no matter how this ends, no matter what she does or where she goes, because that's how it is, how it's always been between them: no matter where the path leads, or what words the witch spoke ten years ago to change him, or what Susanna did to get what she wanted. Through it all, Brother's eyes stayed steadfast and true and always will. This dog will follow her to the ends of this world and into the next.

She knows the truth of it now, standing here at the end and the beginning. It isn't easy to shoot a dog, not even as a mercy and a kindness, not even to spare him the pain and suffering otherwise to come. Not when your souls and shadows have mingled since the day he was wrenched from Mama's womb. Because the real bargain she made, before any other, though the words were never spoken and Susanna did not understand the weight and depth of it before tonight, was to take care of him, of this dog, her brother, till the end of his days, till the end of hers.

It's hard to shoot a witch.

Harder still when Brother starts barking at the old woman's feet, snapping at her hem and sleeves, but still she must take aim.

Hands shaking, she touches the match-cord to the powder.

The crack and smoke of Papa's musket fills the night.

As the tangled bodies of witch and dog collapse in the doorway, Susanna stumbles forward, breathing one word into the silence—a plea and question, both. Kneeling, she blinks away the sudden sting of tears and reaches through the bitter smoke, praying for the warmth of fur and breath, praying for the power of sardonyx and amber, praying that the spell won't break.

AFTERWORD

BEING A WRITER CAN OFTEN feel like a lonely business. There's me and the keyboard and the blank page, and hopefully some words that I find, or that find me. When I started out as a writer back in the olden times in Sweden, it *was* lonely. There was no internet, and I never had any other writers to share and commiserate with back then. But since I came back to writing fiction in 2015, after a long time away, I have found a community of writers and readers and other creative people online and that has meant a lot to this old introvert. Thank you to my online community. You helped keep me going, helped keep the light on, even when I felt I was clawing my way through the dark.

Thanks to Dr. Angela Slatter for everything, always.

Thanks to my family for giving me a reason to get up every morning and lie awake at night.

Thanks to my mom for reading everything I write.

Thanks to my dad for putting Ray Bradbury and Tolkien on the shelves at home.

And thank you to Jake, the Very Big Black Dog, for walking with me in the woods as I turned over new stories, new words, new worlds, in my mind.

PUBLICATION HISTORY

WHEN MAMA CALLS: in *Bracken#4*.

TUNGUSKA, 1987: in the anthology
Tales from Alternate Earths. (Inklings Press).

SEVEN KINDS OF BAKED GOODS: in the anthology *Just Desserts*
(WolfSinger Publications).

DRAGON SONG
Original to this collection.

LONG AS I CAN SEE THE LIGHT: in the anthology *Alien Invasion
Short Stories* (Flame Tree Press)

BLACKDOG
Original to this collection.

AND YOU SHALL SING TO ME A DEEPER SONG: in *Interzone
#280*.

SILVER AND SHADOW, SPRUCE AND PINE: in *Flash Fiction
Online*, March 2020.

SIX DREAMS ABOUT THE TRAIN: in *Flash Fiction Online*, July
2020.

CLEAVER, MEAT, AND BLOCK: in *Black Static #73*.

HARE'S BREATH: in *Shimmer* #39

MOTHERS, WATCH OVER ME: in *Mythic Delirium*, April 2018.

DOWN TO NIFLHEL DEEP: in *Kaleidotrope*, Autumn 2020.

TEN THINGS I DIDN'T DO: at *PseudoPod* #745..

THE GUITAR HERO: in *Kaleidotrope*, Spring 2018.

GOOD GIRL: in *Escape Artists* PodUK 2020 Live Show.

DEEPSTER PUNKS—in the anthology *A Punk Rock Future* (Zsenon Publishing)

THE ROOT CELLAR: in *Beneath Ceaseless Skies* #251.

A STRANGE HEART, SET IN FELDSPAR: in the anthology *Abandoned Places* (Shohola Press).

THE BRIGHTEST LIGHTS OF HEAVEN: in *Fireside Fiction* #69.

METAL, SEX, MONSTERS: in *Gamut Magazine*.

CLEAR AS QUARTZ, SHARP AS FLINT: in *Augur Magazine* 2.1.

IT'S EASY TO SHOOT A DOG: in *Beneath Ceaseless Skies* #260.

ACKNOWLEDGMENTS

PUTTING THIS COLLECTION TOGETHER IN early 2020 was a task that kept my writing light burning at a time when I thought it might sputter and fade. Many thanks to my friend Colleen Heidrich for listening to me and walking with me. Thank you E. Catherine Tobler for whispering to me in the dark when I was struggling. I am especially and eternally grateful to author and witch-queen Dr. Angela Slatter for her unwavering encouragement and friendship, as well as her edits. Without her, this book would not exist.

ABOUT THE AUTHOR

MARIA HASKINS is a Swedish-Canadian writer and reviewer of speculative fiction. Her work has appeared in *Black Static*, *Fireside*, *Shimmer*, *Cast of Wonders*, *Interzone*, *PseudoPod*, *Escape Pod*, *Mythic Delirium*, B&N's Sci-Fi & Fantasy Blog, *Beneath Ceaseless Skies*, *Flash Fiction Online*, and elsewhere. She writes a quarterly short fiction roundup for *Strange Horizons*, and also reviews speculative fiction at her book blog, Maria's Reading.

She was born and grew up in Sweden, and debuted as a writer there before moving to Canada in the 1990s. Currently, she's located just outside Vancouver with two kids, a husband, a snake, several noisy birds, and a very large black dog.

CPSIA information can be obtained
at www.ICGtesting.com
Printed in the USA
FSHW010659190821
83938FS